WHEN KINGS FALL

VICIOUS THINGS, BOOK TWO

LEIA KING

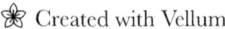 Created with Vellum

Welcome back to Stonewell

See you on the other side, Wildflowers

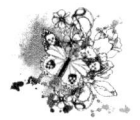

WHEN KINGS FALL Blurb

Six years ago, my life was shattered to pieces.
Now it's happening all over again.

I thought information was true power.
But as awful secrets come to light, it's clear it's also pain.
He's pulled me back in.
He's started something that can't be undone.

Now they're coming for us.
History is repeating.
They want us to crawl.
But we're different now.
This time, monsters will weep and false kings will fall.

Author's Note

This is a dark college bully reverse harem romance with scenes of M/M.

A list of TWs can be found at **www.leiaking.com**

~Mason~

"Anything on Royce?"

"Nothing yet," Levi reported.

He stepped back from his laptop, then bolted from the coffee table and slammed his fist into the nearest wall. "Motherfucker! Argh! *Argh!*"

"We're analyzing right now, it'll come. We'll figure out how he's gonna come at her, even if we can't pinpoint exactly when it's gonna be quite yet," I assured him.

"Yeah," Colt piped up from the couch, where he was far from his usual relaxed self, not leaning back at all this time, and rather right on the edge.

Hell, we all were, more than just literally speaking.

"Mason and you have *Hex* watching the borders, so we'll know the moment they cross over."

"Meaning we can act to intercept before they get to Brianna," I added.

Expecting Levi to pull back from the wall and take comfort in what we'd just told him, the reassurance we'd given, we were both surprised—and worried as fuck—

when he instead started roaring and wailing on the drywall furiously.

"I fucked up! I *fucked* up!"

"Shit," Colt uttered, getting to his feet and rushing over to Levi.

I dodged into his path, stopping him.

It was rare that Lev lost his temper in this sort of way, by hurting himself. It meant that all bets were off, that it was dangerous to approach him and that it would be a bitch of a thing to pull him out of it.

It was hard enough as it was not to show how pissed I was that something he'd done had driven Brianna away from us.

I knew that showing that wouldn't do any good. In fact, it would only make things a great deal worse. Working Levi up, especially when it came to Brianna, was not a healthy idea. Besides, he was already hurting badly, the last thing he needed was an *I-told-you-so* thrown in his face, or a reprimand.

What he'd done had occurred before we'd all grown close together and before he'd agreed to tamper down his reckless and lone wolf ways, so I couldn't get on his back about something caused by a version of him that didn't exist any longer.

Lev was yelling about *breaking us* and the *train wreck that is Chloe ruining everything*, then moving on to say that he was the one responsible, that he ruined everything he touched.

I eased Colt back further, then I came up behind Levi and swiftly trapped him in a body lock, then used all my strength to rip him off the wall.

He fought me, yelling in so much pain that it had me and Colt fighting to swallow down the emotion it was evoking in us both. That wouldn't help right now. Levi needed stability.

2

That was what Brianna had brought to him once she'd stopped running from him, and now she wasn't here with us, it was really destabilizing him.

"I need you, Levi," I spoke as I tightened my grip to a brutal hold that constricted his airflow, so I could weaken him enough to make him stop. "*She* needs you to fix this Royce Humphrey situation."

Slowly, he started to calm in my hold.

When he was no longer fighting me or resisting, I released the pressure around his throat.

"Fuck," he breathed, as I helped him into the armchair adjacent to the couch. "I messed up."

"Lev," Colt began. "As much as it sucks not having her here with us right now because this revelation came out, we also know that whatever you do regarding Brianna is out of love for her, protection, what you figure is in her best interests. We can't fault you for that."

"And this is something you did before we all got together."

"She didn't see it that way," he murmured, shoving a hand through his hair.

"Give her time," Colt said.

I sat down beside him on the couch and told Lev. "She just needs time for the shock of it to wear off. It's raw now. It's why we insisted you don't bombard her with messages and fight to contact her."

"Or, worse, actually show up at her door," Colt added.

"Exactly," I said.

Levi sighed heavily then pulled his phone from his pocket, scrolled for a moment, and handed it to me. "These are all the draft texts I wanted to send her, but stopped myself from doing since we agreed to give her space."

I took them in, Colt reading over my shoulder too.

Levi: I'm so sorry it came out like that.

Levi: It's not as bad as you think.

Levi: I mean, I know it's bad, I can actually recognize that, but I meant it wasn't done for a bad reason. I didn't do it to isolate you or anything. It wasn't like that.

Levi: I truly am sorry, Wildflower.

Levi: What can I do to make it better?

Levi: I can't stand the thought of losing you.

Levi: We can work through this. However you need, on your terms.

Levi: I care about you so much, we all do. Please don't leave.

"Aww, oh my God," Colt said.

I handed the phone back to Levi, still stunned that he'd actually shown it to us, put his vulnerability on display like that.

It just went to show how much he was hurting, and how much he needed us to understand that, to understand he needed us so badly right now.

The thing with Levi Knight was, when he was hurting, he needed a distraction.

Well, in his case, a focus.

And we had one.

Not a good one, a really fucking bad one.

Royce Humphrey and his mercenaries were coming for Brianna.

"Lev, it's actually best that she's distanced herself from us right now. If not, we'd have to tell her about Royce, and that would cause major panic, considering the brutal history there. So, I need you to focus up and put the rest on hold at the moment, so we can deal with this. And then once it's done, if she still hasn't reached out, we'll go to her, all three of us together, and talk it out. We'll fix it."

"We will, Lev," Colt uttered, bolstering my words to him.

It took him a moment to absorb it all.

And then he nodded. "Yeah. Yeah, I can do that." He rose to his feet. "I can find Royce."

"Good, and then we'll run him and his mercenaries into the ground."

"They won't get near her," Levi growled, vehemently. "I'll rip them apart before it can ever come to that."

We all would.

Estranged right now or not, she was ours.

And nobody threatened what was ours.

~Levi~

She wasn't home.

According to the eyes I'd had Mason put on her again, she was studying late at the library.

Trying to avoid us.

Well, me.

Thanks to Chloe's big fucking blabbering mouth.

Clearly it had been some form of payback on the part of that train wreck for me pulling her out of Stonewell U by playing on her mother's issues with her being here in the first place and not attending the elite fashion design institute in the City of Tolhurst like Celeste Anders had desired in the first place for her daughter.

I leaned against my Harley as I waited off the dirt road across from Brianna's apartment.

Again.

But this time I wasn't here to observe her in her natural habitat.

Or, *stalking her,* as some less open-minded people might tar it.

I was here to decimate a threat against her.

Against all of us by extension.

We were at that stage with her now where if anyone came at her, they also came at us.

All right, I'd been in that stage for six fucking years, but now I had Colt and Mason there with me too.

Mason and I had determined that Royce's mercenaries would target her at the apartment, rather than anywhere else. These guys were ghosts, they didn't draw attention, so they'd never come at their targets in a crowded area, or anywhere at all public. No, they'd break into her apartment quietly, then attack from within.

My plan was to put them down while she was in class back at the campus, and then we'd tell her what was going on, give her the whole truth.

This threat from Royce changed things and as bad as it was, it did mean we could finally be done with the secrecy that had been twisting me up.

Her and I had come a long way and I couldn't handle the idea of that being set back, and our closeness being compromised made me sick to my stomach. It was already eating me up inside that the whole Chloe thing had put a dent in things. Fortunately, it was connected to the rest, so once I was able to lift the veil of secrecy, I'd be able to explain why I'd had to do it.

Until then, being cut off from her was something I had to weather for a little while longer.

Movement caught my eye and I watched as a black unmarked van carefully pulled into the lot.

I pushed off my motorcycle and kept myself concealed as I approached the building, keeping an eye on the van as four overly musclebound guys decked out in the cliché all black—jeans and leather jackets—to blend into the night emerged.

They were here.

It was time.

I darted up the opposite entrance to the stairwell and took the steps two at a time toward Brianna's floor.

Fortunately, Mason had managed to empty the building citing a fake gas leak or something—we'd have time to discuss the details later, once this immediate threat was taken care of.

I made it to the fourth floor just as I heard heavy footsteps rushing up the opposite stairwell, coming in hot.

Sliding my tactical knife from the sleeve of my hoodie, I spun it in my hand, then readied a long-practiced fighting stance.

The first one appeared, rounding the staircase, and I reacted instantly, tossing my knife and watching as it embedded in his chest. Unfortunately, not his heart, as Mason had outlawed me taking their lives tonight.

Chaos erupted then, roars and threats spilling forth.

I launched myself at the now injured guy, ripped my knife out of his chest, then slammed my boot into his gut.

The power behind it blew him down the stairs into one of his asshole buddies on the way up behind him and he crumpled into a heap on the landing below.

Another two leapt over them and came at me.

A roundhouse kick that clocked one across the side of the head and had him stumbling back into the wall with a nasty thud took care of one of them, buying me a little bit of time to deal with the other.

He tried to land a punch to the underside of my jaw, but I deflected it easily. His eyes flashed and he tried harder, now realizing what they were dealing with.

That rush that took me when I was street fighting was more intense this time, more raw, because of the stakes involved.

And it fueled everything.

Every move I made, every decision to be absolutely brutal.

Before I knew it, I was beating the motherfucker into the concrete with punch after punch, destroying his face.

As another bolted up the stairs to assist, I snatched his wrist, twisted it mercilessly until I heard that telltale crack and his satisfying cry of pain, then I used it to force him around, wherein I smashed my boot into the back of his knee. As he went down, hitting step after concrete step painfully, the impact knocked him out.

I wrenched the shoulder of another, dislocating it and making him scream.

The fourth came at me and I dodged his blow, then fisted his hair and used the leverage to smash his face into the banister and knock him out cold too.

The two remaining tried to move in to take me together, but as one made his move to snag me, I used it against him and reacted, turning it around and forcing him into a sleeper hold.

I kicked back his buddy and as he staggered down two steps and jarred against the wall, I tossed my blade. He shrieked as it drove through his palm and pinned him to the wall.

The guy in my hold went limp and I released him roughly, watching as he fell into a heap like a ragdoll.

Before I could put the pinned guy out, a whizzing sounded and a tranq embedded in his throat.

He slapped his free hand to it, then Mason was there ripping the knife from his palm. His scream was cut off as he passed out and hit the stairs hard.

I stepped back, wiping sweat off my brow.

"A little slow on the timing, brother."

"Did the best I could with the short notice."

His eyes darted all over at the four guys. "They're all still alive."

"For you. You made it clear you didn't want the mess."

"And major complications, Lev."

"Sure, that." As far as I was concerned, they deserved death for coming at our woman. But Mason and I had a deal, one she had gone to great efforts to broker.

"All right, you deal with this. Call in *Hex* and have these shits transported far from Stonewell. I'll get Colt up to speed and keep an eye on Brianna."

"Yeah," I murmured. "Go. Watch her. Closely, Mason."

"Got it."

"No," I said, grasping his arm. "Do whatever it takes."

"I will," he vowed. He laid his hand on my shoulder. "We've got her, brother. She's ours now and we'll protect her as ours."

Damn fucking straight.

3

~Brianna~

I was exhausted.

It had been almost the crack of dawn when I'd finally arrived home last night.

Again.

For three days and nights running now.

I hadn't trusted that the guys would stay away when I'd really needed them to after that messed-up revelation about what Levi had done.

Urgh. It was beyond invasive and a violation of my freedom and choices, something he knew was *so* important to me.

I couldn't believe he'd actually done this.

So I'd come home really late yet again, and I'd had to get up far too early to go to my first class of the day.

As I finished getting dressed, I checked the text notifications I'd heard as I'd stepped out of the shower.

I was more than a little surprised when I didn't find anything from the boys.

Nothing at all.

Not for three whole days.

There hadn't actually been any contact whatsoever since the night I'd kicked Levi in the balls.

Instead, there were some from Chloe.

Chloe: Are you okay?

Chloe: Maybe I shouldn't have told you. I'm so sorry I upset you.

I shook my head to myself and wrote back.

Brianna: You didn't upset me, you just told me the truth. It was brave and I love you for it.

Chloe: Aww, I love you too. I wish we could be at Stonewell U together still.

Brianna: Me too. But, you know, it's gonna be great for your career at least being where you are now instead at that special design school.

Chloe: Yeah, there is that.

Brianna: Exactly.

Chloe: There you are again always seeing the positive in everything, even when there seems like there isn't any to be found.

I started at her message.

I guess I did do that.

At least these days since my *reinvention*.

But I hadn't done that earlier with Levi after I'd found out he'd kept my friend from me.

Worse, that he'd actually driven her away from me, that he'd manipulated a whole bunch of things to make it happen too.

I just… it had hurt.

We'd come through so much, all his craziness at the beginning, the bullying from Mason and *Hex*, so fucking much.

I'd thought we'd turned a corner, that we were all out of the woods.

I'd thought the trust was there.

More than that, I'd thought it had been solidified between all four of us.

That we were a team.

And I got that this had obviously happened before that had come about, before things had changed between the four of us, before we'd grown so close.

But he still should have told me that was what had happened, that he'd done that.

I mean, I'd forgiven him for other things.

The fact he hadn't told me… it hurt.

And, honestly, it worried me that there could very well be a whole lot more he was keeping from me.

Maybe that Mason was keeping from me too.

Colt, not so much. He was an open book and he didn't have a manipulative bone in his body. That first interaction with us where that had seemed to be in play regarding the duet excuse had been all Levi putting it up to him, so I didn't count it as Colt's infraction, but Levi's.

I sighed heavily and said my goodbyes to Chloe over text.

I needed to get to class.

I grabbed my bag off my bed, then headed out of my bedroom.

I just needed to focus on college until I was able to calm down from the rest, until I could process it.

As I went to open the door, the lights suddenly shut off.

With the early hour it plunged the immediate area into blackness.

An eerie sensation rolled over me, the sensation that I wasn't alone anymore.

A warning screamed at me.

In the next moment, the door was flung open and a rush of movement came my way.

I didn't even get to react when I was suddenly trapped in a bear hold, a hand slapped over my mouth.

I screamed into the palm and struggled wildly, slamming the weight on me against the wall.

They held fast, the impact not even dislodging their grip in the slightest.

My head was wrenched back, making me grunt.

A damp cloth was slapped over my nose and mouth.

And then everything started to fade away.

My fight disintegrated.

My surroundings slipped away.

No! No! Not again.

Not back into that hellscape!

The demons had found me.

I couldn't… I couldn't stop the overwhelming sensation dragging me under.

It was going to take me.

No. No.

It was too late in the next second.

Everything slipped away.

4

~Brianna~

Six Years Ago

CLANG.

Clang.

Clang.

"Brianna? Wake up. Brianna?"

I opened my eyes slowly to darkness.

Seeing as though that was how hours on end had been spent, my eyes adjusted quickly.

And that was when I saw Levi crouched over me.

Crouched? He wasn't in the chair anymore.

I shifted on the ground and realized there was no restriction for me either.

My hands weren't cuffed in front of me as I remembered them being after Malcolm Lynch had finished torturing me for the day earlier.

"What's... what's going on?" I asked, my voice rough and scratchy from screaming and a lack of water.

They only allowed us the bare minimum to eat and drink, wanting to keep us weak.

As if the sedatives they'd started shooting me up with to calm me down since they'd taken my mom from me weren't already fucking doing that as it was.

I went to sit up, feeling pain all over my body as I attempted just that slight move.

Levi was there then, helping me to my knees.

His gaze strayed to my legs and he grimaced, stark concern filling his eyes. "You need a doctor right away."

I followed his gaze to see blood seeping from beneath my ratty dress and dripping all down my legs.

"It's okay. I'll be fine. Just a little sore."

A little didn't even begin to cover it.

It hurt so bad that I had to use every ounce of the limited energy I had left to stagger to my feet, even with Levi grasping my arm and assisting.

I cursed and shoved my hand through my hair, trying to get my bearings and make sense of what was going on.

"How... how are we free of those cuffs?"

"I did it."

"You what?"

"I got a hold of your pick set and I managed to figure it out. You were unconscious on the floor and bleeding, I couldn't fail."

Oh my God. "Thank you."

"No worries. Now, we've gotta get out of here. Malcolm and Royce aren't here right now. I overheard them saying they had to get to a meeting. That other one, Kyle, is here, and their muscle, but with Malcolm not here their guard will be down. I even heard them saying something about drinking. This is our best chance."

I took his words in. "Very good intel gathering. All right, with being dragged around this hellhole a lot, I've been able to map it out pretty well. I can lead us out."

"Good. Let's go."

We made our way toward the door at the far end of the space.

"I'll need a few moments to pick the lock," I told him as we reached it.

I reached out my hand for my picks and grabbed the door handle with my other.

And it gave way.

"It's not locked," Levi spoke.

"It could be a trap."

"Whatever they do to us can't be worse than what they've already done," he pointed out.

"You're right. Let's do this."

I took the pick set from him and pulled out the torsion wrench and the rake, handing them to him, and pulling out the ball pick and snake for myself, then shoving the rest into my dress. "Not the best weapons, but it's all we have."

He nodded and readied them as I did the same.

Then I opened the door carefully, peering outside into the corridor.

When I'd determined it was all clear, we stepped outside. One path led straight ahead, the other to the right.

"Right," I told him. "It leads to the east exit. We only have to dart from the building a few feet before we'll be camouflaged by the surrounding forest."

"Okay," he said, looking all around and trying so hard to hide his fear, his hands shaking with adrenaline.

"We're here together. You're not alone," I told him.

He smiled out at me. "Couldn't have asked for anybody better to be in this nightmare with."

"Right back at you."

As we were making our way down the corridor, one of the doors to the left opened, and a guard wearing one of those awful ski masks stepped out.

"What the fuck are you doing free?"

He came at us in the next second.

17

The hell I was going to let him stop us from finally making our escape from this nightmare.

Despite the fact that every step was causing me significant pain, focusing on the adrenaline of it all was managing to mute it enough where I could function.

And this asshole coming at us added a whole other powerful element.

Rage.

Levi was obviously right there with me on that, because he roared, then slammed the guy back into the wall with a brutal shove—especially for somebody so young and unaccustomed to this down and dirty life. For the most part, anyway.

Until this.

Until these monsters had taken that innocence and shattered it to pieces.

As soon as the guard jarred against the wall, I was there, driving my snake into his throat and twisting it for good measure.

He let out an awful gurgled scream that went right through me in a way that I knew would haunt me for a long time to come.

As well as the sight of blood spurting from his throat because I'd hit his carotid artery dead-on.

I couldn't take the chance of just injuring him and him being able to fight on, or get back up later just as we were on the verge of escaping this place.

Blood splattered over my fingers and Levi's neck and face.

I wrenched the snake out and wiped it on my pants.

"Let's keep going," I told Levi as he stared at the guy sinking down the wall to his ass and dying right before us. "Look away," I said, grasping Levi's arm and steering him away.

Fortunately, he managed to focus and we hurried down the corridor.

We shoved open the heavy emergency exit door together.

We'd just stepped outside when a guard lunged at us from the left.

There was no time to react as he was suddenly wrenched back.

What the hell?

The two of us watched in shock as the roided-out guy with slicked back hair, Kyle Trass, one of the main three here, laid into the ski mask and then smashed his head into the exterior wall, knocking him out cold.

In the next second, Kyle was stepping up to us and holding out a gun.

"The safety's off, so just point and shoot. There's three guards over by the east side exit, the way you're headed. I can't be seen helping you, all right?"

"I… yes," I said, taking the gun from him. "Why do this? Why go against your boss?"

He looked between us, grimacing. "Because what he's doing is demented. Now I sent them off to a fake meeting, this is your chance."

"Fake meeting?" Levi asked. "You set all that up?"

"Yeah, now go. And hurry."

Levi and I took off, running around the side of the building, prepared to make the sharp turn that would lead us toward the cover of the trees.

"There!" I called out, panting from the exertion on my injured body, as I located our path through and away from all of this.

Levi's eyes sparked with hope.

We bolted toward the trees, almost home free.

And then we heard shouting.

I looked over my shoulder to see Malcolm Lynch and Royce Humphrey hurrying out of their vehicles along with four ski mask assholes.

A shudder rolled through me.

No!

They were already back.

I fired off several shots in my panic.

While running and because I'd only fired a gun once in my life prior to this, I only managed to hit one of the ski masks. He clutched his gut and dropped to his knees.

I looked away and followed after Levi.

We were just seconds out from disappearing into the trees when a shot rang out.

A white-hot pain tore through my upper back and I screamed, tripping and landing painfully on my hands and knees.

Levi cried out and stopped running, coming back to me.

"No," I gasped. "Go. Get out... of here."

"I'm not leaving you behind," he said, resolutely.

The shouting grew louder, footsteps closer.

And then Levi did the unthinkable.

He stepped in front of me, forming a human shield.

A fifteen-year-old kid facing off with a group of deranged, grown men.

It was several levels beyond brave.

But I couldn't allow it.

I couldn't allow him to suffer because of me, in the name of protecting me.

"Levi, no," I croaked.

He was tackled to the ground in the next second by Royce and one of the guards.

And then they wailed on him.

My choked screams for them to stop landed on deaf ears.

And then automatic fire ripped through the area.

Screams from the masks filled my ears.

Royce pushed off Levi and spun, his eyes wide.

"Get your motherfucking hands off my son!" a voice of furor thundered.

An older version of Levi flitted across my vision just before all chaos broke loose.

"No mercy, Roman."

My dad's voice?

"No worries there."

I tried to turn to see, but I couldn't.

I was so done.

A shadow fell over me, sending an additional jolt of adrenaline through me.

And then Tommy Dixon was there like an angel of vengeance snarling at the enemy, then smiling kindly down at me. He was my dad's right hand, SAA for Steel Dawn MC.

"You're gonna be okay," he told me. "It's over. You're safe now."

As much as I wanted to sink into his words and let myself believe them, I couldn't.

I had an awful feeling that I'd never be safe.

That I'd never be able to feel that again.

5

~Levi~

Dawn.

That was how long it had taken to conduct the *cleanup* of those motherfucker mercenaries.

I'd taken the help from four of our *Hex* members to drag the assholes into the transport van Mason had procured at impressive speed given the short notice, but after securing them, I'd handled the actual sanitization myself.

Right or wrong, I knew a thing or two about wiping evidence.

I'd left absolutely no sign of them or what had gone down in the stairwell.

Then I'd transported my unconscious cargo a hundred miles outside Stonewell and left them on the doorstep of a cop shop complete with rap sheets I'd managed to pull up on each while *Hex* had taken time to get me the necessary equipment to conduct my sanitization, as well as then taking undue time to haul the fuckers into the van and secure them for me.

Royce was effectively down four soldiers now.

Now I was speeding back home, using the backroads.

There was more of a peace to it than driving down the highway.

And, honestly, I'd needed it *and* the extra time that using the more roundabout route home afforded me.

It was hard to shove my bloodlust back into its proverbial sealed box once it was triggered.

Even when it wasn't triggered actually.

That was what I had my street fighting *hobby* for, to tamper down those urges that had been awakened a few years ago.

And usually that was enough to hold it at bay.

But lately things kept happening where I was being pushed.

First, the farmhouse takedown of some of Mason's *Hex* soldiers after he'd come at Brianna.

And then, last night, stopping that incoming attack at the apartment.

Those were both personal and much more uncontrolled than a street fight that had a ref was.

The last time I'd actually let go and unleashed *everything* had been that night when I'd taken down that gang in the City of Tolhurst.

This was the first time since then that the urge to let that fucked-up part of me loose and give into my bloodlust all the way was growing stronger than the rational part of me that cared about the consequences that would come crashing down upon all of us.

When I'd launched that attack against Mason's soldiers, I'd seen Brianna right after, and being in her presence, having her with me, had taken the edge off.

But now… now she was pissed at me and ignoring my attempts to connect with her.

Now there was no block in place, nothing else to hold onto, this… urge… it was nagging at me something fierce.

I was having to be controlled in all things at the moment.

That just wasn't me.

It wasn't the norm and it certainly wasn't my forte.

It took supreme effort to pull off.

It was fucking tiring.

Majorly emotionally taxing, in fact.

And it was starting to get the best of me.

My hands were shaking around the steering wheel.

I could feel my pulse starting to pound.

A wave of lightheadedness hitting me was the final straw, warning me that I needed to pull over quickly.

It wasn't an anxiety attack this time.

It was a flash.

Of the *incident*.

I saw a turnoff and took it.

The last thing I was aware of as I just about managed to pull the van to a jarring stop was a floodlight of a parking lot cutting through the darkness.

DRIP.

Drip.

Drip.

Blood oozed from my bo-staff as I dragged it along the worn wooden floor of the abandoned mansion that had seen better days.

Worse now after the horrors it had been home to tonight.

Horrors they'd brought upon themselves.

Violence.

Pain.

Death.

And a whole lot of bloodletting.

All in the name of justice and protection.

Of safeguarding those who couldn't safeguard themselves.

This gang of assholes tonight had already maimed, assaulted, and dealt in dirty dealings as it was. I'd made sure I'd stopped it from going any further.

I'd stopped them from becoming like the demons.

They'd been on the same path.

And now they weren't.

I had one target left to deal with—the big boss of the outfit—and then my mission would be complete.

He was staggering a few feet in front of me, looking back fearfully every now and then as he saw me still coming, still pursuing like the predator I was tonight.

I watched him disappear into the last door along the corridor.

Trapped prey.

Invigorating.

The thump of my boots echoed hauntingly through the deathly still mansion.

My combat pants swished and squelched, drenched in the blood of my enemies.

My black tee too. My face, my arms, my hands, even my hair.

Some was mine, I hadn't gotten out of this without taking some hefty hits myself, and I hadn't expected to. My training had taught me well where that was concerned. And because of that, I'd been able to take the hits I'd been dealt.

That was half the battle, being able to get back up after taking a brutal hit—or several.

Sixteen years old and I'd murdered for the first time.

No, more than that… massacred.

I should be disgusted.

I should be plagued by a shit-ton of shame.

I should feel remorse.

But I didn't.

A sense of victory rolled through me.

A feeling of unadulterated power.

"Lev!"

I spun and looked to see Mason striding up to me, his arm around a trembling Colt with his hand shielding his eyes from the horrors we'd just committed.

What Mason saw as unnecessary but I saw as essential brutal justice.

Him showing up suddenly after I'd thought he and Colt were heading out, while I dealt with the remaining guy, and then the cleanup, drew too much of my attention.

The distraction of it had me caught off guard when the door that my final target had disappeared into flew open.

He barreled out.

I registered the gun now in his hand a split-second before he fired off a shot.

I staggered back as a white-hot, jarring pain tore through my abdomen.

As I smacked against the wall, slapping my hand to my shirt that was quickly drenching in my own blood, the big motherfucker decked out in all denim came at me.

A shot rang out and I swung my head to see Mason there, his gun cocked.

The target roared and dropped hard, clutching his kneecap with one hand.

But the other... the other still held the gun.

I heard myself yelling to Mason.

But it was too late.

The target fired off a shot and hit Mason in his left arm.

He lost his grip on Colt and smacked back against the wall like me.

But he still had hold of the gun.

Thank fuck, he managed to fire off another shot.

This time, right through the shithead's skull—a solid kill shot.

"Christ," I breathed, sliding down the wall as the pain overcame the adrenaline coursing through my system.

As Colt ran to Mason, the latter stared out at me.

I saw him register that dark look in my eyes, reading me well as usual.

Something I vowed in that moment as his disgust became apparent that I would never allow him to do.

Because I saw it in there, the upsetting truth.

We were shattered.

And he'd never, ever look at me the same way again.

I SQUEEZED my eyes shut against the memory and came back to reality.

I took a beat to regain my equilibrium.

Once my breathing had leveled out and I'd gotten my bearings, I realized I'd parked in the lot of a diner.

It was actually the one I'd marked on my GPS to take a break at for a few minutes before I continued on home.

I also didn't do well driving—or riding—without eating.

It had been several hours since I'd done so, and on no sleep.

Clearly that flashback was a sign that it was wearing on me, weakening me.

Intending to rectify that, I stepped out of the van, locked it, then went to head toward the diner entrance twenty feet away.

The clack of footsteps in the dark had me stilling in my step.

I heard it again and I followed the sound, spinning in that direction.

Just as somebody emerged from the shadows, the illumination of the floodlight touching them.

My breath caught in my throat as I took in the designer suit, the black curly hair that brushed his collar, and those striking blue eyes that even pierced through the night.

Just. Like. Mine.

Christ. "What are you doing here?" I only just managed to choke out.

The corner of his mouth turned up as he stopped in front of me and shoved his hands into the pockets of his fancy suit jacket. "Not your best greeting, *Son.*"

6

~Colton~

I couldn't believe he'd done this.

We'd all finally been in a good place.

Now his actions, this solo decision he'd made, threatened to ruin it.

It threatened to shatter us.

Mason Hall and his fucking unilateral bullshit!

"He's gonna kill you for this," I muttered as I hurriedly stuffed a bunch of my clothes and toiletries into a gym bag I'd pulled out of the bottom of my closet.

Mason had insisted that we relocate to our safehouse—a place we hadn't set foot in for five years.

"You're being overdramatic."

I stilled, then swung my head over my shoulder as he paced up and down my room typing rapidly on his phone, sending orders to *Hex*, telling our professors we'd need to set up remote learning for a while due to a personal emergency, and what-not.

"Overdramatic? Are you kidding?"

He looked up from his phone. "It's what's best."

"Debatable."

"No, it's not," he bit back. "I'm doing what's needed."

I slapped my gym bag and turned to face him. "That's the thing. *You. You're* doing what *you* think is needed. We're supposed to be deciding things together. Especially you and Lev."

"He's not here and he's not answering my texts. I had to make a decision. I had to act quickly."

"You could've given it more time. A little more, at least. He's on the road and he doesn't text when he's driving, not even at a stoplight or anything. And he doesn't like to pull over when he's in a rush to get to his destination."

"*Or* he's had an episode because of the violent blood-letting that took place at Bree's apartment. He's likely struggling with it. It's been twice he's been a part of something like that in just a couple of weeks. It's gotta be getting to him."

That pulled me up short for a moment.

Shit, that really could be the case.

"Then we should track him and go to him. You have eyes on him, right?"

"No. I had to pull my resources and redirect them because of this situation."

"Okay, then *get* eyes back on him. Or we can reach out to Caterina and have her track him through his phone… ping it… triangulate, or whatever."

"Rina isn't an option. Anything I ask is gonna come with a favor in return. Whenever she uses those skills of hers, it's a risk, given who she is, so she requires persuasion to use them for others. The last favor I had her do me cost me a gala appearance with my father. If I call in a favor on Lev's behalf, he's gonna be pissed. He doesn't like to be in debt. Besides, with the way things are going, best to save favors like that for something more vital. We both know Lev can take care of himself. You're just spiraling because of all the worry and adrenaline this situation has sparked."

I scrubbed my hand over my face. "Fine, but beyond another couple of hours and we take action, we do whatever, call in whoever we need to find him."

"Deal."

He pocketed his phone and walked to me.

Reaching out, he slid his hand to my cheek, stroking softly. "Everything will be okay."

"You don't know that."

"I promise you that I won't allow it to be any other way."

He brushed his lips over mine, but I pulled from his hold.

"Colt, I know you're not on board with the decision I made, but it's already done, and I can't have bad blood between us again when we just got past the last thing. Like you said, Levi's gonna be pissed. I can't have you against me too. I can't fight a fucking war on so many fronts—least of all, internally."

"I am angry at what you've just done, because it risks the great state of things we've been enjoying lately, all of us being on the same page, having Bree here shifting our dynamic to something much better, without so much aggravation between you and Lev. *But* I do get your reasoning. I also know you did it for the right reasons, for Lev too. That's not why I pulled away."

He frowned in thought for a moment. "Is this about Bree?"

"Yes, but not in the way you probably think." I wrung my hands, feeling ill at ease bringing this up, especially while things were so tense and now in a state of flux. But now it had inadvertently been touched on, I had to put it out there. Otherwise, I'd keep putting it off and it would make things a whole lot more awkward between Mason and me. "I just… ever since we brought her into our inner sanctum, ever since we came together… you know, fucked?"

"I know what you mean, yeah. Didn't need to hit me over the head with it."

I rolled my eyes. "You know it's my way."

He held up his hand. "Sorry. Go on, brother."

I sucked in a breath. "Ever since we became a foursome, like a solid unit, I feel weird about breaking off into a twosome with you. Especially without telling her. Even Lev. I feel… guilty, like it's a betrayal of the new bond we've forged."

"I understand."

"You do?"

He nodded. "The idea of it has felt different to me as well, since we established this foursome. I just couldn't put my finger on exactly what or why."

"Because you're so far from being in touch with your emotions?"

He gave me a look. "Yes. That."

"While we're talking about this, there's also another reason why I'd rather we don't fuck separately anymore… at least until we can figure this out." I went to him and took his hand, weaving my fingers in his. "You're different when the four of us are together. You come alive, Mason. You let go in that dynamic. That burden that's there whenever you and me fool around one-on-one isn't there when she's present, or Lev either. It does something to you, eases you somehow." I smiled out at him. "And I love it. I love seeing that from you. It's been so fucking long, brother."

He squeezed my hand. "I know. And I'm sorry, Colt."

"Sorry?"

"That I couldn't get back to the person you and Lev

knew. That what happened, what being under my father's thumb did, changed me so deeply. I used to be free spirited like you." He pulled away and screwed up his face. "And now I'm *this*… this stoic machine. *Killjoy.*"

"Hey, it's not as bad as you're making it out to be. You're my boy, I love you. Lev loves you. I know he gives you a hard time about all this, but if you just look a little deeper you'll see it's because he misses his buddy, the guy who used to be right there beside him wading in the shit with him, letting loose alongside him. It pretty much used to be you two who were tighter than you and me are now. I was off doing my music, honing my skills, and songwriting, while you two were off pulling crazy stunts and running wild. When you… after the incident changed you… that was taken from Lev. He gets it, though, I know he does. And he's still here, still your brother-in-arms like I am." I smiled. "And now there's Bree too."

He surprised me then as he abruptly wrapped his arm around me and pulled me tightly to him. "Thank you, brother. Thank you."

Unfortunately, the moment didn't last nearly long enough as his phone rang, cutting right through it.

"Dammit," he muttered, as he fished it out of the back pocket of his designer jeans.

When he took in the call display whatever he was seeing had that agitation morphing to some serious concern.

He took a beat, the answered, "Mason here. He's… what? Where? Okay, yeah, I'm listening."

And that was all he did.

Whoever was on the other end had clearly told him to stop with the questions and just listen real carefully.

"Yeah, got it."

The call ended and Mason absently stowed his phone away.

When he glanced at me, I didn't like the look in his eyes one bit.

In fact, it sent a shudder down my spine.

"Who was it? Was it about Bree? Is she—"

"Things have taken a turn."

Holy. Fucking. Shit.

7

~Levi~

The diner was dead silent.

There was literally nobody inside.

No patrons, no staff.

I eyed my dad across the ugly brown plastic booth, looking jarringly out of place sitting in a joint like this in his navy striped Brunello Cucinelli suit.

He reached into his pocket and tossed a protein bar down on the table in front of me. "Here. Eat."

How did he know I really needed something to fuel me right about now? "Thanks," I said, not about to look a gift horse in the mouth. I opened the bar and took a bite, chewing quickly as he just stared at me—or more like studied and analyzed me.

Once I'd swallowed, I cut through the silence and asked, "You bought this place out for a couple of hours?"

"No. I bought it, period."

Oh no. That didn't bode well.

Best to just address it directly then, seeing as though he wasn't giving it to me upfront.

"You hate the food services industry from a business investment perspective."

"It's a gift."

I cocked an eyebrow.

"For your girlfriend's father."

Fuck.

I was usually as cool as they came, able to remain calm in the face of pretty much anything, to stand my ground and come out on top.

But when it came to Roman Knight, it was different.

I'd met my match.

I actually had to clear my throat before responding, "Girlfriend?"

"Would you prefer I term her your *obsession?*" he asked, evenly, not missing a single beat as per usual.

"Dad, listen, I—"

"I haven't laid eyes on you in over a year, Levi." He looked me up and down studiously, as I munched on my protein bar. "You've put on a lot of muscle. Not always a good thing with you, because it's beyond being about mere physical fitness. You look tired. Not just due to being up all night running that *errand.*"

Christ, he knew way too much.

He reached out and laid his hand on mine. "You had an *episode,* didn't you?"

Instinctively when it came to that subject matter being brought up, I went to pull away.

But he didn't allow it.

"Son?" he pressed.

"It wasn't about what you think. I just flashed back to five years ago."

"That's what you were experiencing in that van for close to ten minutes?"

He'd been watching me since then?

"Yes."

"You merely put down the threat that those vermin posed, nothing more than your street fighting, so where was the link to that night five years ago?"

"It's still enough to activate my bloodlust."

"Which you have under control. You have for years now." He released my hand and sat back, folding his big arms across his chest. "So, I ask again, where was the connection made in your mind?"

Son of a bitch! I slammed my fist down on the table, rocking it from the force. "You know where and why! You know! That's why you're here!"

He kept his cool, like I hadn't just snapped right in front of him.

In an even tone, he said, "Say it then."

I grabbed the edge of the table in a white-knuckle grip and took some time to control my breathing to tamper down my rage.

Just like he'd taught me to do after the kidnapping— and again after I'd lost it the night of the massacre.

"Because," I managed to answer in a strained voice. "I need to go to that headspace again." I glared out at him. "I won't let you stop me this time. I have to do this. I need—"

"I know what you need, son."

"What?"

"I had hoped that the last year away would have given you what you needed when you discovered just how difficult it is to even get a lock on Lynch for a moment in time."

"You knew that was what I was doing? You didn't buy the internship story?"

"Not to knock the impressive smokescreen that you fashioned, because it was indeed intricate and well-choreographed, but it was also too perfect. So I put eyes on you a couple of months in. That was why when you returned to the location that you'd tracked Lynch too, he'd already moved on."

I started. "*You* let him get away?"

"My man on the ground did. You were outnumbered. Even if he'd stepped in as had been his orders if you hadn't stepped back when you had, you would have failed against that many. Thirty-to-one are unacceptable odds, Levi."

"I could've got off a kill shot."

"And simply walked away with not one of them making you?" He scoffed. "Impossible."

"You don't know what I'm capable of anymore."

"I'm well aware. That's why I'm not simply putting you in the back of my Lexus and driving you back home to put you under close watch."

I frowned. "Wait, that's *not* what you're here to do?"

He leaned forward. "I'm here to make you a deal."

I cocked a highly skeptical eyebrow. "A deal?"

"Relocate to *Boreas* and continue your search for Lynch through his associate, using him as a buffer, but create one of your favored smokescreens and take it further, making it appear as though Royce Humphrey is coming for him, rather than you. I'll feed reports that you've been hospitalized following a failed battle with several of his mercenaries, so that you can't possibly be responsible for tracking Lynch, nor even seen as a threat to him and his organization. I'll have my people draw Kyle Trass into the situation too, to be seen as working alongside Royce Humphrey. Their reasoning? That *Osiris* has become too powerful and Humphrey is concerned Malcolm Lynch will run right over him and try to command him again. Of course, Trass will always follow Humphrey like a lost puppy, so his motivations are clear."

"You'd do all of that for me?"

He held up a finger. "I said a *deal*, not a handout. Besides, we both know you never liked being handed anything, always insisting on working for it yourself. You even bought that mansion in Stonewell from your own funds that you'd acquired from hiring out your ingenious technological skills over the last few years. Commendable, of course. Although, given your obsessions, also oftentimes dangerous."

"Dad, I get it. What's my side of the bargain? Aside from running to a safehouse like a fucking pussy, anyway."

"You mean a responsible young adult who understands what it would do to his father if something awful befell his son?"

I slumped back in my chair. "All right, I'm sorry. Go on."

"In exchange for me allowing this, assisting quietly, and not interfering in your relationship with Brianna Walker, in addition to going to the safehouse until the heat on you dies down, when you locate Malcolm Lynch, you will *not* launch a strike."

"What? No. No fucking way. No deal." I went to rise to my feet.

"Sit. Down," he ground out in that no-nonsense tone. The one that had his employees and business partners alike pissing themselves.

"There is no way in hell—"

"I didn't say you can't be there when a strike is underway. I merely said you can't launch it. You can't head it, you can't devise it. Myself and Curt Walker will see to that."

I sat back down, taken with his words. "You'll do what?"

He gestured around the diner. "Why do you think I

need this gift to approach him with? It's not just this, there is an entire lucrative chain of these roadside diners. All his now. This is sore subject matter for him, as it is for me. I need something positive to open with. Suffice to say, once I am able to smooth things over—especially the part where your slipup with going in hot at Kyle Trass caused you to put yourself, your friends, and *his* daughter in the crosshairs of Royce Humphrey—he'll recognize what I have. That this is our chance to finish what we started before Lynch disappeared off the map and was actually believed to have perished."

"If I agree to this, swear to me that you won't go in without me."

"Son, I know how much you need this… closure. There's so much rage and pain that the trauma of those weeks in their captivity caused you. But the truth is that it's rooted in shame. Shame that you couldn't escape on your own, that you couldn't spare Brianna. No matter how many times I tell you, or your many therapists told you, that it wasn't your fault, that you didn't possess the power to play the hero, that you were just a child, you won't accept it. So, I believe the way to solve that is to overpower the man himself—to put him down."

I stared at him in absolute incredulity. "You're really going to allow this to happen? Allow me to do this?"

He sighed and slumped back in his chair also. "I've tried everything else to help you to move past this. Nothing has worked. You've been pursuing this non-stop since you discovered that Lynch and his two cohorts didn't die that night as we'd all believed. Your instincts are drawing you in this direction. So this is what we'll try." He smiled sadly. "Perhaps it will finally give you and your girlfriend some peace."

"She's not just mine. Mason and Colt are involved with her too now."

"Interesting. I doubt very much that Curt will be pleased about that, so let's keep that aspect quiet until we're well underway with this mission."

"I'm all for not further complicating matters."

He arched an eyebrow. "Since when? You usually barrel through everything."

"Since it's not just me who stands to take the brunt of things now."

"You don't just mean the boys, you mean her."

I nodded. "Whatever it takes to protect her." I could feel him staring at me intently. "Although, that would be made easier if she was actually communicating with me right about now."

"She found out you kept Lynch's survival from her?"

"No. Something else… a miscommunication I haven't gotten the chance to clear up yet."

"So she doesn't know at all?"

I scrubbed my hands over my face. "No. *Christ.*"

"Levi."

"I just… it took everything I had just to get her to admit it had even happened, then to pull her close to me."

"Tell her as soon as I let you take your leave."

"I will. I just wanted something concrete first, a location to move on against Lynch."

"Life isn't about perfect circumstances, or things lining up the precise way you intend. Sometimes you must work with what you have." He shifted his weight. "Also, be careful with how you *protect* a woman like her who was subjugated most of her life by overwrought misogyny. She deserves the right to a choice. *You* don't get to decide what's best for her, she does. If things go south there, then you be there for the fallout to support her. That's the most interference you can have, Levi. Trust me on that. If I'd done the same with your mother, things may have turned out differently." He shook his head to himself. "After you were born, though, I became extremely overbearing in my mission to protect you both. It was too much. She couldn't breathe. She couldn't stand being a part of our high-pressure world, she felt like she was under a microscope, and with no life of her own outside of my shadow and domineering influence. So she ran, she left us. Sometimes good intentions aren't enough, not when the execution is all wrong."

I took the weight of his words in.

"I understand." I reached out and took his hand. "Thank you, Dad. And not just for the advice. Thank you for not reprimanding me for the lie of the internship, thank you for supporting me with something so fucked-up like this. For all of it."

"You're my flesh and blood. I'd do nothing less to give you peace of mind." He eased from me then rose to his feet and rounded the table toward me.

I pushed out of my seat to meet his approach.

And then he threw his arms around me.

Emotion overtook me and I held him to me tightly.

"Be careful. Swear it to me. Swear it."

"I swear, Dad."

And, for once, I would actually hold myself to that.

8

~Mason~

The air moved.

I felt it before it connected.

A palm struck my cheek, a stinging pain radiating across my skin, the force of the blow making my head snap to the side.

I staggered from the surprise of it, then swung my head toward Lev. "Did you just fucking bitch-slap me?"

"You're lucky. The way I'm feeling right now, anything more hardcore and I wouldn't be able to stop with how unbelievably pissed I am at you."

"I told you I had to act quickly."

"Not like this!" he roared, getting in my face.

Colt was there just in time, throwing out his hands either side, one to each of us. "Take it down and talk it out. Lev, you were right the first time, anything more hardcore and you *won't* be able to stop."

This time, Lev didn't simply back down because Colt was there between us.

"You kidnapped a former kidnapping victim! Somebody who's still traumatized by it! Are you fucking serious?

What the motherfucking hell was going through your head when you made that decision?"

"The situation was too hot, we needed to get her out of there. And because of what *you* did, she wasn't speaking to us, so I had to use other methods."

He shoved Colt out of the way, then ran me into one of the many trees lining the driveway of the mountain lodge. "You've hurt her by doing this! You don't get to make the final decision when it comes to her! You don't, Mason! You fucking *don't!*"

I choked as he wrenched me by my pale-blue Henley shirt and slammed me back against the tree over and over again. "You told me," I rasped. "You told me to make sure I did whatever it took. This was it."

He stilled, his fingers fisted in my shirt.

And then he shocked me as he abruptly released me and staggered back, letting out an awful pained cry that echoed hauntingly through the night.

He collapsed to his knees and hung his head, burying his face in his hands.

"It's ruined… it's all ruined."

Colt and I exchanged an incredulous look.

Levi didn't break down.

Ever.

Even when he was upset or hurt, it came through in rage and reckless actions.

Not… this.

As Colt ran to him and knelt down beside him, emotion clogged my throat at seeing Lev like this.

"It's not ruined," Colt was telling him, as I pushed off the wall, adjusted my shirt, then walked to them.

"It is," Levi uttered, in a broken voice we hadn't heard from him since that day we'd come to see him in the hospital after Roman and his team had rescued him six years ago. But Bree… she brought emotion out in Levi that we'd thought had been long lost. She was doing the same to me as well, she was focusing Colt with the duet, and he'd kept that up with altering the makeup of *Mythic Cry* and songwriting non-stop.

She was changing everything.

But with everything good, there was usually an element of bad to balance it out.

And this pain because he was feeling things again that weren't just rage and recklessness of his adrenaline junkie ways was the bad side for him.

"You don't understand," he was murmuring as I reached them and stood there as Colt stroked his back, trying to comfort him. "It took so long and *everything* I had to bring Brianna to me, to draw her close, to get her to trust me. Then with Chloe's revelation that was jeopardized. Now my actions bringing Royce right to our doors. Not telling her that they're even alive, let alone that I was pursuing them this entire time… now Mason doing this and actually kidnapping her… it's fucking destroyed."

I reached down and stroked his hair. "Levi, I won't allow it to be over. I'll fix this. I'll take the blame that's due me and I'll spare you. The rest we can work out."

He looked up at me with pained eyes swimming with emotion. "Why?"

"Why what?"

"Why would you do that?"

"Because you're correct. I shouldn't have made a unilateral decision. Colt was right on. I shouldn't have. I just… the idea of them coming at her and succeeding this time… I panicked."

"You panicked? *You?*" Colt asked, as shocked as Lev clearly was.

"I did," I confirmed. "I was wrong. I was so fucking

wrong. And I'm sorry. Lately… I'm fucking up everywhere. With you coming back, Lev, and starting up *Hex* again, I saw hope for the first time that I could do it this time, that I could take my father. And it's clouded everything, it's twisted me… that desperation."

"Mason," Colt said, reaching out to me as well and rubbing my shoulder. "You're not infallible, not superhuman, we get it. We'll work on it. *Together.*"

I nodded sadly and told Levi, "I'm so sorry. I *love* you, brother."

"I love you too. Both of you." He reached out and took my hand. "But I can't bring it back from this with Brianna. And I just… I can't go back to how it was when I was trying to win her over, before she was in our lives, before I finally had her as mine. I can't return to that emptiness. I should've told her much sooner. I didn't want to hurt her and I didn't think she was ready. But my dad told me that it's not my call to make. I get that now, but it's… it's too fucking late."

"It's not," Colt and I said in unison.

"We'll sort it all out," Colt added.

"No," Lev said, shaking his head. "She'll never forgive me for this."

A shadow fell over the area and a sweet voice rang out.

"It seems like you've already learned your lesson, *lovely.*"

I took her in, her silky, long black hair all disheveled in a sexy, bedhead way, contrasting sharply with the bubblegum-pink robe Colt had wrapped her in as we'd put her to bed in the master suite upstairs when we'd arrived up here a couple of hours ago after I'd gotten that call from Roman Knight telling me that he was on board and reinforcing that we needed to head to *Boreas* ASAP, that Levi would be sent along too.

I stepped back as she went to Levi and smiled at Colt who rose to his feet to give her some room.

She leaned in and sank her fingers into Levi's hair, then planted a soft kiss on the top of his head. "Nothing is ruined. I'm not happy about what you did, but we'll talk it out."

Levi looked stunned as she helped ease him back to his feet.

He was throwing his arms around her in the next moment and holding her tightly.

I walked away and leaned against the tree Lev had run me into earlier, letting them have their moment that Levi desperately needed.

Colt looked on smiling with relief for him. Always such a sweetheart, no matter what.

After a few moments, they eased apart, and then Bree was glaring at me.

I tensed, ready for her to lay into me.

The way it happened wasn't what I'd been expecting at all, though, as in the next second, the glint of something caught my eye, a moment before she tossed a blade through the air.

It tore into the left sleeve of my shirt and drove into the trunk of the tree.

I jolted and looked to see that it hadn't even scraped the skin of my arm, not even a little.

I didn't get to register much more than that when she stormed toward me, then threw one hell of a punch that had me grunting, my head snapping to the side.

She grasped my jaw. Hard.

"When you wake up for the next few days and see a black eye staring back at you in the mirror, you'll remember your mistake, your fucked-up decision to kidnap me like that. It will sink in, just like it will every time you put on this shirt going forward and find that knife tear in it. Repetition is the key to imprinting on your memory." She yanked the knife free and stepped back, spinning it expertly in her hand. "Don't do anything like that again."

"Jesus," I heard Colt utter.

She caught Levi's eye and nodded. "Yes, this is my dark side. A glimpse into it, anyway." She looked back at me. "You came close to bringing it to the surface when you marked me and I had to retaliate. But kidnapping me, of all fucking things, *that* really did it." Her attention turned to all of us, eyeing us in turn. "Good thing, huh? Considering what the fuck has happened?"

Before we could get a word out, she called to Colt, "Mind showing me around?"

"Sure," he said, walking to her in a stunned state that matched mine.

"Thanks." She looked out at me, glaring again. "I need time to calm down, then we'll talk."

With that, she took off with Colt at her side, already starting to talk her ear off about the history of the place, and the amenities we had here.

"Jesus," I breathed, slumping back against the tree.

Levi came to me and inspected my shirt. "Damn, her accuracy is on point. Pun intended." He eyed me curiously. "Didn't know she had that in her, did you?"

"And you did," I realized from his tampered down reaction to it. "You seriously didn't think to tell me that the woman we're falling for is a human weapon?"

"I figured you wouldn't take it so well. You know, pretty much the way you're taking it now?"

I scrubbed my hand over my face. "Actually, with what we're up against, her unleashing this part of her couldn't have come at a better time."

Levi wrapped his arm around me. "Come. Let's get you some ice for that eye."

"Lev—"

"We'll figure it out, brother. It's okay. Like you told me, it'll all be okay."

Things had shifted.

Because of her.

Because of us coming together.

And as antagonistic as they currently were because of certain decisions made, I still actually believed that for the first time in so long that things actually would be okay.

9

~Brianna~

They were alive.

The demons were still alive.

"It took so long and everything I had to bring Brianna to me, to draw her close, to get her to trust me. Then with Chloe's revelation that was jeopardized. Now my actions bringing Royce right to our doors. Not telling her that they're even alive, yet alone that I was pursuing them this entire time."

I couldn't believe it.

It just didn't compute.

Not yet.

I needed time to get past the numbed stage of it, I figured.

That was how I dealt with shocking news—I went into a numbed state until my brain had the chance to process it.

The thing was, I didn't have a lot of time. I needed the boys to fill me in on the details of it all as soon as possible, given that an attack had taken place on my apartment that Levi had managed to stave off.

For now.

Those guys, they didn't stop.

I shuddered. They certainly hadn't when Levi and I had been in captivity.

Maybe going into this talk with the boys, being numbed to it would be better, a way to take things in at an emotional distance, objectively.

Rationally and with logic and reason leading the way.

I sucked in a sharp breath and blinked back to the moment, to the beauty ahead of me.

Boreas.

That was what the boys called this winter lodge in the mountains.

Their safehouse.

Colt had informed me that it was named after a Greek God of the north wind.

He'd also told me that this was where the three of them had retreated to five years ago after what they'd termed *the incident.* It was a bit more than an incident, but I got their need not to emphasize that when they discussed it.

It seemed that them never really discussing it, except when it came up in bursts of frustration for Mason was much more of a detriment to all three of them than actually talking it out and recalling what had happened.

I'd even noticed a little of the weight bearing down on Mason's shoulders easing after he'd confessed to me what had happened back then.

The thing was, he needed to recollect it with Levi. He needed to process it in a bid to let go of the blame he put on him, something that impacted their relationship even to this day.

And *I* needed to take my own advice and process what I'd found out earlier after waking up with one hell of a headache and exhaustion still plaguing me from being chloroformed and transported up here against my will and without my knowledge—kidnapped.

Malcolm Lynch and his two cohorts were still alive.

I needed to know more, not just the outline—not even really the CliffsNotes—that I'd overheard earlier when I'd walked up to hear the boys arguing, then Levi collapsing in so much pain.

I hadn't seen him that way since our captivity and it had cut into me terribly. I hadn't been able to stand it. It was why I'd absolved him so quickly.

But we weren't done.

We all needed to talk it out.

And we had to restore the trust that had taken a hit.

I drew in a calming, centering breath, then took another gulp of my coffee that Colt had made for me in the kitchen after our tour earlier. I needed it to offset the lingering effects of the chloroform as well as a couple of painkillers Levi had given me to dispel the nasty headache that had plagued me.

I looked out at the spectacular view of the snow-covered mountains surrounding the winter lodge on all sides.

"How are you feeling?"

I turned to see Mason standing there leaning against the closest of the three doors that led back into the house from the wraparound balcony. His arms were folded across his chest and he was still dressed in that sexy shirt that clung tightly to his broad, muscular body, the one I'd torn with my blade earlier. The bruising was more prominent now beside his left eye from my punch.

"Getting better by the moment." I raised my coffee mug. "And by the cup full."

"I'm sorry."

"I know you are."

"What can I do to make it better, except swear to you that I'll *never* do anything like that again?"

"Stop making unilateral decisions and moves on behalf of the rest of us."

"Done."

I cocked an eyebrow. "Just like that?" I shook my head. "You can't really make that promise, because of your trust issues—with Levi. When things heat up and the pressure is on, you'll default to the autonomous route because of that. You think involving him and *his* judgment is a risk. You need to talk about what happened five years ago and find out where he was really coming from, how it came to that, and what his thought process was. That way, even if you hate it, you can understand it, and determine how to ensure something like that never happens again." I took a sip from my coffee. "I'm also here to assist with that."

"You help him to see reason. He respects you."

"He respects you too. If he didn't, he wouldn't have come home to you and Colt. He could have also taken *Hex* from you and gone it alone, but he respected your leadership—until you marked me, of course, and lost control because the two of you weren't sharing control of *Hex*."

"You're right, I did lose control," he actually admitted.

I sighed. "Levi just doesn't trust that you won't automatically stop him from whatever he intends to accomplish at any given time if it doesn't toe the line completely. He's afraid, Mason. He's afraid you'll cage him." I smiled sadly. "Like you've caged yourself."

He took a few moments to take my words in.

And then he gave a nod. "Well, we're stuck up here for a while just the four of us, so it's as good a time as any to have that difficult conversation."

"Good." I finished the last gulp of my coffee then walked to him to head back into the house. "Let's have the other conversation now. Time to get me up to speed."

"Yeah. I'll get the other two."

Before he could, I snatched his arm, holding him to me.

Our gazes collided.

"Don't ever fuck with me like that again."

"I won't. I'm sorry, Bree. Really sorry."

I gave a nod. "All right, then let's move on."

"I'd like nothing more."

I went to move past him, but he called out, "Wait."

I stopped and eyed him in question.

"You want me to have that difficult conversation with Levi, I need to know, I need to understand... out front there, how did you forgive him so easily?"

"Simple. Everything Levi does actually comes from a good place. Things get twisted up for him because he's been in survival mode since the kidnapping. All that rage and pain and recklessness, it's him trying to find peace and love. Now he's found the latter in me, you might have noticed the edge has been taken off. There has been a change in him."

"I have noticed it, yeah."

"Unfortunately, it can't be more than that until he feels peace. For him, with this revelations about Lynch still being alive and out there, we now know that peace is putting that sick bastard down. Taking back the power he lost six years ago to him, to the whole situation."

He took my words in, nodding along. "How are you doing with that revelation? I can't even imagine the shock it is for you."

"I guess we'll see when we get into it all in a few moments."

⸻

"MY KNIFE, BABY?" Levi said, as he stopped in front of where I was sitting in one of the armchairs in the living room and held out his hand.

The whole place was so homely with a rustic edge.

The walls were made of cedar logs which had a calming scent and vibe right off the bat. Cozy shag rugs lined the hardwood floors. Gray oversized couches and armchairs had plaid throws and lots of cushions. Rustic rounded wood furniture was throughout the house along with real wood-burning fireplaces.

I reached into the pocket of my robe and handed it back to him within the sheath.

He surprised me then as he pocketed it in his cargo pants, but then drew out another sheathed knife. "This is now yours."

I frowned as I took it from him.

"It's weighted better, sharper too, accuracy unmatched." The corner of his mouth turned up. "Although seeing you wield the other one earlier made it clear accuracy is your jam."

"Seriously?" Mason said from the couch where he and Colt were sitting, Colt lounging back with his arm behind his head, while Mason was sitting on the edge rigidly straight. "Are you doing this to—"

"To what? Twist the knife?" Levi asked, laughing.

Colt burst out laughing too. He quickly slapped his hand to his mouth, took a moment, then told Mason, "My bad. I couldn't help it. Sorry, darlin'."

Mason rolled his eyes at him, but then shot a sour look Levi's way.

Holding up his hand, Levi told him, "No, seriously, I'm doing it for two reasons. One is to take the edge off what happened outside. And, voila, it's already working. The second is because after those skills I witnessed out there, our woman needs a knife worthy of said skills—and her."

"Thank you," I said, pulling it from the sheath and taking in its beauty, feeling the weight in my hand, then spinning it around, enjoying the boys looking on in awe as they saw my skill.

It wasn't something I'd planned to bring out unless I'd had to—which I'd felt like I'd needed to earlier to make it clear to Mason that not only shouldn't I be trifled with, but that I wasn't a porcelain doll that required such an insane level of protection.

Point made. Pun intended.

"This is really sweet," I told Levi.

He beamed down at me. "Glad you like it."

"Weapons as presents. Never thought of that as a gift option before," Colt mused.

"Hey, I know our woman. She likes that," Levi said. "It's not the first time. I know about the 26 you keep for protection."

"26?" Mason said. "As in a *Glock* 26?" He shook his head at Levi. "You're the only one who calls them just by the digits."

"Not the only one, but sure. And, yeah."

"Of course you know about Tommy giving that to me," I said, with a roll of my eyes.

"Your ex?" Colt chimed in.

"Her predatory ex, yeah," Levi clarified.

"He wasn't—" I stopped myself. "Let's get down to it here, all right?"

"She's right, focus up," Mason said, backing me.

"Sorry," Levi said, although I could tell that it was one of those times where he didn't actually feel sorry at all. He was stoked that he'd given me a present.

Mason snapped his fingers in front of Colt's face as he was staring off into space. "Focus, brother."

Colt blinked. "Sorry, I was thinking of gift ideas."

"What? Why?" Mason asked.

"Because I keep getting upstaged by the two of you. First Lev with the butterfly nightlight, then you with the sandwiches gesture, then this knife thing. My duet recording is nothing compared to that."

"You're wrong," I said, stretching out my hand to rub his arm on the adjacent couch. "It was heartfelt and really sweet. Don't sell yourself short."

"Really?"

"I promise."

He smiled out at me and kissed my knuckles. "You really are a cutie."

"Beneath the dark angel thing," Mason countered.

"Don't you forget it," Levi told him.

"Levi," I groused.

"Right, yeah. Getting down to business. Filling you in."

"Start with Chloe and we'll go from there."

He shoved a hand through his curls and sauntered away so he was standing in front of the couch and the armchair, facing the three of us. "All right, so, yeah, it was my doing getting Chloe out of the picture. Out of Stonewell U and the town. *But* it wasn't so I could remove an obstacle."

"Because you're never about that," Mason said with dripping sarcasm.

Levi tossed him a look. "She wasn't an obstacle to *me*. She's Brianna's friend, I didn't *want* to take that from her, that support system. Even though I'm not a fan of her being a fucking trainwreck who you ended up having to basically babysit so often."

"Levi!" I cried.

He held up his hand. "Sorry. Just bringing the honesty."

"Jeez," Colt said, shaking his head.

"Get back to it, Lev," Mason told him. "Maybe, without that sort of thing."

Levi sucked in a breath, then went on, "As I was saying, yeah, even if I had seen her as an obstacle, it wouldn't have stopped me anyway. Even if she'd still been around, I would've found my way to you. You know it as well as I do."

I nodded. That couldn't be denied in any shape or form.

"The reason I did it was to protect her, *because* she's your friend. Your only friend at the time, until the three of us came into the picture actually. I wanted her safe for you, out of the line of fire. I'd planned to tell you about my investigation into those fuckers sooner, but it took so much for you to come around to even admitting the kidnapping had happened, to warm up to me, that I delayed it. Again and again. And once I felt like it was time, I was afraid to screw things up, to hurt what we'd finally started to build. So, in my mind, danger would come our way, retaliation from my pursuit of Lynch, and I didn't want them to go after the only person close to you at the time. So, yeah, I got her out. I figured you'd still keep in touch and maintain the friendship, even if it couldn't be in person anymore."

"Wow, that's so sweet," Colt commented.

"Sweet?" Mason questioned.

Colt lifted a shoulder. "You know, in Lev's distorted way." He looked out at me. "You've gotta get that it *was* super sweet in his mind. He doesn't always think like regular people, he can't help it."

I smiled. "I know, it's okay."

"It is?" Levi asked, his worry about it very pronounced, as he kept clicking his nails, and shifting his weight.

"Yes, I believe you had good intentions. *But* it was extremely underhanded. Although, that was before you and me reached an understanding and you stopped doing that sort of thing."

"I made you a promise and I'm trying my hardest to keep it, even though it really doesn't come naturally to me."

"I know. I know it doesn't. I've seen you trying."

"And?"

"And, keep it up," I said, grinning at him.

"He got off way easier than me," Mason groused.

"Easier?" Levi said, turning to face him head-on. "She cost me a lot of money from a fight, punched me in the face, then kicked me in the balls."

Mason and Colt stared at me wide-eyed.

I shrugged. "Told you I'm not a damsel in distress."

"Damn," Colt whistled.

Mason chuckled. "Well, I feel better now."

"Good, glad we could assist," Levi bit back at him. "Can we move on with filling her in now? You good? Or do you need more affirmations and hand-holding?" He stepped forward. "Want me to give you a kiss?"

"I'm good, but we can keep it on the table for later, seeing as though you brought it up."

"Hmm, interesting."

Colt broke the strange tension between them and planted a kiss on Mason's cheek.

"There. Now moving on, guys."

Mason grinned. "Thank you, gorgeous."

Levi chuckled.

"How long have you known Lynch and the other two were alive?" I asked, unable to hold the question in any longer, as much as I enjoyed their banter that flip-flopped between lighthearted playfulness and aggressive tension.

It jarred Levi and he spun toward me. "Too long." He sighed. "Three years, give or take. Three years ago was when chatter first reached me, but it took a hell of a long time for me to get something concrete beyond whispers and rumors."

"That's why you really left for a year," Mason said.

"What about the internship?" Colt asked.

"A smokescreen. Sorry, cupcake. I couldn't pass up the leads. It took some time following the path I'd found a thread for, but it led me to Lynch."

A shudder rolled through me. "You actually saw him?"

"I did, but I couldn't fucking well act. He was surrounded by thirty of his guys at the time. If I'd moved in, I would've fallen, and there was no guarantee that I could've taken him down with me in the process."

"If he'd seen you, Levi," I choked. "What he would've done to you... oh my God."

"Hence my retreat, baby. So I came back here. I wanted Mason to mobilize *Hex* to give him a taste of power to distract him so I could pursue you, because I knew he'd be suspicious of me suddenly coming back. Just me being back would have him on my back... because of the history of my recklessness, me returning would be jarring to the peace and quiet he'd endured without me here."

"Peace and quiet... more like unbelievable boredom," Colt said.

"All well predicted and deduced," Mason told Levi.

Levi acknowledged his rare compliment, then told me, "I'd heard that you'd come to Stonewell U just after I'd left. The urge to go to you and come home right away was overwhelming. Knowing you were finally within reach and out from under your father's thumb… it was something I'd been waiting on for so long. *But* I wanted to come back and reintroduce myself to you with something major to tell you. That being that I'd taken out Lynch. When that couldn't happen, I pivoted, deciding that I'd come to you and recruit you to my cause, get your help. I knew all about your skills and resources, I just hadn't wanted to involve you if I hadn't needed to, because I also knew about your trauma. And when I came back here, I saw that it was worse than I'd even imagined because you were in such denial that you'd completely reinvented yourself and thrown away the old you—the real you, baby."

"Shit, Lev," Colt said. "You must've felt so alone. I'm so sorry, brother."

"It's okay, I'm not anymore."

I beamed out at him. "No, you're not. Neither am I. Neither are any of us."

"I'm so sorry we were all forced to come here, though, to lay low like this."

"Because of Royce Humphrey. What happened there?" I asked.

"I tracked down Kyle Trass to get confirmation on the name of the organization Lynch was using now. *Osiris.*"

"Apt," I grunted.

"Exactly my thoughts." He sucked in a breath. "I kept the fucker alive in case I needed to use him down the road. While Mason and I were using Royce's network to track Lynch through, making him appear as though he was the one pursuing Lynch with the intent to rip the growing power of *Osiris* out from under his former boss, Kyle and Royce came into contact earlier than their usual monthly check-in call or meeting, and it tipped Royce off to *me.*"

"All right," I murmured, my thoughts wandering now as I felt that numbness wearing off from all the slap-you-in-your-face reality I was being inundated with. "That's everything?"

"My dad is involved now. He's going to reach out to yours and once I get a location, they're going to devise and launch a strike with us in tow against Lynch, and we'll decimate the fucker and his rising organization. We'll take out Royce and Kyle too. In the meantime, while we're at the safehouse and I'm working to get a lock on Lynch again through covert means so my dad and yours aren't linked to it which could risk Lynch targeting them, my dad has put out word that I was gravely injured in that attack I thwarted at your apartment."

"Jeez," I uttered.

"We left the guys alive, Lev," Mason pointed out. "I mean, it's feasible that you took a hit and kept fighting through it, but it's still a reach that Royce might not believe."

"They're not alive anymore," Levi told us. "Roman took care of that."

"What?" Mason said.

"With his underhanded business partners?" Colt asked.

"No. Personally. It was where he was headed when we parted ways and he sent me up here to reconnect with you guys."

"Jesus fuck," Mason breathed. "Roman Knight going the personal route... that's another level."

"Well, this whole thing hurt him too. Like it did Curt."

I rose to my feet, all of it hitting me at full force now. "Okay," I only just managed to voice. "Thanks for the... the report. It's... good. We'll... I need to take a breather."

With that, I rushed out of the room without another word.

10

~Levi~

Five and a Half Years Ago

A LITERAL KICK to the ass had me crashing onto my elbows and knees.

Damn, that was gonna leave one hell of a bruise.

It didn't matter.

I didn't give a crap about the punishment that I took.

I'd take whatever I had to in order to achieve what I needed to here.

What I had to.

Vindication.

Proof that I was up to the task, that I could handle what I had planned.

I swiftly rolled onto my back.

Just in time as his combat boot came at me.

Combat boot—unheard of for the CEO of Knightsridge Engineering. But Roman Knight had really come prepared. I couldn't deny that I was feeling the full effect of that either.

But I did what I'd learned to in that hellscape and pushed it down so I could keep moving forward.

So I could keep fighting.

I twisted away before his boot could connect and used the rolling momentum to spring back to my feet, assuming a fighting stance.

I'd just landed stably when he threw his fist lightning-fast and clocked me across the side of the face.

"Fuck," I muttered, as my head snapped to the side and I tasted blood on my lips.

"I told you that I had it covered, that Curt and I are handling it, Levi."

"It has to be me."

"The most important thing is that the threat is destroyed."

"They need punishment."

"And, believe me, they'll have it. They took my son. They took you from me. That won't stand. They'll be punished severely. And then they'll be disposed of."

"What if Malcom Lynch and his guys go to ground before you manage to track them down?"

"I have my people on it. I'm pulling on a lot of resources to make it happen and to fast-track it. Curt Walker is even waging a war against them, crossing all sorts of lines and former allies in the process."

"It sounds bad. Isn't it going to bring down his motorcycle club?"

"If we don't find them soon, it's possible."

I wiped the blood out of the corner of my mouth. "All the more reason to have him stand down. You find them for me, and I'll deliver justice."

"No."

"Dad, I've been training to—"

"You've been doing it for a few months only, Levi."

"I'm a fast learner. You know that."

"It's still not enough time. You're still a boy."

"I stopped being a boy the moment I was taken by those mother-fuckers."

Emotion plagued his features so similar to mine. "It makes me sick that it happened, and I'm so sorry, son. But I'm not about to let you risk your life in the name of this vengeance. It will be seen to for you."

"No!" I roared, my temper exploding like it kept doing ever since I'd been pulled out of that hellscape.

I'd never been an angry kid before. But what I'd seen and also had done to me, what had been done to her, had caused that in me. I could barely control it at the best of times.

But for what I planned to do, rage would function as power.

Power that would rip those fuckers apart.

"Levi, there's still a lot you need to learn."

"I don't care! I can do this! I can, Dad!"

In the next moment, he socked me in the gut.

I choked and doubled over, but he didn't give me any time to recover before he then swept his leg at my ankles, ripped me off my feet, then reached down and dragged me across the room.

I was gasping for breath as he threw me up against the wall and pinned me to it with his full body weight, looming over me in the process.

I screamed and struggled wildly against him. "Dad, stop! Get the fuck off me! You're not playing fair!"

"There is no fair," he rumbled. "Not in a real-world fight."

I didn't want to hear it.

I didn't want his words to seep into me and undermine my conviction and my plan.

I pushed against him, trying to free myself.

I tried every move I'd learned over the last few months.

Nothing worked.

Nothing could help me to escape.

Nothing could move him.

"You're not strong enough, Levi," he told me firmly, yet calmly, a complete and jarring contrast to me in those moments. "Not yet."

Rage bled into frustration.

And as I kept struggling, kept trying to fight, that frustration was tainted by exhaustion and was stripped away to leave the awful thing I'd been trying to avoid, to shut off, all this time.

Pain.

"I can't… I can't stop it, Dad. It won't… they won't… they won't leave me."

He pushed off me and uttered sadly, "I know."

"I don't know how to let it go without doing this, without hurting them back."

"You will. In time. All this focus on that is toxic, son. Let me help you to put your concentration on the bright future you have ahead of you."

How could I even think about any sort of future when I was trapped in the past, in that room at the abandoned police station.

The shackles might not be physical anymore, but they were still there.

"Have you heard anything else about her?"

"Brianna Walker?"

"Yeah."

"She's recovering at the clubhouse with her father."

"I want to see her."

He shook his head. "It's not a good idea."

"Dad, we were there together, we—"

"That's the issue. She's not doing well, Levi. Seeing you could trigger her and make it all the worse. She needs time, just like you do. Besides, she's under lockdown, her father has round-the-clock protection on her."

"Fuck."

I pushed off the wall and he wrapped his arms around me.

"Let's get you cleaned up."

"All right, yeah."

"*I got you those computer components that you wanted, so you can put all this pent-up energy into that.*"

I forced a smile that I really wanted to feel, but couldn't. "That sounds good. Thank you."

As we made our way out of our home gym, my dad fell into that sad and contemplative state that he had been since I'd been liberated from that nightmare. He was so distraught about what had happened to me and despite his efforts to hide it, I knew him too well not to be able to see through to the truth.

The fact that something that awful had happened to his son was bad enough for him.

He loved and adored me so much and we were so close, I was basically his world. Everything else came second to him, even his multi-million dollar business empire.

But that I'd come back haunted so much by it all to such a degree that I couldn't see past it was another, because it was lingering, it was changing me. And I knew he was so very worried that it had actually damaged me irreparably, that the son he'd known had gone and been replaced by something else.

A shadow of what he had been.

And he wasn't wrong there.

Those demons had taken something from me during that hell.

They'd also infected me.

With fear.

Powerlessness.

Despair.

Rage.

And the hardest thing of all to shake—shame.

Shame that I hadn't been able to stop it, that those things had been done to me.

That those things had been done to her.

The angel among the demons had saved me, she'd sacrificed for me, she'd hurt for me.

All because I hadn't been strong or capable enough to save myself. Or her.

How the fuck did you even begin to figure out how to live with all that?

My dad wanted me to focus on my future.

My friends, Mason, and Colt did too.

But as hard as I tried to push forward, the past and those brutal memories were locked around me constantly pulling me back.

"You were right, Dad. I'm not strong enough to go after them. I'm not ready."

"You don't need to be. It's being handled."

"Yeah, I know. It is, it'll be dealt with."

He ruffled my hair. "I've taken the next couple of weeks off to spend time with you. We'll get you past this."

I smiled back.

But once again I didn't feel it.

And I knew in my bones that getting past it wasn't an option for me.

Not until I was ready to face what had damaged me.

And I would be ready.

I'd build myself up.

I wouldn't stop.

I'd do whatever I needed to in order to get to that place that meant I could come at those motherfuckers.

I'd take back the power they stole from me and shove that shame back down their throats where it belonged.

Because the inescapable truth was, I knew that I'd never feel peace until I destroyed them.

~Colton~

I blocked the doorway to the bedroom we'd assigned to Bree. "Leave her, brother."

Lev's gaze was unsteady as he looked at me, clearly wanting to just shove me out of the way and go after Bree, but resisting because he didn't want to do anything aggressive to me, and likely because he was hesitating on his course of action itself too.

Mason was at my side in the very next moment, reminding him, "You rushed out right after she blew out of the living room and she told you she needed some space."

"Well aware, brothers, but it's been two hours now. She didn't even come down when we texted her for lunch. Sandwiches and chocolate chip cookies—her favorites."

"She obviously just needs some more time," Mason assured him. "Probably at least a couple more hours, maybe the day, Lev."

Despite his calm words, it was clear to me that he was stressed as hell and worried just like Lev, just like we all were.

He even had a box of Cheerios with him and he shoved his hand inside and came away with a handful that he then stuffed into his mouth.

When he caught me looking, he tossed me some and I caught them in my mouth easily. Years of practice where I'd sit with him when he was stressed and binge eating them and I'd have him toss me some wherein I'd catch them in my mouth to entertain him. It always managed to get him to at least crack a smile.

As it did now.

Lev went around me, dodging me in that skillful way of his.

But instead of doing what I'd thought and reaching into his pocket where he always kept a pick set, he just pressed his ear to the door.

And then he stepped back, telling us, "Sounds like she's taking a shower."

"So, let's just leave her to it, yeah?" I said.

However reluctantly, he still gave a nod. "Yeah. All right."

I gave his shoulder a squeeze. "Look, brother, it's been a lot for her. Finding out the likes of Lynch is alive and kicking, even trying to reclaim power, is major for her, as I'm sure it was for you when you first found out. And we get that you want to share that shock and fallout with her, and we're sure you will. But you had time to process it on your own first, you've gotta give her the same."

"It's been a lot for all of us coming up here too, so that's compounding things," Mason added, helping me out. "Being displaced, knowing what's coming, it requires some adjustment. For you too, Lev."

"Yeah, right on," I agreed. "So, let's all take a beat. The rest of the day. Mason, head to the bookshelf in the living room. There's that Dreiser book you were only halfway through last time, *Sister Charlotte.*"

"*Sister Carrie.*"

"Right. And, Lev, head out to the shed. You can finish up that spice spinning thingy you were making for the pantry before we had to leave here earlier than expected last time."

"And you?" Mason asked.

"I've got my old acoustic up here. I'll play a little, write some songs."

"Sounds good."

With that, we went our separate ways, taking the space and processing time and, honestly, the day to just chill and decompress.

And, aside from some intense fucking, the best way I knew how to do that was through my music.

———

I'D BEEN BLOCKED for a couple of hours as I'd tried to clear my head of all the bullshit that was going on, but then I'd managed to sink into my music, finding comfort in that and accessing that inspirational headspace from all the bad and all the worry.

Actually *because* of that.

My inspiration had been our foursome and as soon as I'd tapped into that theme, the words had flowed and the melody had followed easily with an edgy, hard feel, my vocals fueling it with raw emotion.

"*Dangerous, feral, ruthless/ Far from toothless/ Dark horses to the rotten core/ We collided with a ball of sunshine/ Pink bubble-gum, cotton candy/ Vicious things tangling in the night—*"

I pulled up short when I registered movement over by

the big-ass shed where Lev was working within on his woodworking stuff.

I'd been sitting out here in the grass working away within sight of where Lev was at so that I could make sure he didn't succumb and try to head to Bree when she clearly needed a break from it all.

The three of us might have agreed to give her space, but Lev had a hard time sitting back and doing nothing at the best of times, let alone when it came to her.

Although he hadn't actually admitted it out loud, perhaps not even to himself, it was clear as the brightest day to me and Mason that he was in love with her.

Intense emotion like that wasn't exactly his thing—not positive ones, anyway. He was like Mason in that way. So it was hard for him.

I'd made a promise to myself to help him without giving too much direct interference.

I didn't want the two of them fucking things up with her, especially when Mason had already come close during a time when I hadn't been watching out for it.

She brought Lev a lot of happiness, something he'd needed for a long time.

Mason was feeling it too.

And as for me, I was already there and smitten with her. It wasn't a long jump from that to those three special words for me.

I liked what we were building as a foursome and I'd do whatever I could to ensure it didn't get fucked up.

I laid my guitar down carefully as I zoned in on the movement—harder to do now that it was dark outside in that area. I was fine with the lights from the porch a few feet from where I was at offering enough illumination for me to do my thing and make notes in my songwriting journal.

There!

It was Mason making his way toward the shed.

Huh.

I headed over there carefully when I saw him disappear inside.

I was just a couple of feet out when some small talk Mason had started up about the project Lev was working on reached me.

"It's nothing special, but it'll do. It's functional."

"Nothing special, Levi? Those intricate carvings and that detailing would beg to differ."

"It's just a revolving spice rack."

"Doesn't matter what it is, it's how it's made by you."

"You're buttering me up. Why?"

"Of course, that's usually your thing. Feels strange being on the receiving end, doesn't it?"

"Touché."

"I'm not exactly buttering you up, but I am trying to start this conversation we need to have off in a good, peaceful, calm way."

"Conversation?"

"Bree thinks we need to talk about what happened five years ago."

"She thinks we do?"

"All right, I do as well."

"So do I."

"Yeah?"

"It's been long overdue."

"I agree."

"I'm sorry, Mason."

"You're… say again?"

"That night when I went after those fuckers, I had tunnel vision. As soon as I realized Colt had followed me down thinking I was headed for a night out, I should've made a retreat. But… one of them was on the verge of beating me down after Colt's arrival distracted me

and I couldn't… it unleashed my bloodlust. Then you arrived and I saw it as the opportunity to finish the job and take them all with a powerhouse like you joining the fight, even with the element of surprise ruined and my original strategy fucked."

"Hold up, you actually had a strategy?"

"I did. I know you've always thought I just barreled in there like an angel of vengeance. But, no, I had a meticulous plan laid out. I'd known those guys were there for days and I'd taken the time to prepare, and to even create backups for my backups."

"Why didn't you ever tell me this?"

"Because I didn't think it mattered, it failed anyway. And, honestly, you weren't willing to listen, you'd made your judgments."

"I'm sorry."

"No, I get it. Like I just said, I should've retreated. But I just… I couldn't. I knew if I'd walked away with it unfinished after they'd managed to do damage to me, I'd regret it. More than just regret, I knew I wouldn't be able to live with it. With it happening again."

"Hold up. With what happening again?"

"The shame of being overpowered. Of being a victim. Of being helpless."

"You were far from helpless that night, Levi."

"And yet it would've felt that way if I hadn't followed through all the way. But… you taking that hit, getting shot… that's what's haunted me all these years. Traumatizing Colt too. I still see it, Mason. I just… I couldn't pull back once I'd tapped into my bloodlust like that, because of where it's rooted. In shame. Shame for not being able to stop any of what happened to Brianna and me in that hellhole for two weeks straight. The things they did… especially to her… I can't unsee it. I can't let it go. Sometimes I can't breathe with it, with that image of that useless boy owned by madmen. The demons haunt me each and every day."

I squeezed my eyes shut against Lev's agonized words.

"Lev—"

"You think I'm reckless and going after injustice and dangerous fuckers all these years, it sure seems that way, yeah. It was me trying to purge all of that shit from my system when I couldn't get to the culprits, the demons, themselves. But I also planned and prepared down to every little detail. And you may have noticed that I never failed, I was always victorious. As good a combatant as I am, that still wouldn't be possible through going in hot without any strategy. I'm meticulous with it, Mason. Like you. Just the act of actually going after people like that seems reckless on the surface."

"Why did you always have me believe that you were wholly reckless through and through, unhinged with it even?"

"For one, you'd made up your mind about me after the incident. But mostly because I never ever wanted you or Colt involved in anything like that again. I couldn't stand the idea of you being hurt like you were five years ago."

"Levi, I get that. I get all of it, believe it or not. But all this approach has done is driven a wedge between you and me and weakened our brotherhood. Knowing this now, it shows me that my worry all this time, trying to rein you in, it wasn't necessary. We could've worked alongside each other—safely, brother. The incident was clearly an anomaly given your other successes in the same vein. Not sheer luck or from wild brute force as I'd thought. Because of your strategies and planning. That changes everything for me, for us."

"Keeping things off your radar or misdirecting you seemed like the easiest option to allow me to do what I needed to do, while keeping you guys out of it."

"No more. From now on, we do things as one. No more of going it alone, Levi. No more battling against one another."

"I'd like that. It's been a long time—until Brianna came along—since I haven't felt alone."

"I'm so sorry."

"I'm sorry too."

"Brothers?"

"Brothers."

I smiled to myself and peered around to see them now embracing in an emotionally raw hug.

Holy shit.

Finally.

12

~Levi~

Talk about soothing on the muscles.

I'd forgotten just how incredible the hot springs here at *Boreas* were.

Just what I needed to relieve some of the lingering aches and pains from that last fight.

When you fought rapid-fire and brutally at the same time, it took a toll on your body.

Even mine, as fit as I was.

It had obviously been compounded by stress and the fact that I hadn't slept more than a couple of hours in the last seventy-two hours.

Tonight. Tonight, I would.

I hoped.

Making peace with Mason and finally seeing eye-to-eye on something that had seemed impossible for ages, was going a long way toward calming me enough where I could manage that.

Almost.

But there was also Brianna.

She was hurting and there was nothing I could do about it.

Well, nothing she'd allow me to do about it.

None of us.

Mason had reminded me that giving her the space she'd requested *was* us doing something about it.

Of course, that didn't compute with me.

Inaction never did.

But I was all about being a good team player and taking the cautious, smart route right now with things, so I'd managed to resist going to her, and I'd given her a breather.

As much as I loved the feel of the hot springs, actually relaxing for more than a couple of minutes was extremely difficult for me.

So, once again, I found myself texting the boys in our group chat.

Levi: Need me to fetch the first-aid kid yet?

Colt: Ye of little faith.

Mason: LOL. All good, brother.

He'd certainly been all about the *brother* since our peace talk in the shed a few hours ago.

I figured he was so overjoyed—and relieved—that we were in a really good place and sharing a deep under-standing that we hadn't had since the earlier days of our friendship before things had gotten so fucked up, that he was overcompensating with all the friendliness.

No matter, it would just take some time to settle.

Levi: So you actually kept to my frozen pizza idea for dinner then?

Colt: Pretty much.

Oh no.

Levi: Elaborate, cupcake.

Colt: Where's the trust, Hellraiser?

78

Levi: We're talking fire extinguisher territory, aren't we?

Colt: You wound me. Keep it up and I'm gonna need you to take away the sting.

Levi: You want my fingers wrapped around your cock for a bit, just say it. No need for emotional blackmail.

Mason: Don't get him worked up.

Colt: Too late. When Bree is out of her room she's gonna love it. Remember her reaction last time?

Levi: Vividly.

Mason: You fingering my ass got her off too, gorgeous.

Hmm. He was being open about his sexuality again.

It was a very good sign with him.

Levi: Get over yourselves. She just likes seeing other people pleasured. Heightens the freeing experience for her.

Colt: Don't be jealous of our anal play, Lev. Just say the word.

Mason: Not his scene.

Colt: Only doing it to Bree.

Mason: Exactly. So, Lev, we're good here. We'll be out in five or ten. Just have a relaxing time in the springs until we bring out dinner.

Levi: Sounds good. Appreciate it, brothers.

Colt: Always.

Mason: Got you.

I smiled and put my phone down on the slate tile at the side of the springs.

Then I sank back and reveled in the soothing warm, bubbling water, and the peace and quiet, along with the serene snowy view all around.

I closed my eyes and breathed it all in.

"Hey."

I blinked and looked to see what I first considered

could be an apparition, only illuminated a little in the darkness from the lights on inside the house and the pot lights on the stone steps that led up either side of the oval hot spring pool to the entry points to safely climb in.

But the more I looked, the more I realized she couldn't be more real standing there on the heated patio area wrapped only in her bubblegum-pink bathrobe, her black hair all wild and cascading about her face.

And those fucking mesmerizing whiskey-colored eyes of hers glinting back at me.

Before I could get a word out, she wrung her hands in front of her, looking all nervous as she said, "I'm sorry."

I frowned. "Sorry for what?"

"Hiding away for the last day."

"No need for apologies at all. You needed space and time to process all those revelations. We all get it."

"They do, but I know it's harder for you with the root of our connection. For me to cut you out——"

"Brianna, I really do get it. It is hard for me, yeah. But what mattered was what you needed." I smiled. "Not to say I didn't have moments of wanting to break down the door and barge on in to see you, but I managed not to with some help from the boys, because it was about what was best for you."

Her lip curled up into a soft smile. "Please. You wouldn't have broken down the door, you would've picked the lock."

I chuckled. "Damn straight."

"So, *you're* actually out here taking a beat, not keeping busy?"

"Seems impossible, huh?"

"Not impossible, but improbable, yes."

"Well, honestly, I've managed probably four minutes in the total time I've been out here of twenty minutes to actually not do anything. The rest has been me texting the guys and doing my college readings through the remote setup Mason managed to get sorted for us all while we're up here." I stretched my arms above my head and cracked my neck. "The boys are all about me relaxing and trying to clear my head with the work ahead of me regarding tracking Malcolm Lynch. I need to be on point. At my best."

"I can help with that."

"Yeah, I was planning on asking you. I know you had doubts about your coding skills when they came up against mine, but like I said, you can hold your own really well." I grinned. "Plus, I told you I'd teach you a few things and this is the perfect situation."

"While I appreciate that and I'll be right beside you there, I actually meant I can help you with the relaxing."

She opened her robe then shrugged it off her shoulders.

My cock jerked in my board shorts.

I drank in the sight of her in a hot-pink string bikini that was doing amazing justice to her curvy, compact body.

Spectacular.

"Mmm, baby, you come over here within my reach and *relaxing* isn't gonna be the word for what's gonna go down."

"We're with him on that," Colt's voice came from the patio doors.

I'd been so taken with Brianna that I hadn't even noticed him and Mason coming out onto the heated patio area carrying the food they'd prepared.

I noted that they'd thankfully kept to cooking three large frozen pepperoni pizzas.

Although they'd also made what looked like a Caesar Salad.

And I saw a Band-Aid stuck to Colt's left forearm.

"Really? How did you cut yourself *there?*" I asked, gesturing at it.

"The knife slipped out of my hand. No worries, it was just a slight nick, a scratch."

I looked to Mason for his confirmation, knowing well Colt's tendency to downplay his mishaps in the kitchen, because he really wanted to lose his bad cooking rep.

"Just a scratch for real," he confirmed with a grin.

That grin faltered when he stepped out after Colt and took in the sight of Brianna in her hot-as-sin string bikini. "Jesus fuck."

I chuckled. "Not subtle for once, huh?"

"How can I be, brother?"

Brianna's cheeks flamed. "Stop."

"Come here, *Wildflower,*" I said, holding out my hand to her and standing up in the water.

Her gaze heated as she took in my bare chest and my board shorts hanging low on my hips, a swirling red and black design.

Well, her reaction was probably mostly due to my hard-on pushing against them.

It had happened even before she'd shrugged off her robe, the moment she'd come out here.

That was how hard-up I'd been for her.

Because of our *disagreement* before all of this had gone down, it had been way too long since we'd had her.

Judging by the hooded gazes of Colt and Mason as they watched her walk up the stone steps toward me, they were feeling it too, right there with me.

That was proven in the next moment when they both hurriedly put the food down on the patio table, then stripped off their t-shirts.

Mason was wearing a pair of board shorts like me, just plain and pale blue.

And Colt had gone his usual way with a pair of turquoise and tight, almost speedo-like type trunks that emphasized everything rather than serving as any sort of real cover-up.

Brianna's eyes flamed as she took them in, and then she smirked slyly and made her way up to the hot springs toward me, swinging her hips in a sexy fucking way that had the three of us basically salivating over her.

Hell, when weren't we?

As soon as she sank into the water, I was there, pressing my palms down either side of her shoulders and crowding her against the edge.

I slicked my tongue over her neck, then nipped at it, making her throw her head back and essentially give herself over to me.

I was leaving marks all over her throat, her collarbone, her shoulders.

"More," she breathed.

"Your wish is our command, cutie," Colt spoke, dipping into the water then wading over to us, with Mason right behind him.

I eased back and Mason jerked down the cups of her bikini top, then shoved Colt's face into her breasts.

Fuck, yes.

Colt went wild, sucking on her soft flesh, then sucking her nipples, and rolling his piercing all fucking over until she was panting and moaning out and slapping her hands to the edge behind her to steady herself.

Mason held Colt there at his mercy in front of her, fisting his mohawk.

I watched his free hand disappear under the water and then Colt was jolting as Mason shoved his trunks down and started stroking the crack of his ass up and down.

He groaned into Brianna's breasts and pushed back on Mason, silently begging for more.

Mason was all too happy to oblige and I grinned as I saw his eyes aflame.

He was letting go, giving into his wild side, control and all that be damned.

"You're so fucking hot when you're begging for it in this sweet ass," he growled at Colt's ear, a moment before he stuffed two fingers deep inside his ass.

"Shit!" Colt cried into Brianna's breasts. "Yeah, Mason," his muffled words sounded.

The three of them going at it had me fisting my cock roughly.

Mason saw the state of me and released Colt's hair to grab my hand and tug me to him.

He brushed his lips over mine, sending a tremble of need through me at the heady eroticism of it.

I groaned as he licked the shell of my ear.

"Get her tight little ass ready for me."

Mmm.

"With fucking pleasure."

Brianna whimpered as Mason eased Colt away from her, still holding his fingers deep in his ass. He floated back, grunting as Mason held him against his chest and started pounding fast and deep, making Colt squirm as Mason banded his arm around him so he couldn't escape the sweet torment.

"Fuck! *Fuck!*"

"Good boy, take my fingers reaming your hot little ass. You're gonna watch as Lev does the same to our woman."

"Shit," Colt gasped, overcome.

I waded to Brianna and brushed my lips over hers.

She rose to it, tangling her fingers in my wet, curly hair

that was all over the place, and using it to hold me to her as she deepened the kiss.

Our tongues tangled, teeth gnashing, passion exploding between us and the needy atmosphere, the erotic spell enveloping us all, taking us over.

"Grab onto the edge with both hands and let yourself float on your stomach," I told her, somehow managing to summon enough control to pull from our kiss.

Caught up in it all and panting with it, she didn't hesitate for a moment, and turned around and grasped the edge, while letting her sexy body float behind her.

I grasped her thighs and spread her wide for me, then stepped between her legs.

She wiggled her toes at me, making me chuckle.

Laughing in the middle of sex? Yeah, only she could have me doing something like that.

"Ungh," Colt grunted as Mason jerked his fingers free from his ass. "Major tease," he groused.

Mason breathed him in. "Just getting you suitably worked up because I don't want you being sweet and gentle when we have you fill her throat with your big cock. You're gonna throat-fuck her just the way she likes it. Rough and wild, no-holds-barred."

Colt trembled. "Yeah. Shit, yeah."

"Good boy," Mason said, slapping his ass, then gesturing for Colt to sit on the edge right in front of where Brianna was clutching the sides.

Here we go.

Fuck, yeah.

Bring it to her, boys.

As Colt settled himself, his legs dangling down into the water either side of her head, his cock in front of her face, hard and slick with his desperate need, I reached over and smeared his pre-cum over two of my fingers, gathering a copious amount.

His cock jerked at my attentions and he trembled for me, breathing my name all hoarse.

As I pulled away to Colt's sounds of protests, I whispered at Brianna's ear, "He needs your warm mouth, baby. Wrap those pouty lips around his needy cock."

She smirked, then eased forward a little and shocked us all as she suddenly dove down onto Colt's cock, taking him right to the back of her throat in one shot.

"Motherfucking shit!" he yelled, slapping his hands down on the slate steps either side of him to steady himself.

She didn't just bob her head up and down, it was more like slamming it in a desperate, almost violent fury. All this buildup we were all feeling had finally gotten to her and she was succumbing to the glorious wild thing within.

"Yeah, let it all out, dark angel," Mason said, wading to her left side, while I settled behind her. He smirked at me devilishly. "*I'm* sure going to."

I smirked back and jerked her bikini bottoms off.

The moment I did, he was there rubbing his knuckles into her cunt. "Our woman's so fucking ready for us. So wet, she's dripping all over my hand."

She moaned out around Colt's cock and he cursed in rapture as it teased his shaft that was already being devoured so spectacularly by her.

Mason had her jolting as he exerted more pressure, lifting her up right as I peeled back one of her ass cheeks. It put her tight little hole out of the water.

With my other hand, I took the fingers slicked in Colt's pre-cum and teased her asshole.

She shuddered all over and tried to push back on me.

Mason stepped up his torment and started rubbing his knuckles through her slick folds roughly and rapid-fire.

My balls drew tight as it had her bucking wildly and screaming around her mouthful of Colt this time.

"Guys, fuck, you're killing me."

"Don't hold off, cupcake."

"Yeah, we want to see you come all over her face and make her drink you down too."

"Shit, Mason!" he cried as Mason's dirty words had her stepping it up even more and going feral all over Colt's cock, basically eating him alive.

"There it is," I breathed as I eased two sticky fingers into her tight little hole.

As I was taking it easy on her—for now—Mason rammed three into her cunt from beneath the water.

She ripped her mouth from Colt's cock and shrieked out into the night, the rapturous sound echoing beautifully through the surrounding mountains.

"God!" she cried out, fisting Colt's cock now as Mason rammed into her brutally and I thrust my fingers deep in her ass.

"Yeah, fuck, yeah, that's what I'm talking about," Mason uttered. "Take my thick fingers. You feel me stretching you open for me? It's gonna be my cock in here next breaking you open. Ungh, yeah, clench for me. Who's a dirty little slut begging for my fingers deep in her cunt while Lev's twisting his in your ass?"

"Me," she breathed. "Oh, God, me."

Colt got into it like the two of us and fisted her hair, using the hold as leverage to slam her back down onto his cock. "Eat, little slut. Fuck, yeah," he said, sinking onto his back and giving into the sweet torment as she pleasured him.

Fucking fiercely at that.

I changing it up with twisting my fingers, pulling them all the way out, then thrusting back in.

Mason alternated his punishing finger fucking of her cunt with my thrusts, and then she lost it, shuddering, screaming around her mouthful of cock as the three of us tormented her until she couldn't take it anymore.

She came, going rigid and tearing herself off Colt's cock again as she screamed and screamed and screamed the place down, vibrating in our hold with the intensity of her orgasm.

A cry from Colt had Mason and I looking from her to him just as he shot up, grabbed his cock and came all over her cheeks and mouth.

Fuck, yeah.

He collapsed onto his back again, spent.

Mason and I pulled out of her.

And then he moved between her and the edge, wrapped her arms around his neck, grabbed her thigh and thrust into her sweet cunt.

I came up behind her and spread her ass cheeks with one hand, while guiding my cock to her asshole with the other.

I slammed inside in one go.

After my prepping, I was able to drive deep and fill her tight hole completely.

Still, she was so fucking tight, bearing down on my cock in the most amazing way.

That was taken up a notch when Mason started to move and I could feel him through the thin membrane between us.

Brianna's screams filled my ears, combined with the feel of him, and the sight of Colt looking on dazedly, then Brianna's face covered in his hot cum, I lost myself to it all.

I was grabbing her hair and wrenching her head back, then biting at her throat, her shoulder, her back, as I fucked her like a madman.

Mason met my pace, the two of us groaning and cursing as we laid into her.

"Ungh," he grunted. "Yeah."

He reached around and grabbed a handful of my ass, digging his nails in and giving me the bite of pain that I hadn't known I'd been needing.

"Damn," I uttered. "Fuck."

She shrieked and came, everything tightening to intense pressure for both of us.

Pleasure built and built until it fucking well exploded and I came deep in her ass.

A roar from Mason told me he'd hit it too.

I eased out of her, then wrapped my arms around her from behind, as Mason did the same from her front. Colt sank into the water, and then three of us were surrounding her.

"You were amazing," I told her.

"Right back at you," she said, chuckling breathlessly. "All of you."

Hell, it had been beyond amazing.

Because of her, because of the four of us together as a unit.

And I was loving every moment of this dynamic of ours.

I couldn't get enough.

13

~Mason~

Check.
  Check.
  And check.

I stepped back from the security fence surrounding the property, satisfied that it was up to par, that there were no weaknesses in it to be concerned about, nothing needing fixing or damage control since we'd last been up here.

While Levi was the king when it came to computers and also possessing an intermediate knowledge when it came to woodworking, and Colt was the music genius, *I* was very good with this sort of thing. Electronics, mechanics, hardware and components.

I'd already checked things out here several times in the last four days that we'd been up here.

And I would keep doing so.

It was the only way to ensure things were operating smoothly, that there was nothing amiss—to constantly check up on things. And people too. You could never be too careful.

And, especially when it came to this failing, it just

couldn't be allowed. It was the last line of defense before a threat hit us, so it was invaluable defense.

We also had an early-warning system in place a couple of miles out that surrounded the property. I'd inspected those tripwires too and all had been well yet again.

I breathed a sigh of relief.

"Hey."

Jesus!

Adrenaline tore through me and I spun toward the sound of the unexpected voice to see Bree walking up to me through the snow, her sparkling white and silver boots sinking into the softness as she closed the distance between us.

Her fuchsia puffer jacket was a vibrant break through all the snowy white. She had a cute little matching colored hat with bobbles on too that were bouncing with her deep steps through the one-foot deep snow all around. A pair of jeans the same shade as her long, silky hair, completed her look.

It was a far cry from my neutral-colored look that blended into the surroundings of the trees with my brown aviator jacket and a pair of gray distressed jeans, along with my black snow boots.

I closed the distance between us and leaned in, kissing her cheek.

She turned into it, sending a thrill through me as she nuzzled against me for a moment.

Holding her hands between us, I asked, "Is everything okay back at the house?"

"All good, yeah. Just as you left it."

"Lev is hacking away?"

She chuckled. "He is. Colt's looking over his shoulder and asking dozens of questions."

"He's restless then."

"Yeah. Once Levi sets the processes up that he needs to —a program he's writing—we'll get out of the house for a bit, play in the snow or something."

"Play in the snow… adorable."

She started at my words.

I wasn't surprised. It had jolted me too.

I wasn't normally capable of uttering such a word.

I wasn't the touchy-feely type.

At least, I hadn't been for years.

It looked like that was starting to change.

Because of her.

Because of our foursome solidifying, and creating a new dynamic with her at the center affecting each of us.

We were affecting her too.

She was becoming a lot less closed off and diplomatically defensive.

She was showing us her harder, darker edge. First with the knife, then her vicious reaction to me pissing her off and crossing that line with the kidnapping.

And after that adjustment period and what had gone down in the hot springs, she'd been bouncing about the house seeming a lot lighter and more open and free.

Earlier this morning, she'd even come out of the shower and sauntered into the living room beautifully naked and dripping wet and beckoned the three of us to ravage her.

Of course, we absolutely had.

She'd needed to take another shower after we'd dirtied her up.

"You heard me," I said, with a grin, as she stared at me with a mixture of surprise and wonder. Awestruck, basically.

"Well, I like it," she said, stroking my hands with her fuzzy white gloved ones. "Oh, you're freezing! Why didn't you wear gloves out here too? It's nowhere near the heated patio to keep you warm."

I wiggled my eyebrows. "You're starting to do a good job with the heat."

"Mason, I'm serious."

I *was* serious.

About how her slight touch and closeness was warming me.

And not just physically.

Oh, well.

"I couldn't have gloves on with what I was doing and checking out here. I needed the full dexterity."

"You're done now, though?"

"Yeah. Let's head inside."

As I went to do that, she eased her hands from mine and pressed her palm to my chest. "Just a moment."

I was looking on curiously then as she unzipped her jacket and reached into the inside pocket and pulled something out.

I started at the sight of something very familiar coming into view.

The gold leaf of the book gave itself away.

My artist journal.

"I want to talk about this first."

"How did you come to have this?" I asked, reaching for it.

She relinquished it and explained, "I was looking through some of the bags that you packed up here containing components and what-not for a device that Levi needed to soup-up the internet connection, and I came across this. I didn't know what it was until I opened it, thinking it was some coding or program notes he might need."

"I must've packed it in the wrong bag instead of with my clothes, because I'd been in such a rush."

"I'm kind of glad you did, otherwise I never would have seen what an incredible artist you actually are. These designs are inspired." She whistled. "You're majorly talented, Mason."

I rolled my shoulders. "Was."

"No. *Are*. Some of these are recent. You date stamp all the images. And I saw an exact replica of my watercolor butterfly tattoo, along with a bunch of others based off of that idea."

"Every now and then I still get the urge to sketch a little."

"Because it's a part of you."

I shook my head. "It can't be."

"I disagree."

I sighed. "While I appreciate your support, my dark angel, it's just not possible to return to any of it. These sketches are just part of a past that can never become a future."

"You revived *Hex* with the intent to change that. Like you told me, to obtain something compromising on him so you'd finally have leverage to make the existence of that taped evidence he holds over your head meaningless."

"And now with what we're doing here, I'll need something else even on top of that. It'll just be an endless cycle every time I act the way I want to and outside of his plans for me." I shook my head. "It was a futile idea. At least I get to do this with the three of you. Something out there, danger and a twisted thrill involved. As soon as he gets wind of it, though, he'll force me out, force me to withdraw my assistance. But I can at least revel in it for now."

"No," she ground out. "It's not going to be like that. I can help you, *if* you let me."

I cocked an eyebrow.

"With *Vixen*," she told me. Off my look, she said, "Come inside, let's talk."

———

"JUST OVER A DOZEN?" I asked, incredulous.

Levi looked up from his military-grade laptop. "Fourteen."

"Impressive that you were able to determine that," Bree told him.

He winked at her, then returned his attention to his hacking endeavor, while telling me, "Let her help you."

"It'll require your help too," she told him.

Without looking up from typing away like a machine, he responded, "Got you always, baby."

"How about me?" Colt asked, sitting forward in one of the armchairs and bouncing his elbows on his knees, evidence of his increasingly restless state.

Bree pulled her gloves off and stuffed them in the pockets of her puffer jacket, then shrugged it off to reveal a sexy off-the-shoulder top with a pastel-pink and silver crisscrossing design on it beneath. She looked to the side of me at Colt, telling him, "*We've* got this, but any input is helpful too. The melding of minds and all that. I need *your* help with something else after we finish sorting this."

I smiled at her handling of Colt.

His forte wasn't strategizing and planning missions or tasks like it was for Levi and me, but he had other strengths, and she was making sure he wasn't left out. That had happened more than I cared to admit when it had just been the three of us before and usually he'd gotten distracted by something else quickly, or barely had the attention span for this sort of thing to pay it much mind.

But us being here in this safehouse with the shit hanging over our head made it impossible for him to just walk away from it and go off and do his own thing with his band or fuck around with his *Mythic Cry* groupies, as were his usual ways. This time he was feeling it.

"Perfect!" he said, brightly, that sweet side of him warming me.

The smile on Levi and Bree's faces made it clear they were feeling the same way too.

I turned my attention back to her. "So, tell me about *Vixen.*"

"You may have heard of club girls when it comes to motorcycle clubs." She grimaced. "They're unfortunately called a lot of other things too, much more derogatory things, just because they have a biker fetish, or whatever."

"Oh, club bunnies, club whores?" Colt commented.

Levi chuckled. "No tact, cupcake. But, yeah, that's what she's getting at."

"Anyway, yeah," Bree went on. "I developed friendships with some of them over the years. In that time, I got to know women from all different walks of life. Different ideals, professions, dreams, and all of that. I fostered those friendships and it occurred to me that we could help each other. So, I formed *Vixen* on the down low. Steel Dawn MC and my father had no idea. Before I knew it, I had a small network of reliable and resourceful women who had reach in different areas."

"A source of power," I realized aloud.

"In essence. Information *is* power."

"Absolutely," Levi commented, still typing away and fixated on his laptop screen as he pulled that amazing multitasking of his and managed to participate while still immersed in that.

"Now, I have three of my girls in place around Peter

Hall, currently in what I call a *neutral* state. Meaning observation and recon only. If you agree, I'll activate them."

I did a double take. "Excuse me? You have three in place already?"

"I put them in place when you came at me, just in case you proved unable for me to handle one-on-one."

"Damn," Colt exclaimed.

"Hot as fucking Hades, huh?" Levi commented, looking up for a moment, pride and desire shining in his eyes.

I blinked past that and focused on Bree.

"After you told me about your predicament with your father, I kept them there."

"And where exactly are they positioned?"

"One took the place of your father's former assistant who finally grew a backbone thanks to some *persuasion* from my asset, and quit. Your father is a real slimy bastard. He'd been harassing her for a long time and she was too scared to quit and lose her job which she desperately needed to support her twin toddlers. Fortunately, I was able to offer her a lucrative *severance* that will tide her over until another one of my girls is in place to offer her a job at *her* firm—a legal aid outfit."

"Jesus, this is… intricate."

She merely smiled then went on, "I have another asset who is now in position in your mom's society circles, who Shirley Hall believes she's taking under her wing, schooling an up-and-coming socialite. My asset is actually a very talent actor with falsified society ties that somebody like your mom looks up to. She's formed a bond with her. She's been inside the Hall estate several times and she's acquired a very good lay of the land." She tossed her jacket down on the couch, cocked her hip, then told me, "And the third is prepared to bring a big-time case to Peter Hall. She's a real lawyer herself, but she'll pose as someone with a beef against a major corporation that's encroaching on her small business. But I'll require Levi's help to be able to pull off a smokescreen that detailed to make the fake case appear completely legitimate." She cocked her hip. "They're all in prime positions to find the evidence he's holding over you and destroy it, as well as finding dirt on him to secure your position and leverage against him going forward." She smiled. "To free you, Mason."

I stepped back a little and scrubbed my hand over my face. "This is… it's remarkable what you've created here. Are these assets on call and working for you as needed, on a case-by-case basis?"

"Yes. Exactly."

"And how do you finance all this if it's off your father's radar? The guy's made a mint with his small business ventures and chains of—"

"My apps."

"Yeah," Levi cut in. "You hid that well. I only discovered that just before I approached you the first time. You sure know how to hide the coin."

"And you're bothering to study at Stonewell, why?" Colt asked jokingly.

Sort of.

"I don't know everything. My skills need some work still and there's more to learn. Things that I need to learn to be able to keep producing lucrative apps and things."

"Smart woman," I said. "In so many ways. I'm insanely impressed."

"Major praise, especially coming from my boy," Colt said.

She smiled in that shy way when she received direct compliments. "Thanks." She shifted her weight. "I'm not going to do anything without your authorization. Like we all agreed, we're together as a team on everything now. That was the last piece of the puzzle from my end. With the rest of the revelations, everything is out in the open that impacts the four of us in any way. So, it's your call, but I *do* strongly believe that turning down this help would be a mistake for you. They're already in place, Mason. With the link being to me and not to you, there's no risk on your end either. From the way I've set it up, it can't come back on you."

"But it could come back on you."

"Even if Peter Hall gets word of my connection to you, I've ensured that it will be seen as unilateral, rogue action on my part, with you having no involvement in it."

"Jesus, you've protected me really well."

"Of course. We're a team. We're together."

I reached out and cupped her face. "All true. And it's because of that why I can't let you risk yourself like this. Not for me, not for anything or anyone."

"Reality check, brother," Levi called. "We're gearing up for a literal battle here. In comparison—"

"This is my father, Lev. He doesn't stop. He's a vindictive, dangerous fuck."

"Wow, you rarely ever call him out like that. Especially not out loud," Colt said.

I didn't, no. It was yet another way I'd noticed myself shifting, changing.

"He won't be able to touch her, don't worry about that aspect of things," Levi said, eyeing us and pausing what he was doing for a moment.

"How can you be so sure?"

"Because Roman Knight won't allow it."

"What?"

"He knows what she means to me."

"Us," Colt cut in.

99

"Got it, my bad," Levi said, before telling us, "If his old buddy, Peter, comes at her, he'll be there to stop him." Levi rolled his eyes at me. "To rein him in as pretty much the only one who's capable of doing such a thing."

I took his words in, processing them for a moment and weighing everything up.

And then I gave a nod. "Let's do it. Authorized."

She brightened. "Excellent."

"Awesome!" Colt cried. "Finally."

As I beamed over at him, excitement blooming at the idea of having something to hold over the bastard in order to sever his power over me, I tuned into Bree and Levi.

"Your dad knows about us?" Bree was asking him.

"Of course. Why not?"

"The four of us too?"

"Yeah."

"And?"

"And it's fine."

"He's just on board, just like that? Even with who I am? The connection I am to that dark time for you—and him?"

"He wants the best for me and he recognizes how you bring that to me, despite the rest. He's accepted it. Easily, actually. Once we're done with this mission, I have no doubt that he'll want to meet you and all that jazz."

"Wow," she breathed in wonder.

Yeah, Levi and Colt's fathers were a world away from mine.

Sometimes, I figured, you just had to create your own family when your own disappointed you and did nothing but hurt you.

And I had that with the three of them.

The sentiment of it actually took me over, just breaking loose from my usually emotionally tightly coiled state, and the next thing I knew, I was throwing my arms around Bree and nuzzling her hair. "Thank you, dark angel. *Thank you.*"

I could see Lev and Colt looking on absolutely stunned in my peripheral vision.

That was about right.

Things were changing for me.

I was changing.

And the hope of it actually outweighed any worry.

14

~Colton~

"Shit!" I cried as I watched Bree's head snap to the side.

Because of *me!*

"I'm so fucking sorry, cutie, I—"

My words caught in my throat as she turned her head back and she licked blood out of the corner of her mouth.

Her eyes flamed.

Holy shit.

Before I could get a word out to finish my apology, or check that she was okay, despite the savage look in her eyes now present, she snagged my wrist, used the hold to jerk me to her with jarring force, then swept her leg at my knees. She hooked one, then wrenched at it and ripped my feet right out from under me.

I cried out and landed hard on my back on the makeshift gym floor.

She didn't give me a chance to recover before she pounced on me and pinned my hands to my naked abs, and my legs with her knees.

"Damn, cutie," I choked, resting my head back on the

floor, as I laid there staring up at her and catching my breath.

It had turned out that the help she'd needed from me was to get her fighting skills back up to snuff because she was rusty.

With what was coming, that could be an issue.

I mean, the three of us would do whatever possible to protect her during the actual physical takedown of Lynch and *Osiris*, but there were no guarantees in that sort of situation. Not everything could be controlled when it came to a live combat situation like that.

And there was no way she'd accept having to sit it out, considering her personal stake in it and her need, just like Lev, to be there to destroy that psychopath and his organization.

I wasn't naïve enough to believe that this was just about me helping *her* to get her skills up to snuff. Mason and Lev must've told her that *I* was more than just a little rusty too.

I couldn't actually remember the last time I'd thrown down against anybody.

I mean, being brothers with Lev and Mason, I had skills in a fight, no doubt. The two of them had made sure I'd learned when we were younger and all that, making sure I could defend myself if it ever came to it.

But I hadn't spent years honing or increasing those skills like Lev had with his missions and his street fighting, and all that insane level of training.

Mason spent some time training too. Not as much as Lev, but he did box and work out. And with all that power-house muscle and his tank of a build, he had what Lev had termed a *cement block punch*. It was why, no matter how pissed he got at Lev, he shoved if it did end up getting physical, he never hit.

"Do you yield?" she asked, grinning down at me, looking so proud of herself.

I panted, staring up at her and her whiskey eyes gleaming with the satisfaction of winning out here. "We've been at this for two hours straight, damn right I yield, woman."

She chuckled, then leaned down and brushed her lips over mine, kissing me softly.

A serene moan escaped me.

"Good fight," she said then, as she pushed off me and got back to her feet.

She held her hand out to me and I took it, groaning as I got up too.

"Let me see," I said, cupping her face, and inspecting the damage I'd done. "Shit," I groused. "I'm so sorry."

She eased my hand down and held it between us, smiling up at me. "It's honestly nothing. We were sparring, things happen. It doesn't even hurt. Besides, I did damage to you as well." She released my hand, then trailed her fingers over the nail marks across my abs, then sweeping all the way along to my left arm where a purple bruise was forming.

"That's different."

"Because I'm a woman?"

"Nah, cutie," I said, reaching out and stroking her hair. "If anything, that makes you a hell of a lot stronger than the rest of us, especially after all you've been through."

I stepped closer until my slick, bare chest was pressing against her shimmering gray sports bra.

I smiled as I heard her breath hitch.

"It's because you're ours. Even the idea of you hurting in any way makes me sick to my stomach. It's like being slugged in the fucking gut, honestly." I stroked her cheek, my fingers brushing over her soft skin.

She turned into it, her eyes fluttering closed briefly before they fixed back on mine in an all-consuming way that promised to drown me in that sweetness forever.

I broke into the melody I'd been working on up here for the last couple of weeks, singing the lyrics low at her ear, *"Vicious things tangling in the night/ She was made for one hell of a fight/ Fuck it, she was born for this/ Born to be merciless/ Girl's got claws and she'll sure as fuck bite."*

"Is that the new song you've been working on?"

"Yeah, cutie."

"It's about the four of us?"

"Sure is. You get it now? How I see you?"

"I do. Thank you, Colt. And thank you for being so welcoming to me right at the beginning when things weren't as they are now, when they were hard. It was a comfort to me and I won't forget it."

"No worries," I said, easing back and holding her to me by her hips. "It was easier for me to be that way, to see the sweetness beneath the hard outer shell that Mason was seeing, because I don't have to be on top of everything or worried about controlling and protecting us. That's his and Lev's thing. I'm lucky, you know, that I don't have all that baggage that Lev does bearing down on him, or all the expectations that have been burdening Mason. I'm allowed to be free."

"It's a good thing you are, because you balance out the rest from them."

"It's you who does that, Bree."

She cocked an eyebrow.

"You don't see?"

"I see some loosening up occurring from both of them in different ways. Because of this mission against Lynch, and the one against Peter Hall, and the hope it's inspired in them for how things will be once we achieve victory."

"Nah, it happened before that was even known to be on the table. It was you coming into our lives, drawing closer to us. Me providing that balance you talked about wasn't enough, but with you here, the two of us, it *is* enough. And it's changing everything." I beamed down at her. "In the best ways."

I leaned down and kissed her cheek.

I'd intended to leave it at that, but she turned into it, then planted her lips on mine.

I slicked my tongue piercing over her bottom lip and she moaned out, then grabbed my biceps and tugged me closer, curling her tongue around mine and grinding against me, making my cock hard in a goddamn instant.

Holy shit.

I was vaguely aware of rushed footsteps sounding near us as I rolled my hips, making her feel me.

When she spread her legs a little to give me better access, I lost it, pushing her against the nearest wall and feasting on her lips, throat, collarbone, down to the tops of her breasts all sexy and pushed up in her sports bra.

"Your favorite Sled Head is resurrecting now!"

I jolted at the sound of Mason's voice.

Footsteps entered the room a moment later—his heavy ones.

And then his shadow fell over us. "Hot as hell to walk in on, but you're rain checking it."

With a grunt, I pulled from Brianna, then turned around to see him right there in my space looking... excited?

What was happening? "Mason, what—"

"We're snowmobiling. Right now."

"Really?"

"Yeah. I even managed to convince Lev to take a break from his hacking fuckery for a bit. He agreed he needs to clear his head. What better way than hitting the snow-mobiles?"

"Well, his Harley, for him."

"Second best way then." He looked out at Bree. "Have you ridden a snowmobile before?"

She shook her head.

"You're gonna love it." He blew her a kiss, then planted one on my mohawk. And then he turned and hurried out, calling over his shoulder, "Ski runners up in ten!"

"Wow, that was… bracing," I breathed, staring out after him.

Bree chuckled. "He's happy."

I grinned. "Guess we're going snowmobiling then."

"FUCK," Lev exclaimed as Mason cut in front of him on the trail—again.

"My bad!" Mason called over his shoulder. "Needed the room, brother!"

I eyed Lev almost beside me. "Your reflexes were a little off there, huh?"

"Busy thinking."

"You're supposed to be taking a breather."

"I did. For twenty minutes."

Actually, that was a major amount of time for him to just be and shut his mind off. "All right," I said, backing off when I recognized that.

"Brianna?" he called behind him. "Speaking of taking a breather, you done yet?"

I looked back to see she was still talking into her earpiece that Lev had hooked her up with when she'd gotten a call from *Vixen* that she'd needed to take, so she could still come snowmobiling with us.

"Nah, she's still at it," I told Lev.

"Now worries, it's for the good of our boy up there."

"Seems it's already doing him some major good," I said, watching as Mason laughed wildly as he sped along on his snowmobile ahead of us, living it up, getting lost in the moment and the liberation of it in a way I hadn't seen from him in so long.

Just as I was trying to wrap my head around that, he took it further.

I signaled for Lev and Bree to slow alongside me as I realized what Mason was getting ready to do. It had just been a long time since I'd seen him go for it like this.

But there he was in the next moment, working the throttle as he approached a jump ahead.

He hit it right on and went sailing over.

"Whoop!" I cried.

"Fucking, yeah!" Lev yelled.

"Wow!" I heard Bree exclaim as she finished talking into her earpiece and caught up with me and Lev.

"Yeah, he used to stunt all the time," I told her. "When we used to come up here a lot in the old days. And when we weren't, he had a Triumph and spent a lot of time stunting with Lev on their bikes."

She looked over at Lev. "He did? Seriously?"

He grinned. "Sure did."

Things got wilder from Mason then and we watched him shift his weight.

And then his right foot was on the saddle.

His left joined it.

And then he rose up and outstretched his arms as he surfed the snowmobile like a champ.

Holy shit!

I wolf-whistled as he jumped out of it and landed smoothly back in a sitting position.

"Whoo!" he shouted into the mountains, the sound echoing around amazingly.

This was one of the best times we'd had in ages.

I couldn't believe it.

He actually seemed happy.

Unburdened.

Unshackled.

"You think that was wild?" he called back to us. "You ain't seen nothing yet!"

———

HE REALLY HADN'T BEEN KIDDING.

Mason had treated us to a stunt show, going all in after that first one.

It had been breathtaking seeing him like that.

Really amazing.

As we neared the house, just ten minutes out now until we were back, I was kind of sad that it had come to an end.

That was until Mason signaled and pulled over on the trail as we were traveling through the forest, the brush and all that buried beneath two feet worth of snowfall.

He dismounted his snowmobile and then he leapt into the snow and started waving his arms and legs, making snow angels.

"Shit, yeah!" I cried, joining him and making some right opposite him.

"Beautiful artwork," Bree told us with a giggle as she came over to join in.

She didn't quite make it as a snowball shot by her, then smacked Mason in the face.

Mason choked and spat out some of the snow that had

filled his mouth. Then he swung his head and laughed, "You little shit."

Me and Bree turned to see Lev standing there in the snow grinning like a little devil.

A challenging glint lit his eyes as he reached down and smushed another snowy weapon together in his gloved palms.

All hell broke loose then, Mason rolling to his side, then getting to his feet and making a snowball rapid-fire, then tossing it back at Lev.

Lev, with all his fight skills, dodged it easily and stuck his tongue out at him.

I joined in, trying to get him, even as he hit each of us dead-on. *Son of a bitch!*

He avoided all the hits.

Until a snowball smacked right into his head.

He stilled for a moment, shocked that he'd actually taken a hit.

And then he brushed the snow out of his hair and some that had gotten on his face, and turned to see Bree standing there with a hand still cocked at him, the other holding another snowball.

"Like that, *lovely?*" she teased.

"Oh, baby, you're so fucked now."

"Promises, promises," she said, giggling in that amazing way of hers that did things to all three of us.

Lev burst forward and ran at her.

She squealed as he caught her across the waist and drove her down into the snow on her back.

She snatched up some snow and tossed it at Levi as he pounced on her.

It hit him in the mouth too. "Payback for Mason," she told him.

He chuckled and then threw a bunch at her pink puffer jacket.

She gave as good as she got and within moments, Lev's hair was drenched by ice-cold snow.

He shook his head like a dog, then growled in his sexy playful way, "That's it, my *Wildflower*."

In the next second, he unzipped her puffer jacket to reveal her scoop neck shirt beneath, all bubblegum-like. And then he was stuffing snow down it.

"Ah!" she cried, shuddering from the cold and trying to grab at him to stop him.

Mason and I were there in the next moment, attacking Lev with our own snowballs, until he landed on his ass in front of Bree with his hands held up defensively as we doused him.

Brianna sat back up, laughing her head off along with us. "What was that you said? I was *so fucked*?" she teased Lev.

"Yeah, about that," Mason said, a moment before he dove down and grasped her waist. He hauled her over his shoulder and carried her toward some massive rocks covered in snow.

"What are you doing?" she cried, her voice choppy as he ran with her, laughing and having the best time being fun and free, and just letting loose.

Lev and I exchanged a grin as we followed them over just as Mason laid her down on the smooth rock surface on her puffer jacket.

"Blade," he spoke to Lev, holding his hand out behind him as we reached them.

Lev, always one for carrying a weapon—either his knife or bo-staff and sometimes both—unzipped his jacket and pulled one out of his inner pocket.

As soon as he handed it over, Mason straddled Brianna's legs, then started cutting through her sweater.

She went stock-still, her eyes burning into his and I saw them dilate with arousal.

She was getting off on him bringing a little knife play into being.

The sharp blade cut through the fabric like butter.

He didn't stop there, though, slicing through her bra, then brushing the pieces aside to reveal her bare breasts and stomach. They were heaving in her rapidly building need and she went to rub her thighs together, but couldn't manage it with Mason between them.

He drew the flat of the blade along her collarbone and down to the tops of her breasts.

"God," she cried as the cold steel made goosebumps on her skin every place it touched.

"Colt," he called to me.

I stepped over there and leaned down and licked the path he was traveling, taking the cold away and bringing the heat.

I was rewarded by Bree moaning out and arching her back, silently pleading for more.

Mason yanked down her pants, then cut through her panties.

"Fuck," Lev groaned at the act *and* her soaking wet cunt coming into view.

"You boys are gonna kill me," Bree panted.

Mason smirked, and then he nicked at her inner thighs.

She bucked and cried out.

He did it again, making pearls of blood trickle down toward her cunt.

"Nothing like a little pain with your pleasure, dark angel."

Before I could soothe those with my tongue, Mason

handed the blade back to Levi who stowed it away, and then he rubbed along the trails of blood heightening the burning pain for her and making her mewl and buck on the rock.

I saw her cunt getting wetter, though. She was straddling the mind-fuck of the pleasure-pain paradox.

Levi stepped forward and moved opposite me by her head and breasts.

And then he gathered fistfuls of snow and spread it all over them.

She almost shot off the rock face from the intense assault of the freezing cold all over a very sensitive area. Lev's hand to her stomach forced her to take it.

I moved in, licking it up, bit by bit with my warm tongue, the cold on my piercing against her warmth doing amazing things to me in the process.

"Oh God!" she cried, grabbing at my hair, then turning and thrusting her tongue into Levi's mouth.

I looked up from licking her to see the two of them making out all animalistically.

Hot as fuck.

Hotter than that was watching her reactions as we pleasured her and teased the hell out of her.

While my cock was rock-hard and being a needy fucker, I actually didn't want to bring it into play right now.

I wanted to keep doing this, immersing ourselves in her, pleasuring her, making her ours, making her feel everything fucking amazing.

It was all about worshipping *her*.

After what she'd done for Mason.

After what she'd done for all of us.

Our woman deserved our everything.

Hell, she deserved the fucking world.

Mason, in his wild state, took it further and then he slapped a snowball right between her legs.

She released my hair and ripped her mouth from Levi's, shrieking and writhing on the rock. "Ah! Mason, shit!"

He didn't only not stop, he took it up a notch, gathering snow in his gloved hand, then pushing it into her cunt, driving it deep with two snow-covered fingers.

"Fuck! *Fuck!*" she screamed, and Levi and I held her down, Lev even reaching over to hold one of her thighs open, while Mason held the other so her cunt was spread open for his torment.

He shoved more snow into her waiting cunt.

"Let that needy hole melt all that snow," Mason said.

"So fucking cold!" she cried. "Too cold!"

"Nah, dark angel, you're gonna come harder than you ever have." He gestured at Lev, who came forward. "Watch this space," he said, grinning at him.

I pinched her nipples, enjoying her squirming in need as I rolled my piercing over them, then pinched again, driving her crazy.

And then Lev was there as Mason held her thighs open, diving into her cunt, his hot tongue licking up all the snow, his mouth sucking some of it out of her.

It had Bree losing it completely and she couldn't keep still, surging up, grabbing at me, then Mason, then Lev's hair as everything smashed up against the rest.

"I can't… ah! It's… I'm gonna come. I'm gonna—"

We saw the moment her orgasm hit her.

It was so powerful, almost ripping her off the rock as she sprayed all over Lev's face and Mason's fingers.

It kept going and going, her cries of ecstasy tearing out into the night.

When she collapsed, she looked out at us with a sly smile on her face.

"Holy crap, we're doing that again."

We all chuckled.

And then we gathered her to us, warming her and comforting her after all the intensity.

Ours.

15

~Brianna~

I woke slowly to warmth.

An arm was draped over me.

Just one?

I remembered Mason carrying me in here last night to the master bedroom they'd sweetly assigned to me.

I'd been utterly boneless after our intense fuck session out in the snowy woods.

They'd stripped me of my wet clothes and then settled me under the covers wherein they'd all climbed in and surrounded me with their warmth.

The soft clacking of keys caught my attention and I turned toward the source to see it was coming from Levi and his laptop.

He was sitting up in the bed with his arm draped over me.

"Morning," I spoke.

He dragged his gaze away from the screen and his whole face lit up. "Hey, *Wildflower.* There's those beautiful eyes gazing back at me."

He was sitting on top of the covers in a maroon tank

and his go-to black cargo pants, typing one-handed again while his other was on me. He couldn't be within reach of me and not be touching me in some way.

"I'm real, *lovely*," I assured him, getting that it was partly what it was about. "Right here."

He moved his hand and slid it to my cheek. "I know you are. In every way."

I grasped his hand on me, telling him earnestly, "And I'm not going anywhere."

He put his laptop down on the nightstand next to him. "Yeah?"

"Yeah."

"Even when it's time to leave this safehouse?"

"I'll still be with you guys."

"Even if I fuck up again?"

"Still with you."

"Even if—"

I pressed my hand to his mouth. "No. Matter. What."

I felt his smile against my palm.

"Want to know why, *lovely?*"

He nodded and muffled a confirmation into my hand.

I sucked in a breath to steady myself for what I was about to put out there, what I'd wanted to for a while. Gazing at him, I uttered, "Because I love you."

A whole slew of emotions flitted across his face.

Surprise.

Awe.

Excitement.

But most of all, pure happiness.

He eased my hand down and held it between us. "I love you too, Brianna. So fucking much." He stroked my hair reverentially. "Everything begins and ends with you, *Wildflower.*"

"It does for me too."

"Fuck. You have no idea how long I've waited to hear that."

In the next second he had me squealing as he rolled on top of me.

His palms came down either side of my head, caging me in deliciously.

My whole body pulsed at his closeness, his heat, the sexy intensity coming off him.

"Uh uh," he said, gazing down at me. "Not that." He leaned in, teasing me as his warm breath fanned over the side of my neck causing goosebumps that had me trembling in the best way. "*This.*"

He brushed his lips over my throat and then he was planting soft and sweet kisses over my cheeks, my head, on my pendant, my forehead, making me giggle.

It culminated with a cute one to my nose that had my heart squeezing for him.

He eased away, pushing up on his hands. "As much as I want to sink into you, my *Wildflower,* I have no doubt that you're sore from last night. And I need to finish working."

He pushed off me and I sat up, but before disappointment could settle he wrapped his arm around me and tucked me into his side.

He grabbed his laptop with his free hand and settled it on his lap.

"How's it going with that?"

He sighed. "Well, as you know I finally managed to access Royce's backup server a couple of days ago after he disabled the original one I'd hacked into. He's been trying to track Lynch's movements too without alerting the fucker. It strongly suggests they're not on friendly terms, especially when coupled with Kyle Trass hiding and using a false identity. It could've been him not wanting to get pulled back into Lynch's shit—he regretted what went down with our kidnapping—but now it seems like a hell of a lot more than that. So, anyway, Royce has managed to pick up an additional three locations than I had already marked that Lynch has been at in the last few months. But it's still not enough. He can't nail him down either."

"We need to discern some sort of pattern then."

"Exactly. That, along with more chatter and sightings. So that's what I'm doing. I'm also running my own developed facial recognition software but it's going to take time due to the massive ground covered through all these sightings. I've written a program that will bring all of this together and be able to predict his movements going forward. Once I acquire a little more data. I've also sent a message out through the underground as Royce Humphrey pretending there's an urgent need to meet with Lynch. That's a long shot but still worth a try."

"Wow, that's beyond, Levi."

He grinned. "It's what I do, baby."

I grinned back then told him, "I'll bring *Vixen* in on this. I have a handful of them in similar *underground* circles. I'll have them work on acquiring the additional data you need."

"Perfect. Thank you. But are you sure you want to activate more of your girls while you've got the Peter Hall mission in progress?"

"It'll be fine." I kissed his cheek. "Speaking of that mission, where is Mason? And Colt?"

"Colt's working on finishing that song he started up here, the one he's really excited about. Mason is on the phone with one of his *Hex* lieutenants. Apparently there's been an attempted insurrection of some sort since we've been gone, our absence being used as a window to take advantage where they'd never normally have the balls to do so."

"Wow, that's the last thing we need."

"Don't worry, he's got it handled."

"You're sure? Because I can help."

"Believe me, I know you can. But, yeah, Mason's got this one."

"Ok. And thank you, Levi. You didn't say anything about *Vixen* until I was ready to reveal it."

"Of course. I never would. The fact I know every little thing about you was borne from my majorly invasive— what you'd call stalkerish—methods, so it wouldn't be fair to reveal what I'd learned for myself to others. It's always up to you to be ready where that's concerned. Not my call."

"And you like being the one who knows me inside out?"

"Maybe a little. But I'm also happy we have our four-some functioning so well, that we've grown really close, and that you're putting your trust in my brothers too now."

"Yeah, I am too."

A familiar buzzing on the nightstand beside me cut through our heartfelt moment. I reached over and snatched up my phone to find a text there from a surprising sender.

Tommy: How's sophomore year at Stonewell U going, B?

I frowned.

"What is it?" Levi asked, reading the mixture of surprise and suspicion in my expression.

"I'm not sure."

Brianna: Long time, no talk. Randomly on your mind, was I?

Tommy: Saw an interesting set of photos the other day.

Brianna: That was weeks ago. Also, you don't have

social media, so how did you come to see anything before it was all then pulled?

When there was no immediate response, I shook my head. "Unbelievable."

I settled against Levi and held my phone between us so he could see.

"Bastard's watching you, baby. Or your father is."

"With the laser-focus you had on me, how would you have missed that?"

"They could be doing it through a constant on campus, like a professor. They could have gotten to a student in one of your classes and had them report back."

"Jeez. I'd hoped my father had let go of that over-bearing type of watch. You'd think for a man all about loyalty and honor, the promise he'd made me to do so would actually mean something." I shook my head to myself. "Then again, I'm not really surprised. Wishful thinking makes fools out of us all."

"No, baby. Not always. It's vital to have hope." He stroked my head. "To wish, to dream."

I smiled up at him.

Unfortunately, another text came in, cutting through our moment once again.

Tommy: I know you're fucking Roman Knight's heir.

Levi growled low in his throat. "Did he talk to you like that when you were together?"

"No. He's pissed about something. More than being with somebody else. He should've got over that two years ago when we parted ways."

Brianna: Who I fuck stopped being your concern a long time ago.

Tommy: Big girl language, yeah? He been teaching you that?

"Motherfucker," Levi rumbled dangerously. "What's

the number?" he said, easing from me and shifting his weight, his fingers flying over the keys of his laptop in the next moment.

I reeled it off to him.

He cocked an eyebrow. "You didn't even have to look in your contact list, just know your ex-boyfriend's number off by heart, hmm?"

I rolled my eyes. "Please. You know I have really good recall."

He grinned. "I know, just teasing you to lighten the mood that the shithead ruined."

"Don't worry, I've got this," I said, a moment before I responded with another text.

Brianna: Don't be a pussy. Get to your reason for contacting me.

Tommy: Your old man.

Brianna: What about him?

Tommy: Knew you wouldn't respond to his calls or texts, so he's hit me up to do it. Stop what you're doing with Knight. All of it. You don't and that freedom you've had is gonna take a turn.

Brianna: Is that a threat?

Tommy: He doesn't want you getting hurt or going down that road again. He's raging all over the fucking place. Smashed up one of the diners after Roman Knight left and filled him in. The fuck he's gonna get involved in that Lynch shit again, turned the smarmy fucker down flat. Knowing you're going the other way has him worried and pissed as fuck. Stand down, B. Fall in fucking line.

Levi eyed the text, his eyes sparking with that dark fury.

Instead of doing the obvious and moving to handle it, he simply told me, "Give it to him, baby."

I smiled at his faith in me.

More than that, it was a major deal for him not to step

in, because he was extremely protective of me and possessive—aside from with Mason and Colt when it came to me—yet here he was with his response serving as a bolster to remind me that I was empowered now and no longer under the thumb of overbearing men treating me like a porcelain doll.

The boys all recognized that now.

But those from my old life still didn't. *They* actually never would. I had no illusions about that.

Brianna: I won't back down. Do what you need to.

Tommy: You're making a mistake.

Brianna: As you will be if you come at me. Pass that along to my father like the little messenger bitch you've become.

With that, I grunted and put my phone down on the nightstand. "Fuck," I groused, shoving my hands through my hair.

"Nicely done," Levi said, stroking my hair.

"Thanks and—why do you have that dangerous glint in your eyes?"

His eyes darkened too. *Oh no.*

"Levi, what's wrong? You know, aside from the obvious that just happened?"

"He doesn't know how to cover his tracks properly. I was able to track his phone. He's not with your father, not at any of his businesses, or Curt's home residence. He's not at his own apartment either. Where he *is* right at the moment of contacting you just now is at the same industrial estate that I tagged *Osiris* at for a brief period."

"What? No. That can't be."

"Give me a few moments and we'll have confirmation."

"What are you doing?" I asked.

"Accessing the security cameras of several buildings

123

within the area, like I did last time to confirm Lynch being there."

As he was doing that, I mulled over the explanations aloud, "He could've gone there trying to get a lead on Lynch for my father. He might be lying about my father not wanting to get involved with it all alongside yours."

"A possibility," he said, while focusing on what he was doing. "Although, why would he be so adamant about keeping you out of it if they were already down there working the leads too? They'd believe they could get to him before we had any chance. After all, your father severely underestimates you. And to the outside world I'm just a reckless fucker and people don't know I have the means to really do a lot of damage."

"He wouldn't work with Lynch. We were together. There was a bond there. Not like what I have here with you, Mason, and Colt, but it was still personal, you know?"

"I do, baby."

He didn't look the least bit convinced. "But?"

He sighed. "*But* when your father abandoned the club and shut it down so suddenly, it left his club members adrift. A lot of them were pissed that he did that, actually raging about it."

"So you think Tommy might have gone to work for Lynch out of spite or something?"

"Possibly out of necessity to make a living. Lynch pays his guys well to keep them loyal. It's fake loyalty if you ask me, but still. It could also be out of power. Losing the club, there would have been that void there, one he could have been desperate to replace with a different kind of power instead of a brotherhood."

I grimaced. "I hope not. I really hope not, Levi."

"There's another option too, but it will be brutal for you to hear."

"Doesn't mean I don't need to hear it."

I shifted my weight, curling my legs up under me as I faced him.

He stilled on typing away and looked at me, pain for me all over his beautifully rugged features.

"He could have been working for Lynch all along. He could have facilitated what happened to your car that led to the kidnapping. He had an inside track to you, being your main assigned club protection back then. After we were freed, he allowed your hero worship of him to become more when it shouldn't have. He also kept you weak and in denial about what had happened, treating you with kid gloves. It may not have been out of care for you. It could have been coming from his role with Lynch to ensure you didn't become a threat or vengeful after what had happened. He couldn't break you when we were in captivity so it stands to reason that he'd be concerned that somebody who resisted all that he inflicted upon them would be classed as a very real threat to him, especially considering with you being connected to what used to be a formidable and brutal motorcycle club."

"God," I choked. "That's… the idea that it was all an awful manipulation… I can't… no. It can't be, Levi."

"But there were red flags when you were seeing him, yes?"

"Honestly, I wasn't looking. Not at all. Like you said, I *was* in major denial."

"Exactly. He didn't know the real you. It's not a stretch to posit that you didn't know the real him either."

"Maybe."

He took my hand. "Listen, that's just worst-case, just considering a bunch of options. Don't put any stock into it until we really figure it out."

"There's one way to narrow it down right now."

He nodded, of course getting it easily. "Call your father." He stroked my fingers. "It's been two years, are you gonna be okay doing that? I can do it for you if you want. Mason too. Even Colt, he's a real charmer, even over the phone."

He actually had me chuckling despite the subject matter. "I can picture it with Colt now. No, I've got it."

I snatched up my phone and scrolled to my phone book, to a number I hadn't accessed for a really long time.

I sucked in a steadying breath as Levi gave my fingers a bolstering squeeze. And then I dialed.

It picked up on the first ring, startling the crap out of me.

"Baby girl," my dad's gravelly voice sounded down the line. "Is that really you, Brianna?"

I swallowed hard and forced the words out, "Yeah, Dad. It's me."

"I can't fucking believe it. First Roman, now you. After all this time."

"Dad, I—"

"I'm sorry."

"You're… what?" He never apologized.

"I'm so fucking sorry. Your mom… what happened to you… this coming back around now… it's all my fault, being so power-hungry… it cost me what meant the world to me… cost me everything I loved."

"It's too late for apologies."

"Brianna—"

"No. I mean, we're beyond that."

Hearing his voice again was different than the last few times he'd tried to contact me over the years and I hadn't picked up and had instead just listened to his voicemails.

Before Levi had come back into my life and changed things, awakening me and helping me to kill the fear of admitting to the awful past we shared, I hadn't been able to stand entertaining anything from my past.

Not even my dad.

Part of me had blamed him.

The decisions he'd made as club president had been partially responsible for me being taken. He'd made some bad calls when trying to find me too, which had led to my mom going it alone, and her subsequent brutal murder right in front of me.

But now, talking to him, I could stand the pain.

Because that wasn't all there was now.

And because I could admit it and take it, I could also see beyond it, see all the other things regarding my dad and my past that *weren't* associated with those dark and twisted days Levi and I had spent being held captive by those *demons*.

"You mean that?" my dad asked, the need for it to be the case bleeding into his voice.

"I do. This won't be my last call." I sucked in a breath. "But for right now, I need to know something. Did you refuse to work with Roman Knight?"

"It was going that way until he told me that *you* were involved. I told him, of course I'd back you in any way I can, even if it could only be indirectly and from a distance. Why?"

"Tommy told me otherwise. He warned me off doing this, laid down a threat on your behalf."

"Brianna, I haven't been in contact with that shithead since I beat him down two years ago after I found out he'd been messing around with you."

I started. "You knew?"

"Intel reached me, yeah. Gotta say, you covered it up real well. It took the information being handed to me on a silver platter and laid out all undeniably for me to learn about it."

The realization hit me and I swung my head toward Levi. "You told my dad about Tommy and me?"

"Shit, yeah, that was me." He held up his hand quickly. "I honestly forgot to tell you during our revelation session, that's all. It wasn't important compared to all the rest. Sorry. I mean it, not telling you wasn't intentional. There's a lot of intel I acquired back then, a lot I passed on to key individuals over the years too in order to further my quest against Lynch, *and* to protect you. Passing information onto your dad was my way of protecting you from that fucker ex of yours. I recognized that he was keeping you weak and furthering your denial of who you really are."

"Fuck, Levi," I breathed.

"You believe me, right?" he asked, urgently, so worried that I wouldn't, that it would mess up what we had.

Especially this special day where we'd actually exchanged our *I-Love-You's.*

These moments of vulnerability from him, the raw emotion, it told me all I needed to know about his true intentions.

Love and care.

There was nothing nefarious in his intent toward me.

In his mind, he was doing what he did for me, for *us.*

He'd already come a long way with it, toning things down and recognizing the wrong way to do that now, but it would still be a work in progress for a while, given that he'd been doing things the same way for so long.

The point was his intent and that he was trying so hard.

"Yes," I said, rubbing his arm. "I believe you."

"Put me on speakerphone with Roman's heir, baby girl," my dad sounded from the phone, where I'd forgotten to put

my hand over the receiver because of the realization about Levi passing on intel to him.

I eyed Levi in question and he gave a nod.

I put it on speakerphone. "You're on, Dad."

"Thanks. Knight, I had a real good talk with your old man. He's trusting you to keep your word with this mission, yeah? You got it in the bag?"

"I do."

"Are you treating my daughter well?"

"Always. It's impossible for it to be any other way when it comes to her."

I beamed out at him. *Wow.*

"Damn, that's a hell of a response. Good on you. Keep it up or there will be hell, and you know I can bring it. Roman told me you've been researching the fuck out of my daughter and everyone connected to her."

"I know what you're capable of, yes. Cards on the table, I'm also a lot more than I seem."

"Roman made me aware."

"Good, because that's what I'm bringing to this mission. The same with Brianna. She's more than she seems as well. A fuck of a lot more."

"I know that now."

"You do?" I cut in.

"You think I don't watch over you and check in here and there? I've downloaded all your apps."

"You... you have?"

"They're fucking amazing. I'm real proud of you. And what Levi's getting at... I'm sorry I didn't see you had that hard edge and killer instinct in you before. You being my daughter clouded a lot and the way the club worked clouded the rest, you know?"

"I do, yeah."

"But that's all over now. I'm not that same guy, don't

see shit the same, Brianna. I promise you that much. I know what you're worth. I see you now, all right? To prove it, I'm not gonna stop you from doing what you need to do here where Malcolm Lynch and his bitch-ass followers are concerned. I've got you. All the way. Roman and me are working together on this."

Wow. I couldn't… I couldn't believe it.

"She's absorbing it," Levi spoke, when I couldn't summon the words.

"I get it, gonna take some time."

"No doubt. So, where Tommy's concerned, this contact he's just made with Brianna wasn't authorized by you?"

"Sure as shit wasn't. I'll drop my protection so you can see into my phone and whatever else you need to prove it if you want."

"I'll take you at your word."

"Yeah, Roman said you're good at figuring people out… even over the phone like this. It's their tone and conviction or lack of it, right?"

"And patterns in their speech and word choices."

"Damn, that's really something. When this shit is over and my baby girl is up for seeing me again, come along and teach me that shit, yeah?"

"It's a deal, Mr. Walker."

"Call me Curt. You've already earned it, empowering my baby girl again, doing this together to give her the peace she's needed for way too long."

"She empowered herself. I just reminded her of who she really was, that it wasn't all pain to reconnect with it."

"All pain… fuck… never should've gone down like that."

"Dad," I finally managed. "Can I let you go for now?"

I couldn't keep the emotion from my voice for the life of me.

I could hear it in his too.

"Yeah, I get it."

"I'll call you again soon. Really soon, okay?"

"Means a lot. Can't wait. Watch each other's backs, all right?"

"Always," Levi told him.

"We will," I added.

I hung up then and put my phone down.

The second I did, Levi's arms were around me, holding me to him. "It's all right. That was a lot. You handled it really well."

"We'd been estranged for two years."

"I know. Now a barrier has been broken through, it'll be different. Because *you're* different. Actually, both of you by the sounds of it with him."

A small chuckle escaped me. "Yeah, I can't believe it."

"I guess it just goes to show that even people who seem so cemented in their ways can find the strength and impetus to change for the better."

"It would seem so."

"What's up in here?" Colt's voice came from the bedroom door.

We eased apart just as he pounced on the bed, then settled himself on his side with his hand propping up his head. "Well? I'm sensing some big-time emotion." He eyed Levi. "What did you do?"

"Nothing, fucker."

Colt gave him a suspicious look. "You sure?"

"Yes. Fuck," Levi exclaimed, offended.

I laughed at their teasing banter. "It's all good, Colt. I spoke to my dad for the first time in ages."

"Oh, wow. How was that?"

"Intense. And… really nice."

His eyes lit up and he rubbed my legs over the covers. "Amazing, cutie."

"Yeah, it was."

"She's still processing it," Levi said, wrapping his arm around me. "How's the songwriting going?"

"Awesomely. Almost done already."

"Wow, that's gotta be the fastest you've ever written from start to completion."

"Well, I was inspired." He beamed out at us. "By our foursome."

We didn't get to discuss it more, as Mason burst in, looking out of sorts. "We have a problem."

Levi straightened and instinctively tightened his hold around me. "Our joint strategy to quell the insurrection didn't work?"

Mason waved his hand. "That's sorted. And, for the record, your idea for a show of force worked wonders. The *rebellion* was completely stomped out, they're running scared and extremely apologetic."

I smiled at Levi proudly, then at Mason.

The two of them were actually working well together and taking each other's suggestions, being open to it all.

Colt caught my eye and we grinned happily.

Until Mason stepped up to the bed and told us, "The safehouse may have been compromised."

16

~Levi~

"I thought those guys Royce Humphrey sent to Bree's apartment were dead?" Colt spoke. "Taken out by Roman Knight personally?"

"They are," I confirmed.

"This issue happened beforehand. When they were being moved into the transport van for Lev by *Hex*," Mason said. "By the time it was happening, one had regained consciousness after Lev's beatdown. He lifted one of our guy's phones."

"Worse that just *one of our guys*. Your lieutenant," I pointed out. "Well, the stand-in while Chase Arlington is still recovering from my takedown a few weeks back."

"Wait, and you think because Chase had been calling *you* on it, Mason, and now it's missing that Royce has it and he's gonna use it to track us here?" Colt looked out at me. "Can he even do that?"

I scrubbed my hand over my face. "Yes."

"Shit."

"It would take somebody exceptionally skilled, but we

know he has access to that, considering he was able to kick *me* out of his server. Initially, but still."

"*If* Royce even has the phone. We don't have confirmation. That's why I said the safehouse *may* have been compromised."

"So, we move?" Colt asked.

"That could backfire," Brianna's voice came from the door as she walked on in, her phone in her hand.

She'd been on the phone with *Vixen* putting her girls into play with the Tommy situation, and also to try to find confirmation of this phone situation.

My greeting got caught in my throat as I took her in.

She was wearing a sexy pastel-pink strappy tank with a whole lot of lace, and a pair of gray lounge pants, her feet bare.

She was so relaxed around us now and I loved it.

Her next words snapped me back to the immediate issue at hand. "It could be a ploy to get us to move, which would draw attention to us and possibly put us in their crosshairs when we may not even be if we actually stay here."

"I agree. There's not enough intel to go on," I said.

"We need eyes on Royce," Mason spoke, giving me a pointed look.

"If I pull off-mission to focus on him rather than Lynch and *Osiris*, it's gonna set us back."

"If you don't, we could take a hit that could put us down, Lev."

"Fuck," I uttered. "Fine. I'll take care of it."

"What if you bring Rina in on this to work the Lynch angle so you don't have to make a choice here or slow things down?" Colt offered.

"Rina?" Brianna asked.

"Caterina Leone," Colt told her. "A close friend of Lev's."

"A close friend, huh?" she asked, eyeing me curiously.

"*Friend* being the operative word, baby. Although, I've gotta admit, I like this little flare of jealously that I'm picking up on."

"In your dreams."

"Oh, absolutely."

She laughed. "Shut it."

"You know who she is?" Mason asked her.

"I'm well aware, yes. Santino Leone's daughter, a mafia princess. But how could she help?"

"She's an ace hacker just like Lev," Mason told her.

"It's on the down low," Colt added.

"Majorly so," I emphasized.

"Wow, okay. Then let's bring her in."

"I can't. She's dealing with her own shit. *But* there is something else I can do. Nico Marchetti has intel. I can gain access."

"Jesus fuck, no. You can't hack into Marchetti's shit. That's a death sentence right there."

I rolled my eyes. "A bit overdramatic, Mason, even for you."

"Lev. No."

I held up my hand. "All right."

"Contact him directly," he said.

"Yeah, make him an offer he can't—"

"Got it, Colt," I said, with a roll of my eyes.

He grinned.

I eyed Mason, more than a little surprised by him giving the go ahead here. "You're giving me your blessing to go ahead and make a deal with a mafia heir?"

"I trust you. *Now*."

"Yeah?"

"Yeah," he said, smiling.

"I'd have to meet with him in person. He won't make a deal any other way, something well known about the particular bastard."

"I expected as much."

"Go in stealth, Lev," Colt cautioned me, his sweet worry for me clear.

"I will, cupcake. Don't worry."

"You should give Caterina a heads up," Brianna advised me. "Another well-known thing concerning all of this is Nico and Caterina's hatred for one another. Her being your friend, I can't imagine it will go down well. Especially if you don't clue her in. Just explain how urgent the situation is, I'm sure she'll understand."

"Yeah. All right, let me reach out and sort this," I said, giving Brianna a kiss on the forehead, then pulling my phone from my cargo pants to set it up.

Making a deal with the devil it was then.

Wouldn't be the first time.

A DIVE BAR.

Kind of apt for the dirty dealing that was about to go down.

It was also the kind of establishment where I felt the most comfortable.

Unlike the world I'd grown up in, these sorts of places were raw and honest. There was no pretense. People were their real selves, down to the bone. There was no bullshit.

With one exception.

The dangerous fucker I was here to meet.

Deception and manipulation were the name of the game for him.

Good thing I was well-schooled in that just as well as he was.

A couple of bar flies sat up at the front nursing their drinks.

There was another day drinker sipping at a scotch near the middle who I pegged as late-sixties, his shock of white wiry hair standing out through the dim lighting of the place.

I heard that distinctive rumble of a Ferrari outside, signaling the mafia prince's arrival.

He moved quickly—just the way I liked it—and he was stepping into the bar a mere few seconds later.

He located me quickly and strode toward me with confident, measured steps.

I took him in.

At twenty-five years old, he carried himself with the confidence and command of somebody twice his age.

His deep-black hair brushed the collar of his white open-collar shirt, a designer leather jacket over the top, black just like his dress pants. He was a big guy, broad and all muscle. Green eyes the color of sapphires honestly locked on mine as he swaggered toward me, emanating a whole lot of power.

As he reached my booth, his gaze darted to my vodka and he turned his nose up. But a quirk of his lips took its place when he turned his attention to the bottle of Johnny Walker Black and the crystal glass beside it.

Recognizing that I'd gone the extra mile in a show of respect, he gave me a chin lift, then took a seat.

He started pouring into his glass, telling me, "You certainly have my attention."

"That was the goal."

He looked me up and down. "I see you're still dressing beneath your station."

"I like to be prepared."

"You *like* people to recognize that you're always prepared for a fight."

"I am," I rebutted pointedly.

His lips quirked again.

He took a sip of his drink, then sat back against the booth, affecting an air of nonchalance, which I knew couldn't possibly be real given the situation.

He was good, though.

Very good concealing his true feelings and intentions behind that proverbial mask of his.

"Your strategy may not be the optimal one, Levi. In fact, it can be unwise to give everything away up front, to allow people to know exactly what and who they are dealing with."

"It can also be a deterrent. A formidable one."

"Well, our philosophies differ. Something that may change in time as you come to see that your approach can be provocative rather than the deterrent you intend. However, that is not what you've called me here to discuss. So, we'll get to it." He took another sip of his drink, then told me, "I *am* investigating Malcolm Lynch and he is an enemy to me, not an intended asset or partner in any sort of business venture."

"Why is he an enemy? That much I wasn't able to deduce."

I needed to understand his motives here in order to protect myself and my loves.

"As I'm sure you're aware, *Osiris* has become heavily involved in arms trading since its revival. My father intends to partner with Lynch, desiring to acquire military grade weapons, far from the street level weaponry the Marchetti Syndicate deals in. It's both dangerous and the wrong move for us. He's getting into bed with madmen. Should it come to pass it will hurt the family gravely, setting us on a path that will be incredibly difficult to turn back from. I won't allow it."

"Wow, going against Marco... that's a hell of a thing."

"We do what we must to protect what's ours."

"Yeah. Yeah, we do." I took a swig of my vodka. "So, how did you come to acquire intel on these operations? I couldn't find it anywhere."

And I was damned good.

"Only through the fact that it is my father who's doing business with them. All their files were locked down, kept off the internet, only rooted to a local network connection. As I'm privy to the deal that was made, I was able to obtain the information." He pulled something from his pants pocket and I saw a flash drive. "Unfortunately, I cannot get my hands dirty on this one. The stakes are too high if my involvement is discovered."

"Hence, why you need me."

"Precisely. Ensure that Roman is also involved. However, he cannot know of my part. Is that clear?"

"Crystal. Terms of the deal and all that."

Nico Marchetti might have a really fucked-up side, but he was also known for never breaking a deal.

Fortunately, he knew me to be honorable too.

As he held out the flash drive to me, I took it, but then his hand clamped down around mine, stilling me.

"One more condition."

I cocked an eyebrow.

"Caterina is off-limits."

"We're merely friends."

"Your in-person get togethers will stop, effective immediately."

I glared across the booth. "I wasn't aware you had influence over her."

His lip curled into a sadistic smile. "The news is very recent, that's why you're not privy to it."

"What news?"

"Caterina Leone is to be my wife."

I jolted and that only made his twisted smile spread. "You hate one another."

"That matters not."

With his free hand he reached into his inner jacket pocket and pulled out a Tiffany ring box.

He opened it to reveal a spectacular diamond encrusted engagement ring interspersed with turquoise— her favorite color—along with a wedding band that was engraved with *NM*.

He saw me focusing on that and told me, "She will wear my brand. *My property, my wife.*"

I gritted my teeth. "I noticed that *my love* was missing from that."

"Some marriages are based on duty. You are fortunate given your position as heir to a formidable empire as well that your father has allowed you to be free of that obligation."

He stowed the ring away and tightened his hold on my fingers, making me fight ever harder to resist my instinctual reaction to smash his bottle, then jam it into his fucking throat for daring to lay a hand on me.

"I trust you."

Mason's words rang in my head. I wouldn't fuck that up. I wouldn't jeopardize any of it.

"My wife won't be in another man's presence without me by her side. Are we clear? That's my final term of our deal."

"Fine," I ground out. "Just don't fucking hurt her."

"I don't intend to. It's a mutually beneficial arrangement."

How?

How had Rina agreed to this?

To marry this man whom she hated?

I stopped myself.

The immediate mission had to take precedence.

Besides, she was absolutely no fool.

If she'd agreed to this, she had her reasons.

And he was right about one thing.

She'd make damned sure the arrangement *was* beneficial to her.

"All right, you've got it," I assured him.

He relinquished the drive to me and I stowed it away on my person.

He downed the rest of his glass, then snatched up the bottle.

"It was a pleasure doing business with you."

I gave a nod. "You too."

"Until next time, Levi."

"Right back at you, Nico."

He smiled. "*Arrivederci.*"

With that, he turned on his heel and swept out of the bar.

Making deals with devils indeed.

17

~Mason~

My pencil flew across the page.

Something had snapped back into place for me since we'd been up here.

Well, it could've been anywhere, but it was just the fact of our foursome—the positive impact it was having on me.

And my creativity.

I'd flown through five tattoo designs in the last couple of hours.

They were damned good too.

Inspiration and creativity were coursing through me like livewires.

Working on my design journal had started earlier as a means to tamper down my anxiety about what was going on, while we waited on Lev's program to complete to detect Royce's location, and also on Bree's *Vixen* to pull the intel we needed too.

I wasn't used to sitting back and allowing others to take the lead.

But we were a team now, and the two of them were best suited to these particular tasks.

As I'd sunk into my drawings, though, it had become a lot more than sublimating.

I was allowing it to become a bigger part of me again.

I was allowing it back in.

It wasn't time to immerse myself back into it fully.

But the fact that I could see the possibility now was a huge thing.

The reminder that it wasn't yet time, though, hit me as rushed footsteps sounded down the corridor outside my bedroom, and then Bree's voice rang out.

"Mason!"

"In here, dark angel! My bedroom!" I called back.

A moment later, I looked up from my journal as I sat leaning against the headboard of my bed to see Brianna walking in with Colt just behind her, his guitar slung over his back.

"We have a problem."

"That should be our fucking mantra or something," Colt groused.

Bree reached out and fondled his mohawk. "Only until this is all over, sweetheart."

He preened at her words of comfort and her cute way with him.

And then she snapped back into action and walked into the room with her phone in hand.

When she reached me, she held it out and I pushed off the bed and rose to my feet to take it.

The program Levi had left running while he was gone that would get eyes on Royce Humphrey flashed on the screen.

"It's completed," she told me.

"Already?" I asked, even as I saw the startling evidence for myself. "That was a mammoth area to cover."

She lifted a shoulder, pride shining in her eyes.

And a little arousal too.

"It's Levi. He wrote the program himself. He could plug in specific variables to narrow things down and discount unnecessary data."

I studied the screen. "Fuck me, it's found the bastard."

Bree nodded. "The most recent sighting was two hours from here at a truck stop."

"Shit," Colt exclaimed. "There's nothing else around that area—around here—for hours on end. He's gotta be coming for us."

"With his mercenaries too, according to the footage Levi's program was able to pull."

"A dozen of them," I spoke aloud as I took in the program's report.

Another curse left me as I rapidly tried to formulate a plan of action.

I didn't get more than a few seconds to absorb the data as *my* phone rang.

I snatched it up from the bed to see that it was Levi calling.

I swiped it open and hurriedly put him on speakerphone.

His voice came down the line before I could even answer, urgency coming off him in waves, *"Are you seeing what I'm seeing from the program?"*

"Yeah, we've seen it, Lev," I assured him.

The sound of his Harley roaring filled our ears.

"Wait. Are you riding and checking your phone?" Colt asked incredulous, because Lev didn't do that. Ever.

"Yeah, I was worried about you all. I couldn't wait the hours' long drive until I got back to you."

"How far out are you?" Bree asked.

"Too far to get back there and pack up with you. Take care of it now. I'm gonna call my dad and have him prepare for our

arrival so he can secure the estate like Fort fucking Knox and bring us in discreetly so it doesn't bring Royce or Lynch bearing down on him."

"I'm not running from Royce Humphrey," Bree ground out vehemently.

"You sure as fuck are," Levi growled.

"No. This is our chance to end that fucker."

"The risk is too high."

"A dozen of his military trained guys are with him," I pointed out.

"So we split up. Four-to-one can be handled. If Lev can get here in time, it'll be even more possible."

"That's one of the most reckless things I've ever fucking heard. And coming from me, of all people, that's really saying something, cupcake. And Brianna? This is not fucking happening. Do you hear me?"

"He murdered my mom right in front of me. He abused you. Taunted me. Egged Malcolm Lynch on when he was ripping me apart over and over. I can't turn away when he's gonna be here within my grasp! I won't!"

Stunned silence filled the space and down the line from Lev.

"Wildflower, I love you. Please don't do this to me. That many soldiers at his side, you won't be able to come out on top. You very likely won't even get within reach of him at all. But what will happen, is you'll get hurt. For fucking nothing. This is not the time to take that motherfucker."

"Levi—"

"I swear to you, there will be another."

"We'll fucking well create another time to put him down," I told her.

She gritted her teeth, clenching her fists, trying to fight the urge.

Colt was there then, wrapping his arm around her.

"Please, cutie. We need you safe, we need all of us safe and together."

Slowly, she managed a nod. "Okay. Yeah, okay."

"Fuck. Thank you."

Relief rolled through me that it had been stopped at that.

I'd made a vow to her that I wouldn't use extreme methods with her like I had in order to bring her up here.

So if she hadn't listened, there would be no way for me to get her out of here against her will.

I wouldn't risk what we'd built and what had flourished between all four of us since we'd been up here.

"All right, move now. He was tagged by my program via those security cameras at the truck stop two hours ago, but it took time to search through a whole load of them to pick him up, meaning he could be anywhere right now. There's no businesses or homes past that point all the way up to Boreas, so we're blind at the moment. He could be there at any time. Don't risk it. Pack quick and go. I'm riding as fast as I can. Brianna, I'm gonna hack into the GPS on your phone so I can track you guys. Stay together, all right? And, are you okay with that, Wildflower?"

"Yeah. Go ahead."

"Asking permission ? You've come a long way, brother," Colt said. "Proud of you."

"Well, I'm only asking from the three of you. Everyone else is fair game."

I chuckled, thankfully his words adding some much-needed levity to the situation.

"We're gonna move now, Lev. Keep in close contact."

"Will do. Watch your six. All of you."

"We will," Bree confirmed.

I hung up, then turned to the two of them. "Time to move."

―

"THAT'S EVERYTHING," Bree confirmed as I took the last reinforced steel case from her and packed it into her charcoal gray Charger.

It contained Levi's computer—hacking—equipment. The fucking case could probably actually withstand a RPG strike, it was that hardcore, something he'd *borrowed* from Knightsridge Engineering. Lev loved discovering new prototypes there. Roman loved it less when he did, obviously.

The Charger had been the most non-descript, non-attention drawing vehicle we'd had immediate access to at the time of rushing up here.

My black shiny Porsche was an attention-getter of a vehicle as was Colt's satin-blue Mercedes. Lev had brought his Harley when he'd had to drop the van back in Stonewell after transporting the mercenaries, which hadn't been ideal for the snow. But we'd had to make do.

It had helped that Brianna's Charger wasn't listed to her, or her father, or technically connected to her. She'd protected herself there to minimize anyone's ability to track her—at least via her vehicle.

Smart woman.

As usual with her.

"Yeah?" I asked, always needing to double-check with everything.

She'd been in charge of packing up all of Levi's equipment, because she had the know-how there that Colt and I didn't.

Meanwhile, I'd packed her clothes and supplies along with my own and Colt had packed up Levi's along with his.

We were ready to move out.

Twenty minutes was all it had taken, because we'd worked smoothly and efficiently.

Just the way I liked it.

Colt came down from the snowy hill toward the car carrying two gym bags full of clothes, his gold puffer jacket a similar style to Bree's swishing about him with his rapid movements and the way he swung his arms when he was hurrying along—even with bags in his hands.

"Good to go," he told me as he reached us.

"Perfect," I said, taking one from him as he reached us and hauling it into the trunk, while he took care of the other.

I shut the trunk, then unzipped my aviator jacket to withdraw the keys and hand them back to Bree when my phone started buzzing wildly in my pocket.

I pulled it out to see a whole lot of flashing red.

Fuck me.

"The electric fence has been tripped."

Bree frowned. "The fence, but not the early-warning system?"

"Royce must've caught onto it and circumvented it."

"Shit. Let's go. Right now," Colt said, heading for the passenger seat.

He didn't even make it that far as two gunshots rang out, echoing brutally through the area.

The two front tires popped a split-second later, the car lurching.

We all spun around, following the trajectory of the shots and the sounds to see four hooded guys all in black emerging from the trees to our left.

The sounds of footsteps in the snow came from the right and we looked to see another four coming from that direction.

"On your knees, kiddos!" a voice rang out coming from

behind us by the house, and there were the remaining four mercenaries striding around the side of the house.

Royce Humphrey made unlucky thirteen, leading the way.

Middle-aged as opposed to his soldiers who were in their early thirties at most, he was a tall and lanky guy. He was decked out the same as them in all black.

The twelve of them closed in around us.

When Royce reached us, he stroked his goatee and started eye-fucking Bree, so Colt and I stepped in front of her, blocking his view.

Slimy piece of shit.

"All the trouble you've caused me, how you've put not only my operations at risk, but my goddamn life, we should be here to kill you. *But* I need leverage, I need to make sure Malcolm knows it's not me coming at him. And he'll want a gift to go along with it. That's you. You'd think that would mean I'm showing mercy here, but, believe me, death would be the mercy. Once you're in Malcolm's hands, the horrors will truly begin." He looked at Brianna through the small gap between me and Colt. "Isn't that right, *pretty princess.*"

I felt her shudder against us.

"Where's Knight?"

"No idea," I ground out.

"I wouldn't be so hasty, *Hall.* I've got twelve guys here who get off on spilling a whole lot of blood."

"You're not touching him!" Colt yelled.

Royce slapped his hand over his heart sarcasm dripping. "How touching." His eyes narrowed in the next second, switching on a dime like a psycho. "And foolish."

I stepped forward and hissed, "Like I said, he's not here."

He sneered. "No matter. He'll come when we're done

here. He'll try to stop me from handing you over. We'll take him then."

"You aren't taking him anywhere, you piece of shit," Bree seethed, stepping out from behind us and facing her former tormentor head-on, like the brave and impressive woman that she was.

"Damn, you've grown up good. I'll make sure to have a taste before I hand you over to Malcolm."

Everything happened so fast then.

Colt lost his composure at the despicable threats to her and threw his fist.

It slammed into the underside of Royce's jaw, making his head snap back and destabilizing him.

As he stumbled back, he bellowed at his guys, "Subdue them! And make it fucking hurt!"

He stepped back, folding his arms across his chest and looking on sadistically to enjoy the fucked-up show.

And then the guys closed in.

Before they could fully, I smashed my fist into the closest guy, knocking him to the snow in one shot.

I spun as another tried to take a shot at me, and caught his fist, twisting it brutally until I heard a telltale snap that had him grunting. And then I yanked him toward me and used the hold as leverage to haul him around and toss him into two more incoming guys.

As I kicked back another with my boot, I caught sight of Brianna jumping onto the hood of the car, then smashing her foot into a hostile's face, blowing him back.

As another tried to grab her, she leapt up onto the roof of the car and assumed a fighting stance.

Two approached her from either side.

Thankfully, I saw Colt grab one of them and wrench them back, then he smashed their face into the trunk, knocking them out cold.

Distracted by the wellbeing of my loves, my plan to cut a path through the guys was jeopardized when I took a brutal hit to the gut.

Instinctively, it forced me to double over, and then I took a hammer fist to the back of the neck that drove me to my knees in the snow.

One of them rounded me and fisted my hair, wrenching my head back, and about to knee me in the face in a clear attempt to knock me out, or keep beating me until it had the same result.

As they raised their knee, something cut through the air.

In the next split-second, a knife was buried in the guy's throat.

As he choked and collapsed, I looked out to see Bree giving me a chin lift, before she spun into a spinning kick that propelled her latest opponent off the roof of the car and had him landing with a hefty thud on the hood. He ricocheted off it and hit the ground on his back.

As I shoved back more hostiles, the fuckers overrunning us by their sheer numbers, I caught sight of Colt struggling to defend himself against three that had closed in around him.

I ducked and rolled away from those closing me in, coming up by the guy Bree had killed, and wrenching the knife from his corpse.

And then I tossed it at one of Colt's opponents.

It plunged into their chest, right on target for their heart and they lurched, sinking into the snow wheezing.

Colt looked out at me and winked, before ripping the knife out too, then turning it on the other two hostiles.

As much as we were giving it our all, as soon as we took one down, several more took their place.

There were just too many.

The odds really weren't in our favor.

And as much as I hated it and the connotations of weakness and failure associated with it, we needed to call a retreat.

A strategic fucking retreat.

I called out to Colt and Bree, "Head for the house!"

Against all rhyme and reason, we managed to break free with a whole lot of dodging, weaving and ducking.

"Go! Go! Go!" I yelled to Bree and Colt as we reached the door of the house and Colt punched in the passcode on the electronic lock.

They rushed inside and I slid in just in time, slamming the door closed and locking it as two of the hostiles crashed into it.

I spun around to face my loves, the three of us breathing heavily.

"How is everyone?" I asked, looking them over.

Thankfully, Bree looked untouched and Colt only had a mild bruise across his right cheek.

For my part, my ribs were killing me.

The guy who'd kicked me in the gut had done more damage that I'd let on, even to myself, while we'd been in the throes of battle. It was trying to move, let alone run.

Thankfully, adrenaline was helping me out, helping me to push onward.

"All good here," Colt said.

He laid his hand on Bree's shoulder and she jolted, jerking away.

"Sorry," she exclaimed, holding up her hands apologetically. "I just… seeing him again… it's a lot."

"No need to apologize at all," Colt told her.

"I'm so sorry this is happening, dark angel." I gestured to the right. "Let's get you out of here ASAP. We'll head to the house entrance into the garage and make a break for it via snowmobile."

Colt nodded. "Wild idea, but the only way out right now, unless we head through the trees."

"Heading out on foot risks them catching up to us," I said."

"The fact we didn't hear them coming points to them parking their vehicles really far out, so we access the snowmobiles and they'll only be able to chase on foot," Bree pointed out, already coming back to herself despite the shock of a demon from her past showing up right at our door and a massive attack descending on us.

That was our woman.

Resilient.

Courageous.

Fierce.

As the hostiles slammed into the front door, trying to break it down, we bolted through the vast space of the house, headed for the access door to the garage.

We were just thirty feet out when a thunderous crash sounded as we were passing the kitchen.

I swung my head to see several of Royce's guys pushing through the wreckage of the kitchen door and the shattered windows either side, glass littering the linoleum floor like a jagged carpet.

I snatched the knife Colt still had from earlier and rushed forward as they tried to bolt from the kitchen toward us.

Before the closest one could even touch me, I snagged his arm, wrenched his gun from his holster, then pistol-whipped him with it.

As he staggered back, I cocked it, then fired off a brutally close range shot to his kneecap.

A blood curdling scream tore from the asshole's throat

as he collapsed onto the ground, clutching his bloodied, shattered knee and writhing uncontrollably.

"Holy shit," I heard Colt gasp, having a difficult time dealing with the full-on, no-holds-barred brutality. It was a lot different than merely trading punches.

The guy just behind the guy I'd felled hesitated at what had just happened to his buddy.

I took advantage of it, firing a bullet through his left shoulder that had him roaring in agony and falling back.

The third guy let out a battle cry and lunged, but I reacted quicker, caught up in merciless life-and-death mode that was reminiscent of the *incident* from five years ago.

I snagged him and slammed him against the door frame, ducking as the guy threw a right hook. I thrust my fist into his gut over and over in a series of rapid-fire blows that had him choking and doubling over.

I'd just delivered a clip to his jaw that had him crumbling to the floor, when a knife sailed past us, and I watched it tear through the eye of the guy I'd kneecapped, killing him instantly.

I turned to see Brianna standing there giving me a nod.

Commotion from the front door had us looking to see it blasting open and four more rushing in.

I burst out of the kitchen and fired off consecutive shots that put all four down swiftly with a simple kill shot through the skull.

But then more movement caught our attention just a moment before more guys burst from the living room, another couple rushing down the stairs.

Jesus.

They were upon us in moments and I only got to fire off one more shot before I was slammed into the wall, another hostile smashing my hand against it over and over until he was able to yank the gun free and toss it away.

It was chaos then as we were descended upon.

I didn't even get the chance to look out to see where Colt and Bree were.

I was ripped off my feet by a sweep to the ankles and I grunted as I landed hard on the hardwood floor.

I thrust my forearms up as three guys wailed on me until it was all a blur of unadulterated violence.

Jesus. They were gonna take us.

I couldn't stop it.

We were completely overrun.

Just when it looked like it was over, automatic fire rang out, jolting the shit out of me.

The guys assaulting me were downed in moments, torn apart and riddled with bullets.

I pushed back to my feet to see all of them being ripped into with the furious fire.

When it finally came to an end, an eerie silence took over, the only sounds I was aware of being mine and Colt's heavy breathing.

I turned to see him with a black eye and his knuckles bloodied, him sweating all over.

He was still standing, he was all right.

I went to seek out Brianna amongst the mess and check she was okay too, when footsteps at the top of the stairs pulled our attention.

It wasn't her.

Colt and I looked up to see a guy at the top of the stairs instead with a machine gun in hand, decked out in red and black padded snowmobile gear, a crimson balaclava over his head giving off Red Hood vibes.

He nodded at us, then pulled off the balaclava and I started when I took in the sight of Roman Knight.

He rushed down the stairs, taking in all the dropped bodies, and came to us.

"Are you hurt?" he asked, that fatherly concern of his coming forth that he'd always shown to Levi in spades.

"Just superficial," I told him, looking to Colt for his confirmation.

Colt nodded. "How did you... what are you doing here?"

"Figured you could use a hand." He slapped his gun. "Or a few bullets."

Through the shock of it, it took me a few moments to take stock, and then I was spinning around and looking every which way, becoming frantic with it as I uttered breathlessly, "Where the hell is Brianna?"

18

~Brianna~

I flailed wildly as the two guys dragged me across the snow toward the trees.

"Stop! Get the fuck off me!" I yelled.

To no avail.

They didn't answer, didn't speak at all.

They were like robots programmed by Royce Humphrey to do his bidding and nothing more. No sentiment, no thoughts of their own, no fucking humanity.

Not a far cry from their maker.

A despicable demon incarnate.

I was suddenly released roughly and dropped in the snow just before the forest.

They stepped to either side of me, guarding me, making it clear I wasn't going anywhere.

And then Royce stepped out from the shadows, where he'd obviously retreated to when we'd started fighting back and he'd been worried about the outcome of his attack.

He walked to me, smiling cruelly.

I jolted as he grasped my jaw in a painful grip.

I went to respond, to lay into the psychopath, but his

guys either side of me grabbed my shoulders, bearing down and keeping me on my knees.

At Royce's mercy.

Just like back then with him and Malcolm Lynch.

That nightmare.

That horrific abuse.

That degradation.

That pain.

The adrenaline already tearing through me threatened to be undercut by one of my *episodes* that I could feel trying to breach the surface.

The flash slammed into me before I could stop it, taking me down to that dark place.

Royce appeared and dragged my mom in. Her jeans and t-shirt were caked in mud, her leather jacket even torn, and her black hair, just like mine, was matted.

"Baby girl!" she shrieked, staring at the glass.

"She can't see you," Malcolm told me. "I've just had Royce tell her you're here being railed by me like a good little whore bitch."

I couldn't even fight as he tightened his grip on me, then fucked into me like a madman, as Royce slapped my mom hard across the face.

I screamed into his hand as he started beating on her until she collapsed onto the concrete.

"All this fear from you is turning me on. Go on, squeeze my cock, and I'll make it quick for her, no more drawing it out."

I couldn't process any of it, I just shrieked and bucked in his merciless hold.

And then Royce drew a gun.

I blinked back to reality to see Royce still holding my jaw and calling me *pretty princess* in that creepy way that Lynch had.

His free hand was stroking my hair now and trailing

down to my throat, along to the tops of my breasts accessible through my now open puffer jacket.

I swallowed hard as a shudder took me, threatening to spark a full-on *episode* which would completely incapacitate me.

As if it wasn't bad enough already.

I hadn't been able to do a thing back then.

To save my mom.

To stop any of it.

Another flash took me.

As we were making our way down the corridor, one of the doors to the left opened, and a guard wearing one of those awful ski masks stepped out.

"What the fuck are you doing free?"

He came at us in the next second.

The hell I was going to let him stop us from finally making our escape from this nightmare.

As I came out of it, I locked onto the memory.

We had fought back.

I'd gone to that dark place fueled by desperation, rage and terror.

I hadn't been trained to fight then.

I hadn't dealt with anything like that prior to that night.

I'd been a little girl, basically.

Not anymore.

It was different now.

Everything was different.

I was different.

As his fingers started to dip inside my shirt I asked, "Are you really this vanilla?"

It worked all too easily—fragile egos of psychopaths and all that—and he took a step back, finally releasing my jaw as he regarded me with a whole lot of dark curiosity.

"What do you mean?"

"You said you wanted a taste, you should make it worth your while, especially considering you'll be handing me over to Malcolm. You know, I thought you were the softer one compared to him. I guess that was why you were the sidekick. You can't bring the sadism and intimidation like he can."

"You're wrong."

"Yeah, then prove it. Let's do a little gun play."

"What?"

"That's something he threatened to do to me, but never did in the end. You want me a mess when you hand me over, subdued, then that's the way to go. I hate guns, they scare me."

Bullshit.

But I was selling it well.

"Why would you offer me this?"

"You walk away afterward, take me to Lynch like you intended, but call off the kidnapping of Mason Hall and Colton Sharp."

"What about Knight?"

"I know that could never be on the table because he's put you in Lynch's crosshairs by using you to search for that megalomaniac."

"True." He played with his straggly goatee, thinking it over. "Fine, you've got yourself a deal."

Then he was snapping his fingers at the guy holding my left shoulder. "Give me your piece."

I'd already checked that Royce wasn't carrying his own.

In fact, it was what had given me this idea in the first place.

It had been all about causing a distraction.

Now I'd put my deal out there Royce was no longer so on edge and wary of me, because he believed he was going to get what he wanted—one over on Lynch using me to do it.

And as he had to grab a gun from one of his men, it served to make the guy inadvertently release his painful debilitating grip on my shoulder as he shifted his weight to draw it from his hip holster.

It actually ended up with him releasing me entirely as he was focused on giving his boss what he'd ordered of him.

That was all the window I needed to turn things around.

Just as the Glock was about to be passed between them, I snatched it with my now free left hand and spun and pistol-whipped the guy to my right still holding me.

As he fell back, I burst to my feet, executing a brutal push kick that sent Royce sprawling into the forest.

As the guy on the left went to grab me, I ducked, then came up with a harsh uppercut that had his head snapping back.

A sense of coming victory rolled through me.

But I was still shaky from what had happened, the threats of it, and the callbacks to that awful time.

I was basically still trying to fight off an *episode.*

It had me fumbling with the gun to flick the safety off, then take aim at Royce, and Lefty was there smashing his fist into my face and then wrenching it back from my grip.

I stumbled back, but managed to catch my footing.

But then Righty was there with Royce coming back too, the three of them surrounding me.

I leapt up into a spinning kick and blew Lefty back.

But it cost me as Righty shoved me and, as I stumbled, Royce was there snatching up a hefty branch and sweeping it at my back.

I grunted at the brutal impact that sent me crashing onto the snow on my stomach.

I scrambled to get up, but then there was a knee on my back driving down painfully and pinning me there.

I strained to look up to see Royce staring down at me with a malicious look in his eyes as he grabbed at his belt.

No. No. No.

Rapid-fire movement caught my eye, rushing through the dark forest.

And then Levi burst out from the trees and barreled into the fray, roaring like an unhinged animal when he saw what was happening to me.

That was exactly how he laid into them in the very next moment too.

Like an animal.

A feral beast.

And I loved him for it.

He was here for me, just like he had been back then during our attempted escape.

"We're here together. You're not alone," I told him.

He smiled out at me. "Couldn't have asked for anybody better to be in this nightmare with."

"Right back at you."

I blinked and focused through the shock of it all, noting that he was covered in blood and dirt, something that had occurred before he'd even come at Royce and his two soldiers just now.

Screams sounded as Levi broke the knee of one of the guys, then the other's arm.

He was snarling as he snatched a gun, then put a bullet between their eyes in quick succession.

And then he turned his unforgiving gaze on Royce who was standing there in absolute stunned silence.

"Yeah, not a *kiddo* anymore, am I, motherfucker?" Levi spat at him.

As I pushed back to my feet, Levi lunged at him and tackled him across the waist, taking him down to the ground brutally hard.

But in his current feral state, he wasn't even fazed by the jarring impact.

Royce was, though, and he was too slow to react as Levi drew a knife, then plunged it into the asshole's gut.

A shrill scream tore through the night and Royce writhed on the ground beneath Levi.

Levi ripped out the blade, then held it right in front of the demon's face.

Royce lifted a trembling hand. "Please," he gasped, grimacing at the wound in his gut, blood pouring down over his fingers. "Show mercy."

Levi's eyes went black.

"There's no mercy for those beyond redemption," he growled.

Then he grabbed Royce's shoulder and jerked him to him as he drove the knife right through his chest.

As Royce's eyes went wide and he choked, Levi twisted it, then yanked it out, a haunting, gargling scream tearing from Royce.

Levi thrust his foot into his face, knocking him onto his back.

And then he stared, like I was, watching as the life drained out of the sick bastard.

As one of the demons left this world.

Levi staggered back and turned to me, his eyes wide and pained.

"God, what happened to you before you got here?" I gasped as the state of him.

He was bloodied and stumbling in his step and there

was a deep, nasty gash down his cheek that was bleeding all down his face profusely.

"The fucker had called in reinforcements. I headed the six of them off and put them down so they couldn't reach their destination here."

Holy hell.

He sucked in an unsteady breath. "It's over," he rasped. "We're safe."

For now.

From Royce Humphrey and his mercenaries at least.

Levi slumped to his knees, all the blood seeping into the snow and staining it, tainting it.

"Too close," he muttered on a pained murmur. "Christ."

19

~Roman Knight~

My son was in love.

I'd heard as much from him during our impromptu—from his perspective—get-together at that diner a few days ago.

But seeing it right before my eyes was another thing entirely.

I'd come close to giving up hope that it would ever be possible for him.

For him to be able to love like that, or to allow himself to be loved like that.

As a child, he'd been the most gentle and caring little boy. To everyone he'd met.

Even when I'd brought him into *Knightsridge Engineering* more so to prepare him for his role as heir apparent, I'd gone to great pains to only expose him to the legitimate aspects.

The only exception had been my business with Curt Walker. He was a dangerous individual, but he had a soft spot for children on account of having a daughter he absolutely adored. Bringing Levi into that had been a perfect compromise and a way to teach him about the dangers involved in running my empire, schooling him on how to read people, how to strike complicated deals that had high stakes attached.

But beyond that, I'd been concerned that drawing him any deeper into those aspects of my work would dim the bright spark that he'd possessed, that it would taint his beautiful innocence, that it would poison his pure and unjaded heart.

Then the kidnapping had happened and it had destroyed everything I'd guarded him against.

It had destroyed my boy.

There were those in life who never recovered from being shattered to pieces.

For the last six years, that had been the fate I'd thought had befallen Levi.

Until *now*.

I watched from the shadows through to the kitchen as he sat up at the kitchen island while Brianna tended to the injuries that he'd sustained.

It was uncanny witnessing such a thing where he was concerned.

Since he'd been liberated from captivity at the hands of those madmen, he'd never allowed me or anyone else to treat any damage he'd sustained. He'd even learned to perform stitches on himself to avoid it.

He saw it as a weakness.

Even suffering a single hit was a failure in his mind.

It went back to six years ago. That shame that they'd afflicted him with.

Everything went back to six years ago for him.

But now there was finally a positive element.

Her.

Brianna Walker.

Curt's baby girl.

Well, that was how he'd seen her for too long.

She was a far cry away from that now.

I'd seen it for myself earlier.

Although, I hadn't needed to see it to have been able to draw that conclusion. The fact that Levi had taken a liking to her in the intense way he never had before when it came to women had been enough to go on. Only someone strong, self-reliant, and powerful could catch Levi's interest in that way. That type of woman was also the only type that would be able to handle my son.

"Gonna keep lurking, or are you actually gonna make it inside the kitchen, Dad?"

I smiled to myself. *Little miscreant.*

"My doctor is finishing up seeing to Mason and Colton," I informed them. "They're well. Just minor cuts and bruises, fortunately. Although Mason has sustained a couple of bruised ribs, but they'll heal well with a little rest."

"Thank goodness," Brianna breathed, looking pained that it had come close to being a great deal worse.

The boys had insisted that she go first with treatment, absolutely not having it when she'd wanted Mason to get a nasty slice to his arm dealt with first.

It was beyond chivalry. It was a deep affection and adoration that they had displayed toward her.

More than even that. They were a unit. A close-knit team.

It was exactly the kind of support that all four of them needed.

I was aware of each of their individual issues, but together now, with the strain gone that had been there for a good long while, those issues were manageable. They weren't transcended, because that wasn't realistic, or true to life, but they were soothed by their foursome structure.

"Thanks, Dad."

I stepped up to him and Brianna eased back, starting to pack up the medical supplies I'd given her. "Let me see," I said, grasping his jaw and angling his face so I could get a look at the deep three-inch cut across his left cheek. It had been bleeding so profusely that it had required stitches. Very impressively done stitches. "This is impeccable work, Miss Walker."

She shrugged. "Unfortunately, I've had a lot of practice."

"Fixing up your father's club members?"

"During what I called the *transition period* where my dad tried to go to war with Malcolm Lynch and it cost him a third of his club members, before he then shut it all down."

"I see. I'm sorry you had to bear the brunt of that, my dear."

"Nothing compared to what she had to bear prior to that, the thing that caused that ill-advised war," Levi muttered.

He eased from my grasp, and I saw his hands shaking.

It was that rage.

Before I could react to calm him, Brianna surprised me as she was there, stroking his hair and nuzzling his good cheek. "Shh, *lovely.* Today was actually a victory. With Royce out of the way, it clears the path to Lynch. One major complication down."

"I… yeah. It *was* another barrier blown away." He reached out and took her hand, holding it between them. "You got hurt, though."

"Superficially."

"It doesn't matter. Somebody still laid hands on you."

"Then it's a good thing I'm not a fragile little flower then, isn't it?" She beamed at him. "Good thing I'm your *Wildflower* instead."

The smile he gave her... I hadn't seen it in so long. So incredibly long.

He hugged her to him, then eased away and told us, "I need to deal with the flash drive I got from Nico." He went to push off the stool, but I slapped my hands down on the arms. "No. Not tonight."

"What? To say this has skyrocketed in urgency doesn't really cover it."

"I agree. *However,* you're injured and exhausted. You require rest. *Or* you won't be any good to anyone. A couple of days, son. That's all I'm asking."

"One day and we'll see how it goes."

"Fine."

"I see you drive a hard bargain even with your dad," Brianna commented.

I shook my head to myself. "You have no idea."

"She does," Levi admitted, wincing. "Some things may have gone down that gave her an excellent insight to that side of me."

"Poor girl."

"Hey, you're supposed to be on my side."

I ruffled his hair. "Go wash up. Dinner in thirty minutes. In the dining room, not the den."

He gave a nod, then I watched him and his girlfriend head out of the kitchen.

His girlfriend.

She certainly wasn't *just* his.

Colton's parents—Oakley and Lena—would be over the moon about this development, seeing it as an act of liberation and him staying true to what they wanted for him, to live his own life, unapologetic to anyone or anything.

Mason's parents, however, that was a completely different thing. His mother would be horrified and clutching her pearls. It had been bad enough when they'd briefly suspected that he was bisexual. I'd actually stepped in at the request of Levi when he'd seen how afraid Mason had been of incurring his parents' wrath as a result, and I'd managed to refute it and allay their suspicions with a smokescreen—yes, Levi had gotten that from me.

Over the last few days, Peter had gotten word that Mason was away from Stonewell University and he'd thrown a fit when he hadn't been able to get hold of him. I'd contacted Lena Sharp—we'd done a lot of business together over the years and she handled Peter's investments, so he listened to her opinion—and I'd had her run interference. That wouldn't last much longer. Soon he'd put the pieces together and turn up at my door.

I'd have to ensure the kids were stabilized before that occurred.

I'd been observing the four of them quietly through assets that I had in place around their college town. I had little choice with the way Levi had been operating since the kidnapping. It had been the only way to keep him safe and protect him from himself and all that rage and pain that he'd carried on his back like an extension of the torture he'd been subjected to in that hellhole.

Through said observations, I'd recognized how much they leaned on one another, especially since Brianna had entered the picture and soothed their dynamic, offering a balance that they'd needed to cast off the animosity between my son and Mason, due to their differing approaches to most things.

I couldn't allow that to be fractured now that Levi was

doing so well, now that he was more stable than he'd been in years, now that he was on the road to happiness.

Being unable to stop those madmen from taking my son was the biggest regret of my life, my greatest shame. He'd had his happiness stolen that day. I certainly wouldn't allow that to occur again. If it meant striking at Peter Hall, I had no qualms about doing so.

I'd walked the line for years between the dark and the light. Even with those kills I'd made recently, it hadn't rocked me because I was stable. I'd ensured it when my son was born, having been close to drowning in it beforehand. But so much had changed for me and in me when Levi had come along. However, should Peter cause issues and threaten the kids and the unit they'd become, I would become that thing again.

After all, what could destroy a soulless husk of a man like Peter Hall but a heartless monster?

Let's hope it didn't come to that. For his sake and Mason's.

Because I wouldn't stop.

It would be a welcome outlet given that I'd made Levi a promise that I'd step aside and allow *him* to deal the death blow to Malcolm Lynch, when it was something I'd desired for years, ever since I'd discovered he hadn't perished.

But my son needed that release more.

What I desired paled in comparison to that.

I smiled as I heard Brianna giggling and Levi's laughter following.

My God. It had been so long since I'd heard that heart-warming sound from him.

I took a moment, then pulled out my phone to call in my caterer for tonight's dinner.

My limited culinary abilities wouldn't suffice, not for

what was a *reunion* meal to me, something special. Levi was the ace in that area, along with Mason as I understood it. They needed to take it easy though, no tasks, no chores, no pressure.

I smiled to myself.

For the next few days, I'd be afforded the opportunity to reconnect with my son and his friends, *and* my future daughter-in-law.

———

"LIKE A GREEN SCREEN?" Colton asked.

"In essence," Levi confirmed. "A digital one, pretty much. I had to make it look like an office environment when you guys or Dear Old Dad here checked in on me, always insisting on video call."

"What about the office sounds and the people we heard calling to you?" Colton pushed.

"Downloaded background noise audio files that I did some creative editing with."

"Wow," Brianna breathed. "That's another level."

"Don't encourage him," Mason said.

"Aww, come on, brother, you know you love me again now."

"Never stopped *loving* you, Lev. It was just frustrating beyond belief and that was leading the way for a while."

"A bad long while," Colton interjected.

Mason nodded, then smiled over at my son. "Too long."

Levi returned his smile. "Yeah, way too long."

"I'm glad you're on good terms again," I spoke.

"Working hard to keep it that way," Mason told me.

He was sitting beside me at the oval mahogany dining room table, with Colton and Levi opposite. I'd put Brianna at the head of the table between Levi and Mason and the boys had been happy about that. I wasn't one for formalities. Nor for distance. The table was rather narrow so when I sat down to dinner with my guests, we could be close and not forced at a distance by the size of a ridiculously large table.

I looked at Brianna who was sitting there rather quietly appearing to be taking everything in, looking like the sweetheart she was for my boy and his brothers-in-arms, in a bubblegum-pink scoop neck top and a little gray skirt. None of them had arrived with dress clothes because they'd been in hiding at the safehouse with just the bare essentials that they'd packed. So, I'd kept it casual at the table too in just a white open collar shirt and a pair of navy jeans, to ensure they hadn't felt uncomfortable or ill-equipped for dinner at what people perceived as the great Knight Estate. Like I said, formalities weren't my thing. Not when I could avoid something so trivial. However, I did like to dress to impress while outside my home, hence my designer suits and my strange title as a *business style icon* to the outside world and the media. Perception was an interestingly complicated thing.

"I assume you have a lot to do with this peace between the boys," I spoke to Brianna.

"A little," she responded modestly.

"More like everything, dark angel."

Dark angel? Interesting. It spoke to that edge that my son needed in a woman.

"These friendships, this sort of special bond, is a rarity. Something to be cherished," I told them.

"Abso-fucking-lutely," Colton said in that bold and brazen way I was familiar with when it came to him. Definitely his parents' son.

I chuckled and my guests joined me.

"Perfectly stated," I told him.

He was most definitely the heart of their unit.

"So, Mason, I've heard you're returning to your tattoo designs?"

He hesitated and tugged at his pale-blue long sleeve tee. "I was just bored up at the safehouse. It was something to do."

"That's a shame. I was meeting with a business associate a couple of days ago whose son has just opened a new tattoo studio. He's looking for an artist to mentor."

He looked around the table.

Colton was smiling excitedly.

Brianna was looking on hopefully and giving a thumbs-up encouragement.

And Levi was watching curiously.

"Well, it's just a hobby. Law is my career path."

"Come the fuck on," Levi grunted.

"*Lovely,*" I heard Brianna say quietly to him. "You're pushing it too hard."

"Screw this," Colton uttered all of a sudden, then turned to me, revealing, "It's because of the other mission we're working."

I looked between them. "Other mission?"

"Peter has surveillance footage of Mason killing some-body from that shitshow five years back. That's what he's been holding over Mason's head to force him into Law and every other thing he decides he wants Mason doing. Ruining his fucking life basically."

I jolted. "Excuse me?"

Levi cursed and slapped his hand to his face.

"Levi," I pushed. "Why have I never heard about this evidence?"

"It was only me on the tape," Mason explained. "Lev was at the other end of the house at that point. When your cleanup team was there, my dad paid one of them off to hand one of the tapes over."

"A physical tape?"

"Nothing online," Levi told me. "It's why I couldn't destroy it instantly."

"Why didn't you come to me about this? All these years, son?" I looked at Colton and Mason. "You too."

"Dad, you'd already busted your ass to cover up five murders that night. You were at the end of your rope. We couldn't pile on."

"I was at the *end of my rope* because you were hurting, Levi. Not because I was angry or disappointed. I'm not exactly a conventional father, am I?"

"No, you're not." He smirked. "In the best ways."

"I didn't want to risk the hell that would rain down if I let Levi or Colt tell you down the road, Roman," Mason informed me. "There would have been war between you and my father. And he's a vindictive bastard."

"I appreciate that, but there's no need to protect *me*. Besides, I'm sure your father will be along soon enough to attempt to drag you kicking and screaming back to college. Of course, that won't be allowed."

Mason looked mortified. "No. I don't want you getting caught in—"

"This is your chance."

He frowned. "Chance?"

"To stand your ground. To show him you're a grown man. No longer a boy he can push around."

"We need the evidence first," Brianna told me. "I'm working on it."

I arched an eyebrow. "How so?"

She then proceeded to tell me all about a network she'd created named *Vixen*. She certainly had a gift for details and subterfuge because it had even escaped my knowledge and I was plugged in to a great deal.

"Extremely impressive."

She blew past the compliment and reported, "The location of the tape has been narrowed down to two locations by my girls. Either the safe behind the abstract painting in Peter Hall's office, or the other in his study at the Hall mansion. I've called in one of my girls who's a professional thief—a master thief, actually. We're coordinating a strategy to hit each one two days apart, while keeping Hall none the wiser."

"She's damned good, hmm?" Levi said, looking at her with so much admiration and pride.

"I've also had my girl planted at his law office get *him* on tape. It will reach me early tomorrow."

"On tape doing what?"

"The usual with him," Mason grunted.

Colton spelled it out bluntly, "Fucking his assistants."

I screwed up my face. "No line between business and pleasure makes for complications and mistakes."

"Especially with him being a married man," Mason said with clear disgust.

Best not to tell him that his father had been cheating on his socialite wife since before he was born.

I'd caught him once.

So had Lena. He'd even made a pass at her actually.

It was a torrid situation where he was concerned.

I took in all the information, then nodded. "Understood. Then I'll have my contact mentor you covertly until the deed is done. He'll come to the mansion."

"I can't ask you to—"

"You're not asking. And you should have. These shackles your father has forced on you could have been cast off much sooner if I'd known."

It took him a moment, but then he gave me a chin lift and admitted, "I'd like that. Very much. Thank you."

"Good, then it's settled. I'll call my contact first thing and schedule mentoring sessions for once this current situation is dealt with regarding Lynch. In the meantime, continue to dust off your artistic skills in preparation." I smiled out at him. "We'll get you the life that you want." Now I was on a roll, I looked out at Levi. "Speaking of, you and I need to talk after this rest period. About *Knightsridge* and what you want to do where that's concerned."

"Yeah, actually that's perfect."

"It is?" I'd thought he'd been pulling away from it.

But maybe it was just that his focus had been on Lynch and I'd read too much into it.

"I've got ideas, Dad." He winked.

"Oh, fuck," Mason uttered. "Brace yourself for that talk now, Roman."

"Shit, yeah," Colt agreed.

"Aww, stop," Brianna said, fondling his hair.

I grinned at the sweetness.

Then Levi laughed at her reaction, happy, loving-it laughter.

My son was actually laughing! *Again!*

And it was the most amazing sound I'd heard in years.

I couldn't believe it.

The Levi I'd thought I'd lost forevermore was returning.

20

~Colton~

I watched quietly from the door of the guestroom that Mason was crashing in.

There he was sprawled out on his stomach sketching away rapidly.

He had a pair of headphones on, music blaring and I smiled to myself as I heard one of my songs sounding through.

"You opened up my life/ Now I can breathe without it hurting/ I'm finally learning/ Until us/ Until me/ Until you."

That particular song, those lyrics, were really apt for the current circumstances.

Brianna Walker coming into our lives had changed so much, had bettered so much.

And I was so happy that she'd found a way to free Mason.

She'd calmed Lev down and settled him.

She'd inspired my songwriting.

Hell, she'd made us happy again.

Having her with us had fixed the broken pieces, putting them back together in the best way imaginable.

I pushed away from the wall and left Mason to it, loving that he was in his element.

I had another hour or so before I was to meet Bree downstairs in Roman's home gym to do some more sparring. It gave me time to get started on figuring out my set list for my upcoming show in a few weeks. I needed to narrow down my hires too, then start rehearsal. There was a lot to do, made all the more overwhelming by everything else going on, this mission ahead, being here instead of back in Stonewell.

Roman was working from home while we were here and right now he was out in the massive workshop he'd built doing some woodworking with Levi.

It was unheard of for him to take time off work like this, but as we'd all seen, especially over dinner, Roman was overjoyed to have some quality time to spend with his son.

Over the last year, with Levi being away, they'd been estranged. I mean, they'd talked and all that, but Levi had unwittingly put a strain there in their relationship with him faking that internship and wanting to keep his mission against Malcolm Lynch a secret. It must have killed Roman, because he was all about his son.

To the outside world, Roman Knight was a notorious, dangerous and heartless bastard. But that was just a façade, one he had to be putting out there to protect himself and his business, given the kinds of people he did business with.

But beneath it, he was sentimental about Levi and all those he cared about.

His son was everything to him, through and through.

It was really nice seeing them reunite. And it was also killer that Roman had taken such a liking to Bree. He'd obviously seen how good she was for Lev and for all of us.

She was holed up in one of the other guestrooms right now catching up on her college classwork remotely.

I should be doing mine too because I'd ended up falling behind again with everything that had been going on.

But that thing was happening in my mind where I was laser-focused on something else, and I couldn't turn away from it.

Mythic Cry was what I needed to work on now.

Until I did, I wouldn't be able to see beyond this frustrating state of tunnel vision.

I had a few weeks before the show, but still. I hadn't prepared *anything* yet. I was a little ways out from finishing my most recent song too.

I headed down the corridor and walked into my assigned room, going straight for my guitar that was on my bed, along with my notebook where I took down melodies and lyrics that I was working on.

I settled into a cross-legged position with my guitar.

And then I let go, immersing myself in my music.

"Vicious things walking into the light/ Girl's ours now and we make a real sight/ Stay here/ Stay, my dear/ Vicious things like us belong right here."

"COLTON?"

I jolted at the sound of Brianna's voice, and stopped playing, turning around to see her leaning against the door to my room.

"What's up, cutie?"

She smiled with amusement. "Just wondering if you're coming to spar."

"Yeah, of course I am. Why?"

"We were meant to start over an hour ago."

I put my guitar down and pushed off the bed. "What? Seriously?"

"Seriously. It's okay. You just lost track of time enjoying your music."

She really let us off too easy sometimes. "No, it's not okay. It's rude and bullshit. I'm sorry, Bree."

She came to me and laid her hands on my chest over my leopard-print shirt. "Stress makes it worse. Your trouble focusing. Right?"

"Yeah," I said, stroking her hands on me.

"Is playing helping?"

"It was getting there."

"Will you show me?"

"Show you?"

"Teach me how to play a little?"

"Really?"

"Yeah, I mean, I've always wanted to learn to play an instrument, but I never did it in the end."

"Sure, yeah, come," I said, taking one of her hands and leading her to the foot of the bed. I let go and reached back, snatching up my guitar.

Then I maneuvered it so that it was on her lap, but I was able to move her fingers for her. "Let's start with some basic chords. Let's go E-minor. It's one of the easiest to make." I set it up for her, then showed her how to strum.

She had a little trouble picking it up, hitting the strings too hard and jarringly with not much rhythm.

"I suck at this," she surmised.

"Nah, you just need practice."

"I have no rhythm."

"We both know that's not true. You've displayed some hella good rhythm in certain other areas."

Her cheeks heated.

"I meant in combat, dirty girl. Although, now you mention it, yeah, in fucking too."

She giggled and it rolled right through me in the best way. "Show me that C chord again."

I showed her with my fingers and she replicated it perfectly, then followed the progression I'd taught her from that.

"Nicely done, cutie." I pulled a pick from my pocket and handed it to her. "Try strumming with this, instead of your fingers."

She fiddled with it until she got a nice grip, then she started strumming.

"Much better. Damn."

"Thanks. It feels better this way."

She worked on the progression then, using a strumming pattern I'd shown her too.

As she did that, I asked, "So, any word on the *Vixen* mission? The Peter Hall one, I mean?"

"Yes. His office was a bust. The surveillance tape wasn't in there. My girls are moving to his home soon."

"This is a major deal what you're doing for Mason."

She lifted a shoulder. "I'm in a position to do it, so how could I not? He needs it. Badly."

"Yeah, he does. This is gonna change everything for him." I reached out a slid my fingers into her hair, making her moan at my soft touch, and she stopped playing. "*You've* changed everything for all of us, Brianna."

"You've each done the same for me as well."

"You saved our brotherhood. You know? It's always meant everything to me, so seeing it straining was heartbreaking for me. But everything changed when you became a part of us. You're like the missing link or something. It fits so well now. So, thank you."

"I love being a part of it, with you guys."

Gazing into her eyes, I stroked her hair and confessed, "I love you, cutie."

Her eyes lit up. she put my guitar down, then wrapped her arms around me. "I love you too," she breathed at my ear. "You're such a sweetheart."

"My tongue piercing is a part of that love, right?"

She eased back, giggling. "Oh, definitely."

We both burst out laughing.

And it was fucking perfect.

21

~Levi~

Nico Marchetti had been investigating *Osiris* for a good couple of years.

He'd had eyes on him from the moment his father had first brought up the possibility of dealing with that fucker, Malcolm Lynch.

The mafia prince was certainly on the ball.

All this information that he'd compiled was incredible and it had the means to bridge the gap with mine. *But* it was also a whole lot to sift through to get to that point. He hadn't left anything out, not one little thing, even what I would class as *irrelevant data.*

"Fuck," I muttered, slumping back in my desk chair in my old bedroom from my childhood and shoving a hand through my hair.

"Hitting some roadblocks?"

I'd been so immersed that I hadn't even heard the approach.

I spun on my rolling chair to see my dad standing at the threshold.

"You can come in," I told him, amused at him hanging

back there. "I'm not a bitch-ass teenager anymore forbidding you from coming into my space."

He chuckled. "No, you're certainly not." He gestured at all my equipment set up. "You're a grown man taking control of the situation, of your own life."

"Ah, I forgot," I said, grinning. "You're where I learned that whole buttering up thing from."

His lips quirked. "You got me." He folded his arms across his chest. "First, though, how's that going?"

"There's a hell of a lot here. It's going to take time to go through. There's a ton of raw data."

"The fact he hasn't seen to this data at all highly suggests that he never intended to go after Lynch himself. He was always looking for someone else to do his dirty work. He wasn't doing you a favor. You're doing him a favor."

"It doesn't matter. This is dirty work I'm more than happy to do."

"For the last time, I'm hoping."

"Dad—"

"It's time, son. After this, it's time to stop."

I scrubbed my hand over my face. "I want to. I just don't know if it's possible."

He perched on the edge of my desk, facing me and folding his arms. "Why not?"

"Because I touched something dark, Dad. Six years ago. And I've only delved deeper since. If I don't have these outlets, I don't know if I can keep it under control."

"You can."

I arched an eyebrow. "How can you be so sure?"

He'd said it with so much conviction, like it wasn't even a question.

"Because I know you. The real you beneath all the rage, pain, and shame. I know your strength, Levi."

I started shaking my head. "Dad, no."

"*Yes,*" he said, vehemently. "After all you've been through, all that's been weighing you down, you've carried it, and you haven't faltered. And here you are now doing this, leading the way, the man they look to in order to achieve the impossible."

I smiled. "Well, when you put it like that."

"You also have Brianna now to soothe that darkness, Levi." He laid his hand on my shoulder. "It's different now. So much has changed for you, and it's time to accept that, and not continue waiting on tenterhooks for the other shoe to drop. This is your new reality now. She's not going anywhere and neither are the boys."

"With this strike against Lynch coming up… it's… it's a clear risk, Dad."

"We will mitigate the risk in every possible way. We have great minds at the helm here who will strategize the strike. This isn't like five years ago. You need to recognize the difference and keeping reminding yourself of that."

"All right, yeah, I hear you."

"Good." He ruffled my hair in that way he could never resist doing, as he rose to his feet. "Now, while your program is constructing all that data, it seems like a pertinent time to discuss *Knightsridge Engineering.*"

I relaxed into my chair and kicked my feet up on my desktop, settling in. "I'm still in college."

"I convinced you to attend Stonewell University to give you structure and a focus in a bid to curb your reckless tendencies and thirst for danger and darkness, your vigilante activities. You're overqualified to be there. All that you'll lack if you leave now are the credentials, which aren't even an issue, given that I can waive that as owner."

"I want to finish out my studies."

"Because of Brianna?"

"Partly. Getting her degree is important to her. Even during all this upheaval, she's been finding time to study and do her readings and projects. She didn't think she'd have the opportunity to do any of that because of her background as club princess, so it means a lot to her. And life is good at the mansion."

"You can move to another house in Tolhurst for you all to share. Here for a while if you wish." His lip curled up. "Or longer than a while."

"Nice try. But my plan is to finish up at Stonewell and then claim my birthright as your heir apparent. Until then, though, I've thought about interning there, having you mentor me so I can be fully prepared by the time I'm done with college."

"Really? You mean that?" he asked, his eyes bright.

It was what he'd wanted for a long time, but other things had always gotten in the way—namely my instability. Then me taking off for a year and becoming estranged from him and everyone because of my obsession to bury Malcolm Lynch.

I grinned back at him. "I do, Dad. If you'll have me, of course."

"I can't think of anything that I want more than you there right beside me running *Knightsridge*."

"Perfect."

Footsteps sounded and we both spun around as Brianna strode into the room, urgency radiating off her.

I shot out of my chair. "What's happened?"

"I just got confirmation from *Vixen* that Tommy was working with Lynch. Actually *is* working with him currently. He was spotted with one of the known members you identified of *Osiris*, outside a gambling den, the two of them looking mighty cozy."

"Christ."

"My girl was also able to tag Tommy when he left the place late last night. The *Osiris* member never surfaced unfortunately, so there must have been an underground route out of the place. He was surrounded by his muscle too, so she couldn't even drop him either. So we missed the opportunity to bring him in for questioning and get a real-time location on Lynch out of him." She ground her jaw. "It would have saved this massive undertaking you're dealing with of trying to pinpoint his location when he's always on the move."

"We can still bring Tommy in. You said he was tagged."

"He won't break, Levi. He was trained not to by my dad. A bunch of the club members went through the same training when they were prospects. It was a dark time back then."

"You'd be surprised what I can achieve."

"*No,*" my dad spoke. Well, growled vehemently. "Absolutely not. Remember what we just talked about. Torturing somebody would seriously strain your ability to walk away from this sort of thing. It would taint you, Levi."

"Yeah, you're not doing that," Brianna told me. She walked to me and took my hands in hers. "It would haunt me forever if I knew you'd done that for me."

"Okay. Besides, we have enough things haunting us, don't we?"

"Things we're on our way to cast off now."

I nodded.

"I recall what you told me about Brianna's text conversation with Tommy," my dad said. He looked at her. "Based off of that and his attitude there, I'd reason that he would be filled with twisted delight to tell you all about his illicit activities with Lynch and how he deceived you and your father."

"He's right," I said.

She nodded. "I need to find out for sure. I need to know what happened. I need the closure, Levi." She pulled away. "I can't allow him to get off scot-free just because our real target is Lynch."

"You're not going anywhere near that motherfucker on your own."

"I know. I came in here not just to notify you, but to ask you to go with me."

"If he's working with Lynch, it's unlikely he'll be alone," my dad warned.

I thought he was going to fight against us doing this, especially with the big strike coming up where we all needed to be at our best, *and* because he'd already managed to bite the bullet and accept me doing one majorly dangerous thing as it was.

Instead, he told us, "I'll send one of my units. You can start by trying to handle it on your own, but if things go south, they'll move in and extract you safely."

I gave him a chin lift.

"What about Mason and Colt?" I asked, Brianna. "Have you filled them in yet?"

"Mason is immersed in his tattoo designs, I don't want to upset that now he's finally back down to it. And Colt is stressed about *Mythic Cry* and having focusing issues. He's behind several weeks with his college work. They'll stay here. We'll be in and out, back before they know it."

"Brianna—"

"Levi, this is extremely personal to me. I wanted to go alone, but I'm bringing you in because I know you guys would never allow me to go solo on this."

"And because you know you couldn't get this past me."

The corner of her mouth turned up. "There's also that, yeah."

"By the way, I was going to say that I agree with you about keeping it to just the two of us. Just this time, though. We do the rest together as our foursome."

"Agreed. Just this one time."

"Good," I said, walking to the closet and reaching inside for my riding jacket. "Then let's ride, *Wildflower.*"

22

~Brianna~

A strip club.

Sultry Sirens.

That was where Tommy was spending his night.

I really hadn't known him at all.

Not the true him, anyway.

Just the façade he'd put on to win me over and then keep me close.

To weaken me, I suspected. To keep me immersed in my trauma.

He'd claimed he hated this sort of place.

He'd never even looked twice at any of the club girls.

And whenever one of the club members had strippers in the clubhouse for their birthdays, he'd never participated.

Just not around me, clearly.

"Shithole," I murmured as Levi and I passed through the doors and into the place, hair metal blasting through the club.

His hand slid into mine in his protective and possessive way.

But that was all he did.

He'd let me go in first, he hadn't tried to talk me out of doing this.

Despite his need to ensure I was safe and well and all of that, he was also working hard just like Mason and Colt were not to be overbearing about it or to take away my agency.

My leather jacket with the studs and pink stripes across the hard black leather swished with my rapid movements like my ponytail as we made our way through the place.

Levi was decked out in his go-to cargo pants and packing heat, just in case, and wearing his well-worn riding jacket too.

We'd come down here on his Harley.

I had a little something on me too, the blade he'd given me stowed in my inside jacket pocket.

"This is the second time in a few weeks that I've set foot in one of these seedy places," Levi commented, his eyes bouncing off all the topless women serving drinks, some performing lap dances, others up on the stages working their moves on the golden, glittering poles.

There was no fakery with him. he could barely stand it.

"Second time?" I wondered.

"Yeah, it was that night I went to see Kyle Trass. He owns one now."

"Huh. Want a lap dance while we're here?"

"From *you*, yes. But in private. I don't want anyone seeing you in your throes-of-passion state. Only me, Mason, and Colt get to see that. Our eyes only, baby."

"*Throes of passion state,*" I chuckled to myself. "You're too sweet."

"Keep my sweet side to yourself for tonight. This fuck-er's only getting my scary and fucked-up side."

I leaned into him as we continued scanning the place

for Tommy. "You'll give me a taste of that sweetness later?"

"Damn, Brianna. You're not making it easy to remain focused and on-mission."

I pulled away smiling. "Sorry, just you and me going on mission together is hot as hell."

"Yeah?" he said, briefly tapping into that sexy teasing tone of his.

"*Hell,* yeah, lovely."

"Fuck, woman." He stilled suddenly, then pointed. "There's the motherfucker."

I followed his gesture to see that long, dirty-blond hair skimming the shoulders of an off-white tank, that hawk tattoo on his right shoulder.

He was with one of the strippers, her hand delving into the back pockets of his jeans as she led him to one of the back pleasure rooms.

We headed over there and Levi hung back as we'd agreed, while I stealthily entered the dimly lit room.

The *pleasure* had gotten underway quickly.

Now that was an aspect of him that was the truth then. He'd always been wham-bam-all-done whenever we'd been together.

I couldn't see his face because the girl grinding on him was blocking the view.

But then I heard his voice as he fisted his hand in her hair and held her painfully to him as he hissed, "While we're in here, you're Brianna, got it?"

Revulsion rolled through me.

It got worse when she nodded, he shifted his grip to her ass, then told her, "Call me Big Daddy, bitch. You got me?"

"Yeah, okay," she said quietly.

As the names thing hit me, I realized that the girl had

long, flowy black hair like me, and my compact build. She was also decked out in all pink.

A shudder rolled through me—he knew about that change in me then.

Her shiny pink booty shorts ground back and forth on his lap as he lounged in the velvet chair with his eyes closed, his hands spread over her breasts that were encased in a silky hot-pink bustier.

"Harder. Roll those hips for Big Daddy. Please me like the whore that you are for me."

Eww.

In the next beat, I drew my knife, took aim, the tossed it.

It cut through the air violently and embedded in his right thigh.

He shrieked and the girl gasped and jumped off him.

She spun around and took in me there. "Go, I'll take care of this creeper."

She nodded frantically and gave me a grateful smile, then rushed off, past Levi who was outside guarding the door.

Tommy eyed me incredulously. "What the fuck? How are you here?"

"That was one hell of a show," I said, sauntering toward him.

His eyes were all over me, flaring with erotic need.

"Yeah? You think so? Finish it with me. Show me how jealous seeing another woman with me made you, B. Take it out on me."

Urgh.

When I reached him, I yanked the knife out, then smashed my fist into the side of his face, making his head snap back. "A *sick* show, you piece of shit! How fucking dare you?"

He went to push out of the chair, to come at me, but I spun my knife in my hand, making the threat clear.

"What the fuck is your problem?"

"That's *my* question. You're working for Malcolm Lynch."

He paled. "How do you—did Knight find that out for you? Little interfering shit."

"I found it out."

"What?" He scoffed. "No. Don't bother protecting him."

"I'm not. There you are, though, completely discounting me and underestimating me. Is that what Lynch ordered you to do? To gaslight me? To keep me down? To have me reeling in what happened?"

"Yeah, all right? That was the deal." He smiled nastily. "And it worked. Like a fucking charm."

"When? When did you start working for him?"

"Six months before the kidnapping. He needed somebody on the inside."

"You betrayed me! Betrayed the club!"

"It wasn't personal. Just money. A hell of a lot of money. Well, and getting to fuck the club princess. That was a big time achievement I was real proud of. You being so scared and submissive after Lynch fucked you up was a treat too." He winked. "I like them pliant."

Something caught my eye in my peripheral vision, a moment before Tommy shrieked as a knife plunged into his groin, driving deep through the denim of his jeans.

He collapsed to his knees, shrieking and shrieking non-stop.

Levi bolted past me and took him in a sleeper hold, slapping his hand over his mouth to silence his screams. "Take your punishment, motherfucker."

Before I could get over the shock of him suddenly

rushing in here and doing *that* to Tommy, he reached underneath Tommy's jacket, then he was tossing me a gun.

"He didn't leave his Desert Eagle at the door. The woman who ran out of here warned me."

"Shit," I breathed.

He smiled at me. "Got you, baby. Always." That smile faded as he glared down at Tommy flailing in his arms in horrific pain. "You want to do the honors? Or should I?"

"The knife to the dick was satisfying enough for me. More than I could have hoped for."

"Well, the punishment fit the crime. He hurt you, played you... he's working for the monster who tortured us. He can't survive that."

"No," I ground out, glaring at Tommy with a dangerous cocktail of fury and vengeance. "He can't."

As much as I knew that to be true, and that he was too dangerous to be left alive with his close association with Malcolm Lynch, *and* knowing that we'd tracked him, what we were capable of together, I still fucking well hesitated as I stepped forward to finish him with my blade.

Levi, knowing me so well and being his amazingly attentive self to my needs, noticed right away and recognized what it meant.

He yanked the knife from Tommy's groin, then jabbed it into his eye, killing him in an instantaneous move.

Releasing him, he got to his feet and spat on his corpse with absolute disgust.

He dialed Roman's unit waiting in the wings hidden outside to shut the strip club down for the night so they could come in and conduct their cleanup and bury the body—literally and figuratively.

And then he was there, wrapping his arms around me. "He's gone. That chapter of your life is over. The lies and manipulation have died along with him. It's brutal justice. It was necessary, my *Wildflower.*"

My Wildflower.

That was what I held onto in order to fight off the chill that ran through me as the cold, hard reality of taking a life started to sink in all too quickly.

I shored up my conviction.

He'd suffered because of his own crimes.

I'd been used and abused and so much of that in my life had come down to Malcolm Lynch and his acolytes.

Tommy Dixon was just another one of them.

And now he'd been defeated like all of them would be soon enough.

"I love you," I breathed to Levi.

"I love *you.* No one will ever hurt us again. It's our time now, Brianna. All ours."

It really was.

And soon we'd both be able to feel that once this last mission was completed.

Soon there would actually be peace for us after all.

23

~Mason~

I swam beneath the surface of the warm water, seeing Colt in the distance.

He was sprawled out on one of the sun loungers sipping at his daiquiri and soaking up the sun in his tiny swim trunks.

It was the calm before the storm for us.

Before everything came to a head.

Before the strike took place and we were awash in violence and bloodletting.

And unlike my usual protocol where calm and relaxation was concerned, I was making sure I enjoyed the brief downtime and soaked up every second of it.

While Colt was with me on that, Levi had gone the other way with keeping himself really busy. He'd compiled all the data into his tracking program to discern patterns of movement and dealings for Malcolm Lynch, and now it was only a matter of time before it churned out what we needed—the location of that son of a bitch. So, in the meantime, Levi was at *Knightsridge Engineering* with Roman learning the ropes. Or at least on track to doing so.

Bree was due to come out here any moment with us. She was just finishing up a call with her dad. She'd told us all about her first contact with him in years wherein she'd promised him she wouldn't be a stranger anymore. And she was keeping that vow.

I picked up speed and power and then, when I was close enough, I surged up, dousing Colt all over.

He jumped up, now drenched, and put his glass down.

"Oh, darlin', you're in for it now," he warned.

In the next second, he was leaping at me.

I laughed and caught him, then ducked him under the water.

That laughter got a whole lot wilder when he resurfaced and his perfectly-styled mohawk was all flat and soaked.

He splashed me, getting it all in my eyes.

As I was wiping it away, he shoved my head into the pool, dunking me right back.

And then we were pretty much wrestling in the pool, getting lost in the moment, the lightheartedness and the fun ridiculousness of it.

"Wait," I choked as I resurfaced again after accidentally swallowing a ton of water. "Need a second to catch my breath."

He swam into me and guided me back against the edge of the pool.

He linked his hands around my neck, then leaned in and licked up the droplets of water all over my cheek and throat, down to my pecs.

I groaned and threw my head back at the glorious dual sensations of his hot, wet tongue and his stud teasing my skin.

"Catching your breath now, darlin'?" he teased.

"The exact opposite," I rasped. "No complaints here, though."

"Is that so? Even though this pool is in a common, public area of the house? Even though the staff could see us and one actually just walked by the patio doors and looked out here?"

I smiled out at him. "Even then, gorgeous."

"Wow, I'm loving this," he said, stopping his teasing in his other kind of excitement and regarding me in awe. "You're getting so uninhibited, so much more comfortable in yourself."

"I know. Amazing, huh?"

"It really is, brother."

Movement in my peripheral vision caught my eye and I turned my head to see Brianna strolling out with her favored Strawberry Chocolate Martini in hand, clad in her pink string bikini with a sarong slung low on her sexy little hips.

Colt followed my line of sight. "Lose the sarong and get in here with us, Bree!" he called over.

She came to us and sat down on the edge, dipping her legs into the water. She was really gleeful as she took us in. "I have amazing news!"

We both waded over to her.

Colt tickled her feet in the water and made her giggle. "What's that, cutie?"

I stroked her thigh, trying to make it soothing rather than erotic, so she could focus on this news she had to tell us that had her so excited.

She was clearly feeling better. The last couple of days ever since her and Lev had returned from that quick take-down of that slimy fuckboy, Tommy, she'd been down and withdrawn.

Lev had told us exactly what had happened and it was no wonder.

Despite the need to what had happened and the down and dirty world she'd grown up in, Brianna Walker had a gentle heart, a kind soul. It sometimes slammed up against what needed to be done and the dark that loomed over her and us all, and there was conflict in that, and upset for her. But she'd obviously begun to process it now. Soon she'd hopefully be talking about it with us and we could help her the rest of the way through it.

When Roman had first given Colt and I the news that Lev and her had headed down to do that without us, I hadn't exactly been pleased. But then he'd explained why they'd made that call.

I'd seen beneath the surface with it too.

Lev hadn't wanted Colt to be there to witness a murder like that.

He didn't do well with that sort of thing. He was the gentlest and most innocent of us all—in that respect, at least.

When this strike happened, I'd be running interference to ensure he was shielded from the worst of it. I didn't really want him going at all, but he'd insisted, wanting to support Lev and Bree with it just like I did. I couldn't deny him that.

But at least he hadn't been there on that strip club mission. And I'd needed to stay behind to ensure he hadn't freaked out and tried to haul ass down there to help.

Fortunately, it had all worked out well and exactly to plan all around.

"After talking to my dad, I took a video call from Sandy, a member of *Vixen.*" She looked at me. "The master thief on the Peter Hall mission."

I tensed. "And?"

"*And* she got the tape. She destroyed it right in front of me, as per my request and I saw for myself via the video call that it was the only copy. It's been confirmed beyond a shadow of a doubt."

Colt grinned from ear-to-ear. "It's really happened? Hall's leverage over Mason has gone? For real?"

"It has," Bree confirmed, beaming.

"Jesus," I breathed, sinking back against the edge of the pool.

I couldn't… process it.

Colt jumped at me and threw his arms around me. "You're free! Free!"

I held him to me and looked out at Brianna. "Thank you. Thank you so much. This has… it's changed everything for me."

"You don't need to thank me, Mason. I want you happy alongside the rest of us."

"I was trapped and now I'm not. Because of you."

Colt released me and I waded to Brianna, between her legs.

Stroking her thighs, I gazed up at her in utter reverence. "Coming into our lives, it's changed everything in so many unexpected and unbelievable ways. You're amazing and we love you. *I* love you."

"Aww, shit, Mason. That was awesome."

Bree's whole face lit up. "I love you, too. You. Colt. Levi. All of you."

Colt and I wrapped ourselves around her.

Unfortunately, the moment was cut far too short when her phone rang.

She grumbled and retrieved it from beside her. "It's Levi," she told us. She put it on speakerphone and answered, "Hey, lovely. We're all here listening. How is your day going at *Knightsridge?*"

"*Wildflower. Boys*," Lev's voice sounded between us. "*The day's been great. But I'm not calling about that. We've got a problem. It's your shit of a father, Mason. Lena couldn't hold him off any longer and he now knows you're here. She just told my dad that he's on his way to sort you out. Brianna, any update on the Vixen mission yet?*"

"A fucking ace update," Colt answered, unable to contain his excitement. "They got the tape. It's destroyed."

"*Yeah?*"

"It's gone," Bree confirmed.

"*Perfect fucking timing. Yeah, Mason?*"

I was having trouble absorbing everything, all these monumental things in quick succession. "Yeah," was all I could manage.

My father was coming *here?* Now?

I was free? Out from under his thumb?

It didn't fully compute.

It hit me then.

Because it wasn't true.

At least, not all the way.

Roman's words from the other night played on my mind, coming right to the forefront.

"*This is your chance.*"

"*Chance?*"

"*To stand your ground. To show him you're a grown man. No longer a boy he can push around.*"

Never had truer wise words been spoken.

Of course that was what needed to happen to make this fully real.

It was time for my father to meet the true me.

⸺

I COULD ALWAYS TELL the moment the old bastard was near.

The air became thicker, filled with a whole lot of toxicity.

The hairs on the back of my neck stood on end.

My pulse picked up.

Adrenaline spiked, my body automatically readying for a fight.

And most of all, a sense of shame took me over prior to even laying eyes on him, prior to him even being in my space.

No matter what, no matter how well I was doing, what I was achieving, he stole that sense of accomplishment and feeling good about myself away with just a few damaging words, and sometimes, even just a single derisive look.

The power he had over me was staggering.

It was disturbing.

Hell, it was absolutely disgusting.

"It's gonna be okay," Colt said, rubbing my arm, as we watched the Rolls-Royce pull in.

"After this, it'll all be smooth sailing," Bree assured me, before planting a kiss on my cheek.

Colt grinned, then kissed the other.

As he pulled away, he laid his hand on my shoulder, "Now, go and tell him how it's gonna be from now on."

I nodded and steadied myself.

And then I stepped out of the mansion.

The Rolls came to a stop and then my father climbed out.

Surprisingly, my mom followed.

She usually stayed out of our *discussions* and gave my father all the power there.

Hell, she'd given him her power in every way a long time ago.

I took her in first. Caramel-brown hair just like mine was cascading about her face in ringlets, done up to the nines. She was dressed in her usual flashy and fashion-forward way in a sleek asymmetrical black and silver dress and a pair of Vivier pumps, it all fitting with her whole socialite thing.

It was a direct and shocking contrast to my father's appearance.

He was wearing one of his ugly brown designer suits, which he considered classic, but was really a lack of imagination. And that, there, was half the trouble between us. He couldn't handle my creativity. To him, it was a threat, something that lacked control and incited rebellion.

Fuck me, he'd come so close to making me a carbon copy of him in the control department—let alone the whole lawyer-in-the-making thing that I'd always hated—and I'd put that on Lev and Colt, even Brianna at first, because I'd been so afraid of the consequences if I didn't do him justice and channel him in everything that I did like he wanted.

Like he'd ordered and then enforced through collusion.

And the leverage that he no longer had.

Unbeknownst to him.

At least, for the moment.

That was about to change.

Everything was about to change.

My father shoved a hand through his perfectly slicked back gray hair, a sign that he was right on the verge of flipping out, because he didn't tend to touch his hair at all once it was set perfectly with all that gel. His espresso eyes that I'd inherited flickered with malice.

I could feel Colt and Brianna just a few feet behind me at the threshold of the mansion entrance doors.

It was enough to give me the initial bolstering that I

needed as I sucked in a breath and walked out to meet my parents halfway.

I'd only just made it to them when my father bit at me, "What on earth are you playing at, boy?"

"I'm going to need some context."

His eyes flashed. "Excuse me?"

I stood my ground and rebutted, "You heard me."

"Mason!" my mom chastised, backing him up as usual like the weak-willed thing she was.

I ignored it and pushed my father, "Get to your point."

"You know exactly what I'm talking about, you little shit. Why haven't you been in school for days on end? And why did I finally find out from Lena Sharp that you'd left with her son? Are you vacationing together like a... like a couple?" Disgust marred his features. "I thought you'd made it clear to him that you were just friends, that you didn't and would never share his proclivities?"

Unbelievable.

They would never accept me.

No, there was absolutely nothing to worry about saving here.

It was time to burn it all down.

"Colt and I actually spent time fucking on a regular basis. Now it's all four of us who fuck around together. We have a girlfriend in the mix too that the three of us share beautifully."

"Oh my goodness," my mom choked, literally clutching her pearls right in front of me, her disapproval and nausea not hidden in the least.

My father took a step forward, his eyes narrowed. "This won't stand, boy."

"That's just it, I'm *not* your boy."

"You will fall in line, Mason. Or else, I'll—"

"Leak that surveillance tape of me murdering somebody?"

"Murdering? What are you talking about?" my mom asked.

My father held up his hand to her. "Quiet. It's nothing for you to worry about."

She shrank back. "Sorry, Pete."

Urgh. Pathetic.

"And, yes, Mason, that is the consequence of defying me and veering off the life plan I've laid out for you."

"Your life plan, not mine."

"That doesn't matter. You will follow it, return to college right now, and get back on track. You won't return to living with Colton Sharp either seeing as though the unfortunate connection between you clearly can't be quelled without me taking action. You'll return to the frat house without him. Levi Knight is off the table too. Him and his father are the last sort of influences that you need. And as for this girlfriend of yours, whoever she is, that's done with too."

"She's a biker princess. Or, she was. Of the Steel Dawn MC. Heard of them?"

"Certainly not," my mom said. "We don't consort with the likes of those sorts of people."

"Which you well know," my father seethed.

"You mean honest people? Raw and real?" I gestured between them. "A far cry from the two of you who are so concerned with appearances and some dictated grandiose scheme you have laid out for me that doesn't for a moment take into my preferences or even my free fucking will that you'd hurt your own son over and over, using him like a pawn rather than your flesh and blood."

They didn't even hear me.

Not at all.

Especially not my father who waved his hand dismissively.

"Enough of this foolishness. You will return to college immediately."

"That won't be happening. I have other commitments."

"There are no *other commitments*, boy. You will return and get back on track, *or* I will take everything from you."

"By releasing that tape, yes?"

"Yes," he hissed.

I signaled behind me at Bree and Colt.

My father's eyes widened as he noticed for the first time that we weren't alone.

That *I* wasn't alone.

They made their way over, Bree looking the epitome of her Barbiecore self in her pink houndstooth jacket and matching skirt, along with a pair of thigh-high gray boots, and Colt bringing his bold style forth in a pair of black leather pants and his zebra-print shirt only buttoned at the middle. His mohawk was out in full force too, while Bree's hair was cascading about her face in beautiful silky waves.

I'd already seen my father turn his nose up at my get-up of a pair of ripped blue jeans and a distressed gray muscle tee. My hair was also wild as fuck as I'd only run my fingers through it since we'd dried and gotten dressed from our pool fun earlier.

"What is this?" my father demanded.

"This?" I said, wrapping my arm around Bree on my left and holding Colt's hand on my right. "This is a real family. *My* new family."

He glared heatedly at Colt, then frowned at Bree curiously.

Colt stared daggers right back at him, giving as good as he got.

Bree turned her nose up at him.

That was about right.

"Enough of this nonsense."

"We're done here," I told him.

"Done? What are you talking about?"

"I won't be returning to Stonewell U. I won't be walking away from Colt, Brianna, or Levi. I'll be returning to the career I wanted, my artistic career that you tried and failed to beat down. Once my business is concluded here, it will be put into effect."

"The hell, it will. You better—"

"Better what? Fall in line. Nah. Like I said, we're done here."

"I will release—"

"You have nothing to release."

"Excuse me?"

"Oh, my bad. Haven't you checked your safe lately? The tape is gone."

He looked utterly stunned for several moments, while my mom murmured questions as to what we were even referring to. As usual, she had no idea what was going on with her own son—or her husband. She much preferred living inside her socialite bubble.

"You little shit. If you think that's all I can do to—"

"You should worry about what *we* can do," Bree cut in.

She was pulling out her phone then and scrolling in the next moment. She looked at my mom. "It's unfortunate you're here for this, but on the other hand, you should know who your husband really is. You might want to review that prenup once we're done here."

And then Bree held her phone up between us for us all to see.

A video had started playing, most definitely NSFW, especially not safe for *his* work.

It depicted my father fucking his assistant, the one who'd suddenly up and quit, bouncing her completely stripped naked on his cock while he was fully suited accept for his pants being open, as he spewed some dirty talk that even Colt would find disturbing. I actually looked over at him and he was cringing.

"What is it with all the Daddy talk lately, by the way?" Bree mused aloud, sarcasm dripping.

As my parents started arguing, my mom apparently completely unaware that he was actually a cheating bastard, Bree looked out at me and Colt. "It's an extreme turnoff, FYI."

"Shit, yeah," Colt said.

"Absolutely right there with you there, dark angel, don't worry."

"Lev can't stand it either," Colt assured her. The corner of his mouth turned up. "He'd never speak that way to his *Wildflower.*"

She chuckled, then went to put her phone away, but my father grasped it, stopping her.

Before any of us could react, Roman's Lexus raced into the courtyard.

Levi emerged first with Roman just behind him.

I took the opportunity of the distraction to slam my hand into my father's chest, knocking him back from Bree.

"Your little biker princess is going to hand over that video," my father seethed, stumbling back a step. He spun to see Levi and Roman rushing over. "And here's the notorious gangster and the son he allows to run wild."

"Pete, what an expected, yet incredibly unpleasant surprise," Roman spoke, stopping between him and my mom, while Lev came to us.

"All right?" he asked us, studying the three of us.

Before any of us could answer, my father lunged at Bree, wanting her phone.

Levi went to react with those lightning-fast reflexes of his, but I guess with all this build-up and the adrenaline coursing through my system, it gave me an extra edge, and my fist was flying at my father.

It slammed into his face with *cement block* force, knocking him straight to his knees.

The satisfaction of it, striking the bastard, and bringing him to his knees… it was another level.

He went to curse me out, but I loomed over him, growling, "Get the fuck out of here. As of this moment, we have no relationship. I'm no longer your son." I gestured between him and my mom. "Get out of my sight. And don't fucking contact me again."

"You're cut off!" he yelled, getting back to his feet, while rubbing his face.

Bree, Colt, and Lev gathered close to me then, and Bree told him, "It won't even touch him. He won't be destitute and he won't even feel it at all. He has us."

A few more mutterings came from my father and some hesitation because he clearly couldn't wrap his head around losing out here.

So Roman took matters into his own hands—literally —and dragged my father back to the Rolls, my mom following with her head bowed in a whole lot of shame.

My father was shoved into the driver's seat and some heated words were spoken by Roman that we couldn't make out, before they finally drove away.

When they were out of sight, a long breath of relief left me.

It was done.

The shackles were cast off.

I was free.

24

~Colton~

I woke up groggily and plagued by one hell of a hangover.

The first thing I noticed beyond my pounding head and weariness was a hand wrapped around my dick.

Blinking to clear my muddied vision, I looked to see that I was sprawled out butt-naked on my front, my dick in Mason's hand as he slept on his back in a pair of boxers, his arms stretched out, the other flung over Bree's breasts over the covers.

She was the only one wrapped up in the covers, but it wouldn't have matter warmth-wise if she hadn't been because Lev was wrapped all over her at the far end of the bed to me, his boxer's robe loosely tied around me and only just covering his dick and a small part of that sexy ripped torso of his. His arms were covered more than anything else.

It looked like Bree was in just her bra and panties from what I could see—and what I remembered.

I had a very specific memory of us licking her through all that hot-as-sin lace and making her come just from that. It had been hella erotic.

Mason's idea.

He had some dirty ones, that was for sure. He just hadn't flexed that muscle for a while. But now he was, I was beyond excited to be a part of it.

Not just sexually-speaking, but for the whole thing.

Now he was free, it changed everything.

And we'd sure celebrated the fuck out of it last night.

Keeping my dick nestled in the warmth of his palm, I craned my neck over my shoulder and took in the place.

We were in the room that had been assigned to Bree, and it was a real mess right now.

Liquor bottles were everywhere.

My rumballs were over the floor and spilled across the dresser.

There were two burned out cigars that I recalled Mason and Lev smoking up a storm with.

A serving tray full of half-eaten sandwiches was on the coffee table in the seating area in the corner, alongside the crumbs left from a stuffed crust pizza—Levi's favorite kind.

Our clothes were all over the place and mixed up.

Levi's hoodie was flung over a lampshade,

Bree's dress was hanging over the chandelier high above in the ceiling.

Damn.

The stale smell of smoke and booze was thankfully eased a little by Bree's sweet and refreshing coconut scent cutting through it.

I looked over at her and how cute she looked while she was sleeping.

Lev was right up there with that too.

And Mason usually slept with a scowl on his face, but right now he had a smile spread over his face and he looked so peaceful.

With Peter and Shirley Hall finally out of his life I wasn't surprised.

"Grind into my hand again and I'm gonna eat your dick."

I jolted and looked to see Mason's eyes opening, that smile widening.

"I didn't realize I was doing it. It's not my fault that your hand feels so good." I grinned. "And was that supposed to be a threat, because, come on."

His eyes hooded, surprising me.

It wasn't usually easy to get him going.

I was used to that layer of inhibition and shame from him at the outset, meaning he rarely made the first move and only really took the lead when he was already consumed by pleasure, his brain on lockdown.

He tightened his grip around my cock and started stroking me.

A long groan left me and I worked my hips, grinding harder into his hand as pleasure built.

"Ungh, Mason, yeah."

Playfulness danced in his eyes.

And then he abruptly removed his hand.

"What the—"

He cupped my cheek. "Greedy boy. I was just giving you a little pleasure to offset the hangover that I can see all over you."

"Taking it all the way would've done that a whole lot better," I groused.

"Yeah, that was mean," Bree's voice sounded.

I rolled onto my side to see her sleepy eyes looking our way.

Mason reached out and played with her wild hair. "If I'd made him come, with the way he's feeling, he would've passed out for several more hours, and we'd end up wasting the day away when there's very few left of this calm before the storm until we're in the heat of dangerous battle and then, after, heading back to Stonewell with college and me starting work on building a new career from scratch again."

"Hey, I thought your *Killjoy* ways were done?" Lev said, waking up too and nuzzling Bree's shoulder from behind.

She turned into it and gave him a sweet kiss on the cheek.

"I was even working on a new nickname for you outside of that and the *Hex* one," Lev told him.

"That is all done with," Mason assured him. He slapped my ass, making it bounce, then told Lev, "We just need to save it for the shower is all."

"Mmm, I'm liking that," Lev said.

"Me too," Bree added in, her eyes hooding.

Mmm.

In the next moment, we were all pushing off the bed.

A squeal came from Bree as Lev lunged at her and grabbed her in a fireman lift.

Mason and I laughed as we headed for the bathroom, following him in.

I walked to the large glass spa-like shower with the gold trim that was big enough to fit three sets of us inside, and I switched on the shower, getting it nice and hot.

By the time I turned back, Mason was butt-naked and helping Lev strip Bree of her pink bra and panties, all that sexy lace skimming down her soft skin. She was giggling and chasing their lips, to which they happily obliged.

I got in on the excitement and grabbed her hips and carried her into the shower.

As soon as we were inside, I eased her under the water and palmed her breasts as I leaned in and slicked my tongue over her jaw and throat, teasing her with my stud.

"Colt. Your briefs," Lev called as he and Mason entered the shower.

"Nah, forget it," Mason said, making me smile because he wasn't bringing his usual worry and control to the party.

He proved that even more in the next moment as he dropped to his knees, shifting between Bree and me, then mouthed my cock through my underwear.

"Ungh," I groaned, throwing my head back.

"God," Bree exclaimed, watching Mason and getting off on the eroticism.

I turned my head as Lev was suddenly there licking and biting my shoulder, before moving up and crushing his mouth to mine.

I heard Bree cry out and I looked to see Lev had thrust two fingers deep inside her cunt while teasing me.

He eased off me, then lowered himself to a crouch in front of Bree, twisting his fingers inside her as he then dragged his tongue through her folds.

"God, Levi! Yes!" she cried in that hot *sex voice* of hers, deeper and raspier than her usual tone.

And so breathy and sexy.

I watched him edge her, lapping up her taste as his tongue explored every inch of her folds. Then he dipped his tongue inside, sliding deeper slowly and making her really feel him. it had her clawing at the shower wall behind her, her thighs shaking at his teasing.

He eased his tongue out, then spread her slickness all over her clit, before then sucking it into her mouth.

"Fucking shit," I breathed.

Watching the sight of her being pleasured, combined with Mason mouthing me through my underwear had my cock straining painfully against the tight fabric.

"Mason," I pleaded.

He grinned up at me, then yanked my underwear off me, tossing them in the corner of the shower.

A tremble of need rolled through me, thinking I was about to feel his mouth on me skin-to-skin, but then he rose to his feet and guided me over to the shower bench instead. "After Levi makes her come her brains out, we're gonna slam her dripping cunt down onto your cock, gorgeous." He slapped my ass cheeks in turn. "And you're gonna grind nice and easy into her, torturing her sweet spot."

"And then?" I breathed, taken with his words.

"And *then*, you'll see."

"Tease," I uttered, before he slapped my ass again, then had me sit on the bench.

He stood there and grabbed my cock, stroking me in a barely-there teasing way, not giving me enough for the pleasure to climb any higher, but keeping me there in a state of desperate desire.

A strangled cry from Bree had me looking out to see Levi holding her steady with a palm to her stomach as she convulsed and came all over his tongue.

She was still in the throes of it when he and Mason exchanged a look, and then Levi was carrying her over to us.

The next thing I knew, they were sliding her onto my cock, her back to my front, reverse cowgirl style.

She cried out as I rolled my hips and sank deep inside her slickness.

"Mmm... fuck, yeah," I groaned as she clenched down around me.

"Colt," she breathed, resting her head back on my shoulder as I ground into her slow and deep.

She tried to buck against me, to thrust back and make

me give her more, but Mason interrupted before she could, easing us back on the bench.

And then Lev was climbing on.

The next thing I knew, he was rubbing his cock through her folds, then dipping inside.

"Oh shit," I choked, realizing what he was gonna do.

My balls drew tight, shudders of pleasure shooting through me as his cock slid along mine as he eased inside her cunt too.

"Ah!" Bree cried. "Oh fuck."

"Want me to stop?" Lev asked her, always checking with her in his awesome way.

"The opposite," she gasped out. "Please. I want you to fill me. So full, so fucking full," she started murmuring, lost to the moment.

Mason walked over and crouched down by her head, gliding his cock along her cheek, wiping his pre-cum on her skin.

The degradation of it had her clenching down around mine and Levi's cocks and bucking her hips.

The motion jerked Lev in deep all of a sudden, messing with his careful approach.

"Shit!" she cried at the sensation.

He stilled and I rocked just slightly.

Lev started teasing her clit, softly stroking in a teasing way that had her moaning out and loosening enough around us so he could start to move.

"Yes! God!" she cried. "More! Please, more!"

"Damn, that was quick, cutie. Figured you'd need more time to adjust."

"Nah," Mason said. "She likes a little pain with her pleasure." He glided his cock over her nose, her eyes. "You like feeling the burn, don't you, dark angel? Look at you taking two big cocks in your cunt. Still not enough is it? Always so greedy."

"Yes!" she cried, his words driving her crazy.

Dirty bastard. I loved it when he got like this.

Mason grasped her jaw and she opened her mouth involuntarily—just like he'd intended.

And then he shoved his cock straight down her throat, pumping hard and fast and fucking viciously right off the bat. As she gagged at the sudden intrusion, his eyes rolled back in his head. He pulled out, then stuffed his cock back down her throat.

Her eyes were so glazed and consumed by it all and she relaxed, taking him deep over and over, despite the ferocity of his thrusts.

At the same time, Lev and I started alternating ours, picking up our pace until we were fucking the hell out of her cunt.

It was such a tight fit, every motion was insane bliss.

I could barely breathe through it, let alone hold on for the long haul.

Mason reached underneath us and I felt him shove a finger into her ass, twisting and curling.

It was one insane stimulation too many and she bucked like crazy and came all over our dicks, screaming the damn shower down.

"Damn!" I cried as her pulsing cunt milked my cock and I came inside her.

"Motherfucker!" Lev roared as he felt it over his shaft, pushing him over the edge.

He pulled out and came all over her stomach.

A moment later, Mason shot his load down her throat, saving a little to paint her breasts until she was covered in us.

Ours.

I eased out of her and pulled her onto my lap. "Okay, cutie?"

She leaned back against me, a dazed smile playing on her lips. "Perfect."

We chuckled and then Lev and Mason wrapped themselves around us too, holding her and giving her that comfort that we made sure we always did after an intense fuck.

I RUFFLED my hair with one of the super-soft hand towels to dispel the extra moisture. I couldn't fix it into my mohawk until it wasn't dripping all over the place.

"That was one hell of a party last night." I smirked. "And this morning," I said as I made my way back into the bedroom.

Mason was pulling his jeans back on, going commando. Damn, I loved seeing the old him, the real him coming out in all these different ways, some subtle, some brazen.

Bree was wrapped in a fuzzy white robe that Roman's staff had put in every guestroom for us, and Levi was in just his boxers as he towel dried Bree's hair while the two of them sat on the wraparound couch in the seating area.

I plopped down beside them, bouncing them a little, especially Bree, and earning a giggle from her.

"Sure was, cupcake."

"Mason deserved it," Bree said. "What happened yesterday was a major cause for celebration."

"What happened because of you, you mean, dark angel?" he said, taking a seat on the edge of the coffee table right in front of us.

"I might have destroyed his leverage, but you did all the rest."

"It took guts to stand up to that motherfucker," Lev said. He grinned. "And to use your *cement block* punch on him."

Mason winced. "Yeah, that wasn't planned. But when I saw him touch Bree, all bets were off."

"Good thing you reacted, because he would've died right there like a fucking bitch if *I'd* gotten there first."

"Lovely, it's okay," Bree said, stroking his arm.

Mason took her hand. "No, it's not okay. Even a slight touch from him is unacceptable."

"Creeper of the Century," I bit out.

That guy had always freaked me out with that, the twisted vibe he'd had.

At least now we wouldn't have to deal with it anymore.

Bree was on the same page, telling Mason, "It doesn't matter now, it's over, he's out of your life."

"Yeah," Mason breathed, amazement dancing in his eyes. "I'm still wrapping my head around it all, what it all means as well. So many changes." His whole face lit up. "All of which I'm looking forward to."

I tossed my wet towel on Mason's lap.

He shook his head at me and I thought the usual sort of reprimand was coming for when I was messy.

But then he grinned and placed it on top of his head and sank back against the couch, folding his arms across his chest and giving me a self-satisfied look.

I burst out laughing. "Shit, I love it, gorgeous!"

"Me too," Lev said, smiling.

Although, it was fleeting with him lately. The smiling and joking around. He was really stressed about trying to track down Malcolm Lynch, feeling the pressure of it.

And worse, the desperation.

He wanted it so badly.

He *needed* it.

Like Mason with his father, defeating Lynch was the key to Lev finally being at peace.

Once it was done, all of us would be in good places. There'd be nothing holding us back or eating us up from within.

I leaned against him and kissed his cheek. "Almost there, brother. Then *Hellraiser* can come out and play one last time."

"Well, it won't be completely the last time. I'm still gonna do a little street fighting here and there. But for fun."

"You are?" Bree asked.

"Yeah. Why? You don't like that?" he said, eyeing her curiously.

"No, I do. I actually think it's a good outlet. I know your dad wanted you to give it all up, but the street fighting isn't the same. It's a sport to you basically. A fucked-up sport, but still. It'll help to offset giving up all the rest." She shifted to face him head on, curling her legs up under her. "And I'm gonna come down and cheer you on when you start back up once we get back to Stonewell."

"Cheer me on, hmm? Is that instead of kicking me in the balls?"

"Well, we'll have to see. It depends if you really piss me off again, right?"

"Oh, baby, you're so fucked."

He lunged at her then, driving her down into the couch and tickling the crap out of her, making her giggle and shriek.

Unfortunately, before Mason and I could join in on the fun, Lev's phone chimed with a sound I hadn't heard from it before. He must've set up a special alert.

He stilled.

Then he was pushing off Bree and darting across the bedroom to one of the nightstands. He snatched it up. "Christ."

"What? What's happened?" Bree asked.

"We have a situation?" Mason questioned.

"Shit," I uttered, worriedly.

But then Lev smiled.

His eyes darkened.

That dangerous look rose to the surface.

And then he told us, "I've found Lynch."

25

~Brianna~

I finally eased apart from my dad and the hug that had seemed to go on for ages.

I mean, I was all for it now that we were no longer estranged, and we were in a good place, but we had business at hand to attend to.

It was why he'd been called down here to the Knight mansion by Roman.

"It's really good seeing you in person again, baby girl," my dad said as we made our way toward Roman's study where he and the boys were already gathered.

"You too, Dad."

"We're never doing that estrangement thing again, yeah?"

"I'm sure we can find a different way to handle it the next time we piss each other off," I teased.

He smiled.

But that was short-lived when his gaze dropped to my all-seeing eye pendant.

"When did you start wearing that instead of keeping it in your wallet?"

"A couple of years ago." I took in the pain all over his face. "Do you need me to take it off while you're here?"

"No. I'm glad you wear it. A part of your mom. Her last gift to you. Laying eyes on it after all this time was just… I guess I wasn't expecting it." His lips lifted. "But then again, just looking at you is seeing a big part of her too. You're so similar in looks." He registered my baby-pink off-the-shoulder top with my matching pink heels. "Although, all this pink is new."

I chuckled. "Yeah. It somehow became my thing."

"I see."

We reached the study and I stopped for a moment. "Are you ready to do this?"

"Baby girl, I've been ready for fucking years. It couldn't come a moment sooner." He reached out and laid his hand on my shoulder gently. "Neither did you putting that fucker, Tommy, to ground. I'm real proud of you."

It was an odd thing for a father to be proud of his child for—killing a man. But from his perspective he meant it as me being capable of putting down my enemies like a boss. Also, he wasn't exactly a conventional parent.

There was certainly a lot of that going around.

We stepped into the study, all maroon and fancy mahogany wood.

Roman and the boys were gathered around a rectangular mahogany table, Levi and his dad on one side staring at one of Levi's laptops, while Mason and Colt were on the other viewing a second. They were all standing, emphasizing the urgency I could already feel coming off them.

I was right there with them on that.

It was about to happen.

We were so close to finally ending Lynch once and for all.

"Curt," Roman said, looking up to see my dad walking in with me. "Good to see you again."

"Long time, yeah?" my dad responded humorously with sarcasm because it had only been a few weeks since Roman had approached him after Royce Humphrey's first attack.

"Indeed," Roman responded with a smile.

"Sorry it took me a while. It's a ways to my storage facility that's housing my old shit from the club days. Namely, what we're gonna be needing for this strike later tonight—equipment and arms."

"I appreciate you handling that end of things. It would've taken me a couple of days to access that sort of thing."

"Well, you've got the whole legitimate business thing to contend with."

"So do you, Dad," I reminded him.

After all these years since disbanding the club, he still thought of himself as dealing in the down and dirty, but he'd cleaned up his act extremely well.

All right, what was about to go down tonight notwithstanding.

But sometimes we had to make exceptions.

Sometimes we had to become the very monsters we sought to fight.

"So what do we have here?" my dad asked as he approached the laptop by Levi and Roman. "Where's this piece of shit holed up?"

I walked over to Colt and Mason and studied their laptop, taking in the location and the floorplan.

Just as I did, my dad echoed my thoughts.

"A fucking penthouse? Bought out the whole building too? This shit really does think of himself as some kind of king."

"A king whose reign will end tonight," Levi seethed.

My dad smiled at him proudly. "Damn straight, Knight."

My dad and Roman exchanged a smile. "You did good with this one," he told Roman.

"Seconded regarding Brianna."

Just as Colt reached out and stroked my hair in an automatic sort of sweet reaction when I was near, my dad looked over at me at Roman's compliment of me, and noticed. He frowned and Colt withdrew his hand quickly, realizing what he'd done, despite our talk beforehand to not demonstrate affection in front of my dad.

Fortunately, he looked away without saying anything or calling it out, and turned his attention back to the laptop.

"It's a twenty-five story building," Levi reported.

"It will pose a challenge accessing the penthouse floor as a result," Roman said.

"Not if you draw him out and take care of putting him to ground outside," my dad commented.

"This building is located on a busy city block. We wouldn't be able to cover it up... too many witnesses," Mason pointed out.

"The strike needs to happen inside," I said.

My dad took in that information, then asked, "He's putting up *Osiris* here in this building?"

"Correct," Roman confirmed.

"How many are we talking?"

"We've clocked it at twenty, including him," Levi informed him.

"That's not the total number of members of that fucked-up outfit."

"No, it's not. We're talking forty-six in total and that's only until he recruits more, which is something he does every couple of months. The rest are in the process of being moved into the building. He wants them all close. For protection as much as convenience," Levi reported.

"I'll take out the remaining guys if you can get me a location."

Levi nodded. "Now I know where Lynch is, which was made possible from this bold move and the expensive purchase of this building under a pseudonym he used on the phone while we were in captivity, I'm tapped into everything there. All incoming and outgoing communications. I'll get you a location from there."

"Dad, you can't take down twelve guys. I mean, even in your heyday that would still be asking a lot."

"I've already got my old club members on standby. Five of the closest brothers to me who owe me a favor or two. I was figuring on bringing them in on the Lynch takedown, but you need somebody to take out these stragglers too or *Osiris* could survive even without their fucked-up mastermind."

"Wow, you certainly came prepared."

He smiled. "Wasn't gonna risk disappointing you again."

"Dad, no, that's not what—"

"It *is*, it's what happened back then. But I appreciate you saying the words anyhow."

My chest squeezed. "That's all in the past. And after tonight, the rest will be as well."

"Yeah, it damn well will," Levi said.

"Son," Roman spoke. "For the four of you to even reach Lynch in the penthouse, you'll need a distraction. Making it up twenty-five stories will take a toll and with that many hostiles in place, they'll cut you down before you reach our chief target. You need the element of surprise."

"A sneak attack," my dad said. "I'll be there to *covertly* cut down any of the hostiles who try to flee, but the risk regarding the rest is too high, unacceptable to me. Letting you do this is one thing and difficult for both Curt and I to accept, but we understand where you're coming from and how badly you need to be the ones to inflict this damage, to defeat that which has haunted you, to reclaim your power that was taken during that awful time. *But* allowing undue risks wasn't part of that agreement."

"I know. We won't move in recklessly like that, Dad. We'll brainstorm a way around it."

"Aside from a fake gas leak, which it's highly doubtful he'd buy, anything bigger would risk exposure and alert half a city block worth of witnesses," Mason said.

"More like several blocks' worth," Levi countered.

"There's a way to do this," Roman said.

We all fell into concentrated silence, trying to determine the way to go with it.

My mind was racing a million miles a minute, but it was compromised, like I was sure Levi's was with the satisfying thought of ending Malcolm Lynch.

"Why don't you use that guy you knifed through the hand, Lev?" Colt piped up. "Kyle?"

Levi's eyes sparked and he went to Colt and grasped his shoulders. "Fucking spectacular idea, cupcake."

"Yeah, we can work that," Mason said. "Have it where he's freaking out because Royce was murdered, then Tommy, and he's thinking he'll be the next one to face yours and Bree's wrath, Lev. Have him go to Lynch for protection, begging to join him again as part of the deal."

"You gotta offer him something big to get him to fake all that," my dad pointed out.

"Protection," Roman said. "He's been in hiding for a long time. Levi found him. His former protector is dead. That fear of reprisal for what happened six years ago from

Lev, myself, and Curt, is his weakness. It can be used in our favor."

"I'll throw in my brand of protection too," my dad told Roman. "You up for doing it on your end?"

"He did help the kids out in the end."

"Too late, though," Mason groused.

"I'll do it," Roman said. He looked at Levi. "You've gotta be able to back off too. It ends with Malcolm Lynch. Forget about Kyle Trass. He's a useless and pointless target anyway."

Levi looked to me for my agreement too and I gave a nod.

It was what was best for the circumstances.

"All right," he told Roman and my dad. "I'll leave him be after this."

"Good," Roman said, pushing away from the laptop. "I'll retrieve him immediately. In the meantime, gear up."

We all nodded and gave our confirmations as Roman headed out.

My dad pulled his phone out and started contacting his former club members who were still loyal—or who owed him a favor.

As he did that, Mason went over some rules and procedures for Colt taking part in this, something he was being lighthearted about compared to how he'd normally be.

"How are you doing?" Levi asked, coming to me.

I reached out and rubbed his arms. "My mind is kind of awhirl, honestly. It's hard to focus on all the details for once with the thought of seeing the defeat in that bastard's eyes pushing to the forefront, then watching the light go out of those fucking eyes. I just... after all this time we'll finally take back the power he took from us. It's a lot to process, to wrap my mind around."

"I feel the same way."

"Yeah? You seem so together, so focused."

He leaned in and whispered, "It's mostly fake. But all I can see is the spectacular end result through all these details and all this strategizing too."

"Maybe focusing on it for right now is best to get it out of our systems, so we'll be able to focus up once we're out in the field and initiating the strike against the depraved demon."

"Solid approach, baby." He smiled down at me. "You see why I didn't want to tell you that he was alive until I had something on him, some way to track him?"

"Yeah. Yeah, I do. Everything you've done has been what you believed was best for me. The lengths you went to, the sheer effort… it means so much to me."

"Why you love me so much, hmm?"

I slapped his chest playfully. "Arrogant shit."

"When it comes to you and how we all feel about one another, absolutely."

A throat cleared and Levi and I eased apart as my dad came to stand before us. "It's sorted. Got the guys mobilizing now."

"Perfect, Dad."

"Nice work, Curt."

"So, what's the deal here?" he asked, gesturing between me and Levi.

"Deal?" Levi asked.

"Roman told me how possessive and protective you are over my daughter, yet then I see one of your friends touching her in full view of you and you didn't do a thing, didn't react one little bit?"

Uh oh.

"I'm not that way with Colt and Mason. I trust them implicitly," Levi said, thinking on his feet as usual, as he tried so hard to cover for me.

231

No.

I couldn't allow it.

Our foursome relationship was the best thing that had happened to me.

It wasn't something to be concealed or buried.

It deserved celebrating.

They deserved to be celebrated as the loves of my life.

"We're all together," I blurted out, the sentiment of it all taking me over.

To my astonishment, my dad burst out laughing.

"What?" I asked. "What's happening? Are you having a break from the shock of it?"

"Ha, no. It was the look on your face." He stroked my hair for a moment. "Well done for telling me. Proud of you. Hell, I'm proud of you for a lot of things. Especially you coming into your own, all this strength coming off you."

"You already knew," Levi surmised.

"Roman thought it would be a good idea to prepare me. He told me a few days after that meet-up we had."

Mason and Colt gravitated over, the two of them along with Levi basically flanking me in a sweet and bolstering way.

"It was a lot to take in at first, so Roman made the right call giving me a heads-up. But it didn't take me that long to realize that this is a real good thing."

"You really believe that, Dad?"

"I do. You're happy for the first time in ages. Content. Powerful. Secure in yourself. Roman explained that it works all ways with you four, you're all helping one another, you're a hella good team. And look," he said, pointing at Levi, "You're with a guy who rides, loves motorcycles and is a brutal bastard in a fight." He pointed to Colt. "You're with this rocker who plays the kind of music I'm into." He moved to Mason. "And you're with a future tattoo artist, also up my alley." He grinned. "Got the whole fucking package right here, don't you, baby girl?"

We all laughed.

"Thank you, Dad." I threw my arms around him then.

He held me to him, his voice breaking with rare emotion as he uttered, "Missed you. Missed you so much, Brianna."

I tightened my hold on him. "I missed you too."

As we pulled apart, he looked out at my boys. "Keep treating her right and we'll stay all good here, yeah?"

They all gave him their word.

I beamed out at them all.

I couldn't believe how far we'd come.

The way things had started down in Stonewell with that seemed like another world now, one whose existence was fading fast with every passing day.

Because now there was this.

Our new reality.

And I couldn't love it more.

26

~Mason~

Roman burst on into the living room holding the guy we intended to use for all he was worth in a headlock as he dragged him in, his head covered with a black hood.

He released him in front of where we were all gathered on the black leather wraparound couch —aside from Curt who was continuing to make arrangements with his guys on the phone out on the patio as he smoked up a storm. According to Bree, he wasn't a regular smoker, just a stress smoker.

And this mission ahead of us certainly qualified.

So much so that I was going to have to go back to my former *controlled* persona just for tonight. I couldn't risk it any other way. Not with this. Not with the stakes and not with how much it meant to the mental health of Lev and Bree.

Roman released the guy roughly and ripped off the hood.

And then Kyle Trass stared up at all of us from his knees, blinking rapidly and trying to process what was happening.

"What the——" His gaze landed on Levi. "You didn't fuck me up enough to——" He caught sight of Bree then, his shock increasing tenfold. "Brianna, fuck. How are you… what's happening?"

"You're here to do us a little favor," Roman told him.

Levi rose to his feet and shoved his hands into his pants pockets. "Come on now, Dad, don't be concerned about scaring him. Fear is a powerful motivator." He walked to Kyle and loomed over him, that dangerous side of him coming out. He growled, "It's not a little favor. Malcolm Lynch is involved."

"No," Kyle said, his naked fear staggering. *Whoa*. "No, I can't."

"You seem under the impression that you have a choice in this," Levi said. He shot out his hand and fisted it in Kyle's hair. "You don't, motherfucker."

Kyle looked over his shoulder at Roman standing there with his arms folded as he leaned against the bookcase observing and supervising. "Roman Knight," he breathed. He turned back to Levi. "Your dad kidnapped me right from my office at *Ravage*. My security guys and my employees are gonna figure out what went down and they're gonna come for me."

Levi scoffed. "They won't be able to follow my dad's path and track you. I've run interference."

"You… what… you can do that?"

"Yeah, and I'm just that fucking good, so keep that in mind before you decline to cooperate *freely* again." He gestured at me and Colt. "Not to mention, my boys here are right on the edge, knowing that you're one of the sick fucks involved in kidnapping me and Brianna. They want to rip your fucking head off. And me? Well, you already know that I have no limits whatsoever. Not when it comes to those who hurt my loved ones."

"I'm not a threat to you. I could've come after you for impaling my hand and attacking me on my own territory, but I didn't. I considered it justice for you after what went down at the abandoned police station six years back. You know I feel bad about it, real bad. I even helped you both."

Bree rose to her feet then. "Not soon enough. Not by a long shot."

Kyle's attention went to her, pain all over him. "I'm so sorry... what they did to you... I can't even... there are no words."

Levi smashed his fist into his face.

He grunted, his head snapping to the side.

"Don't make her relive it, motherfucker."

Kyle wiped blood out of the corner of his mouth. "I'm sorry. Look, back then I couldn't do much until they left that shithole for a bit. I was on the chopping block too. Malcolm had threatened me with castration for fuck's sakes. He didn't like my constant protests about what went down with you two."

"If that's the case, he's useless to us," Colt piped up. He shoved a hand through his mohawk. "Shit."

"He can turn it around," Roman spoke, having just been there watching, clearly wanting Levi to handle this by himself, knowing he needed to.

Levi looked out at him and something unspoken passed between them before Levi ordered Kyle, "Get up."

He staggered to his feet, looking all around at us worriedly.

Except at Brianna.

With her, he had that pained look mixed with what looked like a whole lot of guilt and regret. He was having a hard time holding her gaze for more than a few moments at a time.

That part was shame.

Exactly what he should be suffering from feeling.

He'd recognized that what had happened to them had been wrong and so incredibly fucked-up, yet he'd just stood back out of fear for himself, while two kids had been tortured and also traumatized for life.

Bree stepped forward and stroked Levi's arm, giving him a nod.

He recognized her need to handle it now too and took a step back to allow her room with the bastard.

"You feel bad about what happened, I see it all over you."

"I do and I'm so fucking sorry that—"

Bree snapped her fingers. "Stop." She took another step forward until she was right there in front of him. "You want absolution, this is what's going to happen." She slapped her hand to her hip and told him, "You'll contact Malcolm with the promise of vital intel concerning Levi's vengeance crusade against him. You'll emphasize the gravity of the situation regarding Royce Humphrey's murder, citing Levi now having formed an army that completely wiped out him and his merry band of merce-naries. You'll tell him that you'll trade intel that will enable him to come at Levi and his army and stop him before he comes for *Osiris*. It will be in exchange for Malcolm's promise of protection for you, as well as you agreeing to work for him again, emphasizing that you've become a successful businessman and you will bring him in on your plan to franchise *Ravage*."

Kyle took her words in, then sighed heavily. "Look, sweetheart, I get it, and I actually do want to help you, to absolve myself at least in some small way to take some of the edge of the guilt I've been carrying since all that shit went down. *But* I'm not gonna be able to do any of that if

I'm dead. As soon as Malcolm realizes I've double-crossed him, he'll come for me."

"He won't be able to do that," she assured him.

"How's that?"

Levi stepped forward. "This isn't just about justice, it's lethal justice. A sick fuck like him can't be allowed to live."

"Jesus fuck." He pinched the bridge of his nose. "Okay, but how can I know the same fate's not gonna happen to me, that you aren't gonna turn this *crusade* of yours on me the moment Malcolm is buried?"

"That's our end of the deal," Bree said,

"We'll let you go, leave you alone," Levi clarified. "It will be done."

Kyle raised an eyebrow. "That's… a hell of a thing."

"With Lynch dead you'd be completely free and clear," Roman spoke.

He took a moment to absorb it all, then he gave a reluctant nod. "You've got me. Only fucking way to survive."

Damn straight it was.

After what he'd been a part of, he was fucking lucky that was even on the table for him.

"All right," Levi said, folding his arms across his chest. "So, for your part, we need the cameras downed in the elevator."

"What? How the hell am I gonna convince a paranoid fuck like Malcolm to do that?"

"Make it clear what a paranoid fuck *you* are. You have intel he needs, valuable intel. It gives you leverage to get in the door in the way *you* feel comfortable. You can also make it clear what I'm capable of, that I have the ability to tap into his entire surveillance system and work it to my will."

"Shit, he'll probably down the whole thing after he tells Lynch that," Colt commented.

"I'll take care of it," Kyle assured us.

Levi stepped into his space and growled, "Make sure you do, or the deal's off, and I guarantee you won't make it out of there alive."

Kyle nodded vehemently.

With that, Levi stepped back and wrapped his arm around Bree.

He looked out at us and gave us a chin lift.

Things were in place.

The time had come.

It was on.

27

~Levi~

I stood on the periphery of a battle I'd been craving for six whole years.

I could almost taste the coming victory on my tongue.

We'd already defeated so many of our enemies, men who'd thought themselves kings.

Royce Humphrey, Tommy Dixon, Peter Hall.

Tonight, the last twisted king would fall.

Brianna, my dad, and I stood with Kyle as he made the call to Malcolm Lynch to confirm the shutdown of the security system in and around the twenty-five story apartment building. He was actually bringing it really well and playing up his paranoia and fear to a T.

It was frustrating waiting for it to happen, knowing how quickly and efficiently I could see to it on my own. But if I cut it myself, it would alert Lynch that an attack was imminent. Given how important the element of surprise was in this particular case, we couldn't have that.

As we were waiting in the shadows of an alley opposite our target location, four of my dad's guys who he'd been able to bring in on this on short notice—part of his security unit—were over on the other side at the south side of the building with Mason and Colt waiting on our word to move in once the security system was down. They'd be taking the stairwells and putting down all *Osiris* members who they encountered.

I stared at the live feed of the penthouse where our chief target was located. I'd accessed his system through a covert backdoor route, a weakness I'd identified in the system—far too easily—to get a lay of the land. I'd been able to give Mason's team the precise current locations of the *Osiris* members scattered throughout the building, while I'd also been able to determine that there were six members stationed on the penthouse floor with Lynch.

Curt Walker was tapped into us via COMMs waiting on our word to move it too so he could take out the remaining members located elsewhere, their locations I'd been able to determine with ease now that everything else had fallen into place.

We couldn't have him move in before we did, because any one of the shitheads could notify Lynch that they were being set upon, which would alert him to the fact that something major was up, thus ruining our element of surprise.

Finally, I watched as the security system I was viewing on my phone went dead.

A moment later, Kyle was off the phone and telling us, "He's shut it off. We're good to go. He says there are two of his guys who'll be waiting at the lobby elevator bay to escort me on up."

"Good," my dad said, then looked at me and Brianna. "That will be your window. I'll take them out, you head on up to the penthouse."

"Sounds good." I slid my hand into Brianna's and looked out at her clad in all black like we all were, along with all of us sporting bulletproof vests. The leather pants she had on were really working for her—and me. I'd had to shore up my focus when she'd first come downstairs in the mansion wearing them. *Christ almighty.* "Ready for this, my *Wildflower?*"

She nodded vehemently, her ponytail swinging every which way. "Let's end this."

And end it we would.

Then we'd finally be free of the demons that had haunted us for far too long.

I tapped my earpiece. "Move in."

In the next second, I had Kyle leading the way across from the alleyway and approaching the parking lot of the building where the elevator bay was, the three of us following behind.

As we made our way over, I saw the shadows moving toward the other side of the building near the stairwell entrances—Mason's team going for it.

Excitement thrummed through me that this was finally happening, that we were so close. It slammed up against a whole lot of adrenaline, putting me in that same hyper aware and unforgiving state that I entered when I engaged in my street fighting *hobby.*

As we reached the elevator bay, two *Osiris* members bolted from around either corner.

We'd known they were there, so we were prepared.

Brianna reacted impressively quickly, snagging the closest one's arm and using his weight against him to haul him into the wall. As he jarred hard against it and ricocheted forward, she swept her leg at his ankles and ripped him off his feet. I was there in the next beat, slicing my tactical knife across his throat.

Before we could work in sync again, we spun toward

the second guy to see my dad dropping him, the guy with a blade buried in his chest, right through the heart.

"Save your energy for up there," my dad told us.

Kyle looked on in a whole lot of shock.

"Focus up," I snapped, jarring him back to himself.

He didn't have any other option then as the elevator doors opened and two more guys came into view, dressed in cheap black suits like the other two we'd just taken out.

As soon as they saw that Kyle wasn't alone, they realized Lynch had been played, and they launched themselves at us.

I pushed into the elevator, dragging Kyle with me, and slammed one of them into the wall. As he threw his fist, I deflected it, snatched his wrist, then used the hold to twist him around, then slam my boot into his back, sending him flying out of the elevator.

My dad was wailing on the other one.

And then a knife shot through the air and tore right through the left eye socket of the guy I'd just kicked out toward my dad.

I spun to see Brianna's arm still in throwing position.

She caught my eye and slicked her bottom lip with the tip of her tongue.

Hot as the fires of hell. "Fuck, baby."

"Go," my dad said, as he disposed of the other guy. "I'll be here. None of them will get out."

I nodded, then held the elevator door open as I tapped my earpiece to communicate with Mason. "Status?"

"Four down, approaching tenth floor."

"Nice. Everyone okay?"

"All good."

"Keep me posted."

"Will do."

I disconnected, then looked out at my dad. "The team is ahead of schedule."

He smiled. "Be careful, Levi."

"Always," I said, winking.

"He means always *starting now*," Brianna clarified to reassure my dad.

"Exactly." I ushered Brianna into the elevator.

My dad gave me a nod, and then I punched in the button for the penthouse, the doors closing in the next moment.

"Shit. Shit. Shit," Kyle was murmuring.

"Keep it together," I said, pulling another blade to go with my other and readying both, while Brianna spun the knife I'd gifted her around down by her side.

"Just play your part and you'll be fine," she told him, the spinning growing faster and wilder.

I nudged her with my shoulder. "Hey, you okay?"

"Fine, yeah. Just gearing up."

"Brianna," I pushed.

"Just worried how I may react to seeing the psycho again for the first time in six years since the time in that hellscape."

"I know. I feel some of that too. Try to keep your focus on the mission and the fact that he'll be gone soon, that it'll finally be done."

"You weren't weak," Kyle spoke suddenly.

"What?" Brianna questioned.

"You were both kids when Malcolm hurt you and traumatized you, but look at you both. You're strong, independent, successful. You're powerful. You don't need to fear coming face to face with him, or even feel anxious about it, *he* needs to fear you both. Just so you know, he's done similar things to others before—just his actual enemies, not the children of them like he did with you—and they *were* broken. Grown adults." He smiled sadly. "There's no place for shame here. You two are something else. Strong, resilient as hell, and fighters to the core. *Now*, let's go get your lethal justice, shall we?"

Brianna and I stared at him in stunned silence.

Definitely hadn't expected that.

I saw a little smile grace her lips and she gave him a chin lift.

"All right," I said. "It's appreciated."

It was as much as I could muster. He might be repentant and all that shit now, but he'd still been there back then.

The elevator was just a couple of floors out, so Brianna and I took position, our backs flat against either side of the door to remain out of sight when it first opened.

I'd discovered that Lynch's protocol when somebody entered the penthouse was to have four guards flanking the elevator. We couldn't risk them shoving us back in, or that welcoming committee descending on us in such a tight space and jeopardizing our mission to get access to Lynch directly.

The elevator dinged just as Kyle sucked in a breath and wiped his sweaty palms on his suit pants.

The door whooshed open and Kyle fed us intel, uttering aloud in a casual tone, "Quite the welcoming committee. Four of you. Where's the big boss at?"

"Living room. Come on through," one of the guys answered.

Kyle walked on out and I listened carefully as their footsteps disappeared down the corridor. I slapped my hand to the elevator door so it didn't close, and when I'd determined they were far enough away, I inched out and shot a look the way they'd come.

"All clear," I told Brianna.

We stepped out together and crept along the corridor, following their path.

Voices caught our attention and we peered around the wall, finding the living room.

Kyle was standing there in front of a tacky bright-red pleather wraparound couch with two of the four guys dispersing and walking off through to another room to the right through the double doors I'd seen on the floor plan. It was a game room with video game equipment visible along with a massive flatscreen TV, a pool table, and even a bar. One such method to keep his guys happy. Until he gathered more power like before and then treated them like shit, as he'd done to Kyle.

The remaining two guys took a seat on the adjacent armchairs and Kyle shifted a little, moving to the side.

I realized why in the next moment as it revealed who he was standing in front of, the person who'd been blocked from view by him at first.

Christ.

There he was in the flesh.

Malcolm Lynch.

He was sporting that same dirty-blond buzz cut. Those beady eyes were as creepy as ever. He was dressed in an ill-fitting black pinstripe suit this time, his linebacker form filling it out.

I felt Brianna shudder against me and I turned to her, nuzzling her neck and whispering, "We've got this, *Wildflower.* No more haunting after this, no more shame, no more shackles." I kissed her cheek.

"Yeah," she murmured. "Yeah."

"Time to let it all out."

She nodded fervently, then nuzzled against me. "I love you."

"I love *you*," I whispered back.

I heard Kyle uttering the spiel we'd worked out, right down to every little detail.

I saw Lynch relax into it as he listened to what he was saying, his eyes lighting with malice as Kyle gave him the fake key to my downfall.

Despite his nerves, he was pulling it off really well.

Until he wasn't.

Until he fucked up.

His nerves got the best of him and he tried to push it along too fast, the plan to ascertain the location of all six of the *Osiris* members up here, then contain them while Brianna and I took Lynch out. We only had four so far.

Kyle asked for privacy, gesturing for Lynch to empty the room of his soldiers.

"Hell," Brianna grunted.

I cursed under my breath as Lynch stilled, then suspicion lit his eyes.

"Why the insistence on us being alone?" He looked Kyle up and down. "If you came here under false pretenses, to harm me or something, you shouldn't come packing heat. My men frisked you and found zilch."

He pushed to his feet.

When his soldiers went to rise with him, he signaled them to stay where they were, as he focused on Kyle. "Is that it? Is that why you really came here? You were always far too sympathetic to the kids back then. Now Royce is dead, you thought you'd go for broke, huh? With him gone there's nobody to keep you hidden and as a ghost, so you figured you might as well set out on a suicide mission and try to take me out before I took you out?"

"And you call me the paranoid one."

"I call you the weak-ass one, Kyle."

Kyle held up his hands as Lynch advanced on him. "It's nothing like you've said. Just… chill."

"Chill?" Lynch gritted out. He snapped his fingers behind him and his two guys rose to their feet. "Nah, the heat's about to get turned up all the fucking way. You're nervous. Even for you. Something is off." He pulled his phone out and typed for a moment, before stowing it away.

Not five seconds later, the missing two guys burst out from a closed door that I recalled was the kitchen.

"Fuck," I whispered.

"We can't retreat," Brianna said. "I won't, Levi."

"The plan's gone off the rails, but I'm always a fan of improvising and cutting another path through. Ready to move?"

"Absolutely," she responded resolutely.

In fact, she beat me to it, bursting from our cover and crossing the threshold into the living room and tossing her blade through the air.

It ripped into the shoulder of one of the guys standing in front of the couch, driving right through his flesh and embedding in the pleather behind him, pinning him to it. He roared and flailed.

And then all eyes were on us.

Through the rest, all I saw were Lynch's soulless fucking orbs of depravity.

He looked at his soldier in pain and then turned away, not giving a fuck, his attention on me and Brianna.

His lip curled as he took us in. "You've grown up well." He raked his eyes over Brianna none too subtly. "Especially you, pretty princess."

A snarl escaped me before I could even begin to reel it in and then my blade left my hand almost of its own accord. *Motherfucker!*

It buried itself in Lynch's left shoulder, blowing him back, a satisfying grunt escaping him.

All hell broke loose then.

Kyle ran away to the edge of the room as the four guys descended on us and the other two burst out from the game room.

"Beat them down, but keep them alive. We're gonna play again like the old days."

Piece of motherfucking shit!

His callback to that nightmare and the threat to make us live to repeat it was so fucking despicable, it triggered my bloodlust full-force.

And this time, I didn't even try to hold it back.

Not one bit.

Pulling my bo-staff from the holster at my belt, I snapped it down so it extended fully, and roared as I sprinted into the room, headed for the closest two by the kitchen.

In my peripheral vision, I saw Brianna toss her blade at the guy trying to help Lynch and his buddy also still pinned to the couch. It ripped into the throat of the shit, blood spraying every-fucking-where as she hit his carotid artery dead-on. Dead being the operative word, because he'd meet that fate any second. *Nicely done, Wildflower.*

I jabbed my staff into the gut of the closest one.

As he doubled over, I spun and swept it at the side of his head, making him stagger into the wall beside the kitchen door.

The other cheap suit with him came at me and threw his fist.

I brought my arm down, deflecting it easily, the asshole relying way too much on his humungous roided-out form, rather than precision. And then I swept my staff up, driving it into his chin and making his head snap back.

Before the two of them could fully recover, I was between them, jabbing and sweeping my bo-staff back and forth and taking them both on at once.

Cries and curses rang out, blood sprayed, cracks of broken bones filled my senses.

Music to my fucking ears.

And fuel to my bloodlust.

It was all a blur of rapid-fire violence and blood-red within moments as I gave into it, tearing into the mother-fuckers like a wild beast.

Punish! Destroy! Slaughter!

It took me some time through it to realize that the two of them had stopped moving, and I looked either side of me to see them downed as I was crouched over them, smashing my bo-staff into each one in turn.

They were so bloodied and beaten, their features were barely discernible.

My staff and hands were slick with their blood.

A snarl sounded, pulling me from the carnage I'd wrought, and I pushed to my feet just as another soldier ran at me.

The moment he hit, I angled my body as I grabbed at his tie and used it as leverage to haul him over my shoulder and into a floor-length mirror. He crashed to the ground, disorientated.

I was about to move in to finish it when a cry from Brianna broke my focus and I instinctively spun around to see her being thrown onto the pool table, one of the guys about to leap on top of her. *Fuck!*

I went to start over there, only to see her snatch up a pool ball and smash it into her opponent's face, shattering his nose and making him stagger back. Then she reared back and used the momentum to spring to her feet on the table. She spun into a spinning kick that smashed into the piece of shit and had him falling back against the double doors.

I didn't get to see her finish him because me being

distracted cost me as the guy I'd left conscious jumped on my back.

Roaring, I slammed all my weight backward into the kitchen door.

It gave way and his grip broke around me as he hit the floor.

I dove for the knife block on the counter to my left, ripped out a butcher's knife, then drove it through his chest just as he was trying to get up.

Another one down.

I pushed out of the kitchen and frantically searched out Brianna.

Relief sung through me as I caught sight of her tossing a knife at a fucker running at her.

It plunged into his eye.

And that was the end of that.

He stilled, then dropped hard, dead instantly.

"Can't keep your focus with the pretty princess around, huh?"

I jolted at the sound of Malcolm Lynch's voice and spun to my left.

A fresh wave of adrenaline shot down my spine as I saw him standing there, a gun trained on me.

He grinned wickedly, then fired off a shot at me.

I cursed as it plunged into my chest, the force of it, and at close range too, blowing me off my feet. I grunted as I landed hard on my back.

"Levi!" Brianna screamed at the top of her lungs. "*No!* Levi!"

Before I could fully process it, he was there standing over me, taking aim at my head.

I saw Brianna running toward me in my peripheral vision.

But she was out of her knives.

And her screaming protests went completely ignored by Lynch who was staring down at me with twisted glee.

"Thought you could best me. Thought you had the balls to fucking well stop me?" He scoffed. "Fucking kid."

The air moved and I saw Kyle suddenly there with a pool cue in his grasp a moment before he swung it at Lynch, ripping him away.

Lynch crashed into the coffee table and the weak-ass glass thing gave way under his weight. He cursed and brought his hand to the side of his face that was now bleeding from Kyle's strike.

"Christ," I breathed.

"Got you," he said.

"Go. Get out of here."

"What?"

"You're done. Thank you."

He hesitated for a moment, looking out at Lynch and seeing Brianna frantically running over to me.

"Appreciate it, Levi."

And with that, he took off, free of this shitshow.

Brianna reached me in the next moment.

"Oh my God! Oh my God, Levi!" she was screaming.

As she skidded to her knees beside me, I caught sight of Lynch staggering away, wiping blood away from his face with the back of his hand.

No!

Brianna's hands were on my hoodie then, pushing it up frantically.

"I'm good," I croaked. "It's okay," I tried to tell her.

But she wasn't having any of it and she accessed my vest.

A choked sigh of major relief escaped her as she saw the bullet embedded there, having been stopped by the vest. Even at close range. It was one of *Knightsridge Engineering's* ace products. Lightweight and massively resistant.

Getting hit close range still shocked you like a bitch of a thing, though, and I could feel a hell of a deep bruise forming that I'd feel for days.

But none of that mattered.

Especially not right now.

She helped me to my feet. "You're sure you're okay, lovely?"

"Okay enough to function *and* to put down that motherfucker."

"He's trying to make a run for it."

I sucked in a breath and shoved a hand through my hair, taking a beat.

That was all we had time for, because I heard Lynch's heavy, frantic footsteps all the way down by the elevator.

"Let's go," I told Brianna.

And then we were running out of the room and veering down the corridor.

There was no way he was escaping our wrath.

He was dying here tonight. By our goddamn hands!

Reaching the elevator, he slapped the button to call it.

I smiled when it didn't come right away.

My dad had clearly been on top of it, keeping it down at the bottom for precisely this reason, so Lynch couldn't get away from us.

He spun and I caught sight of something in his hand, concealed for the most part.

And then a sadistic smile played on his lips a moment before he opened his hand.

A motherfucking grenade.

No.

"Oh my God," Brianna breathed.

"Are you fucking crazy?" I yelled over to him.

His lips pulled into a sadistic grin. "You already know the answer to that."

He pulled the pin.

"Go! Go! *Go!*" I yelled to Brianna, snatching her arm and dragging her with me to the closest stairwell entrance.

I slammed my hands into the emergency exit bar and the door gave way just as the grenade went off, the blast sending us careening down the steps.

The fiery heat and the smell of smoke was the last thing I was aware of before everything went black.

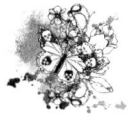

28

~Brianna~

Madness.

Utter fucking madness.

The sick bastard had gotten worse over time.

I hadn't thought that possible.

Yet, he'd just demonstrated proof of it.

"Hell" I choked, as I pushed up on my hands from my sprawled position on the stairwell landing.

"Hell? Your wish is my command, pretty princess."

I jolted at the sound of that maniac's voice and as I managed to stagger to my feet, I caught sight of him climbing through the wreckage of the stairwell door.

That paled in comparison to the sight of Levi on his stomach halfway down the stairs passed out. He was bloodied and covered in debris.

I remembered then, him throwing his body over mine to cover me from the blast.

"Levi!" I cried, scrambling toward him.

A gun cocked, stilling me.

Lynch stood there smirking. "Let him sleep. It will buy us some time alone together." He licked his lips in an utterly disgusting way. "It's been too long since I've had your pretty princess pussy, wouldn't you agree?"

Urgh. A fully body shudder took me. "You're demented. Don't take another step."

"*I'm* not going to, you are."

I snatched up a sharp piece of rubble and readied it. "Take your chances then."

He laughed, a nasty unhinged laugh. And then he took aim at Levi's unconscious form.

"No!" I screamed.

That laugh sounded again and he pulled his aim away. "I'll shoot your boyfriend to death unless you be my good little bitch like before."

"What?" I croaked.

"You're gonna turn around and press your hands to the wall. Then you'll pull your pants down to your ass and arch your back. You'll maintain that position no matter what." His eyes rolled back in his head. "No matter how I use you."

"You're beyond sick."

"And you've got serious delusions of grandeur thinking coming at me would play out any other way than this, thinking you could overpower and win against *me*. I ruined you, you see. You're still that girl held captive by me, the girl I turned into my bitch whore. And you always will be. You're fucking well damaged. So, how about you just accept that and lean into it? Spare your boyfriend in the process. Drop the piece of concrete, turn around and obey, pretty princess."

I swallowed hard, my fingers tightening around the piece of sharp debris in my hand.

He took aim at Levi again. "Now!" he bellowed. "The least you can do is open to me after the shit storm you've caused tonight! Now do it, become my whore again!"

He took a step toward me, but pulled up short at the sound of rushed footsteps coming from down the stairwell below. He swung around with his gun just as two of his *Osiris* members appeared.

"Perfect timing," he said, turning his aim back to me, then gesturing with his free hand at Levi. "There's still a path through the wreckage up there. Take him in there and haul him over the balcony. Make sure you get a nice video of it so we can send it along to Roman. It'll break that fucker and the whole Knight dynasty will die tonight. Then we'll swoop in while it's ripe for the taking."

"No!" I screamed, as the guys hauled Levi up between them and started dragging him away.

I lost control and bolted forward, only to be pistol-whipped by Lynch.

My head swimming, I fell back against the wall, and he fisted his hand in my hair, shoving his gun against my throat, as he used the painful hold to drag me through the wreckage and back into the penthouse.

I struggled and every time I did, he pushed the muzzle harder into my flesh.

"If you're a good girl once we get to the couch, I'll taste you first before I bounce you on my dick."

"Call your men off! Call them off now!"

"Huh, not being a good girl." He ripped me around by my hair and then I was tossed onto the couch right near the balcony where the guys were opening the doors and struggling to haul Levi's deadweight out there. *No! God, no!*

I tried to bolt off the couch to go to Levi, but Lynch pounced on me and shoved his gun to my forehead.

"Pull down your pants. *Now.*"

The fear rolling through me slammed up against my absolute terror for Levi.

"Stop them and I will."

He grunted and called out, "Five minutes! Leave him!"

I strained to see them putting Levi down on the patio, then the two of them coming back into the room.

"That comes at a price. They're gonna watch as I tear you apart." He hissed at my ear. "Change of plans. Gonna break your ass open this time. Can't fucking wait."

Don't freeze up. Don't freeze up.

I could feel an episode coming on, trying to claw its way to the surface.

I was beyond triggered right now.

But if it overtook me I'd be done for, Levi would be done for, and it would all be over.

I was jolted back when I felt him shifting behind me and I heard the sound of his belt opening.

In the process, his grip inadvertently loosened on his gun.

That was all that I needed.

I slammed my head back, smashing it into his fucking face.

He roared and flailed and I took the opportunity to dislodge the gun from his grip.

In the struggle, though, it went spinning across the floor.

He went to dive for it, but I roundhoused him into his guys.

"Stop her! Don't just fucking stand there!" he yelled.

I saw one of them brush his gun in his holster.

And then a shot rang out and drove through his skull, killing him instantly.

I spun to see Mason standing there beside Colt.

"Oh my God," I breathed with major relief.

That escalated even further when I saw Levi moving out on the patio, coming to.

He lifted his head, frowning and looking around, trying to get his bearings.

I saw the moment he realized what was happening because his eyes went utterly black.

He zeroed in on Lynch with his belt undone.

And then all hell broke loose.

Levi barreled through the open patio doors and tackled him to the ground.

Mason broke from Colt and launched himself at the remaining *Osiris* member. "Thought you'd gotten away from us. Your fatal mistake," he said, as he delivered rapid-fire blows of his *cement block* punches.

"Shit, are you okay, Bree?" Colt said, suddenly beside me and looking me over, rubbing my arm in comfort.

"Fine. I'll be fine," I said, distracted by the sight of Levi in an animalistic fury as he unleashed all over that sick bastard.

He reached across the floor for a moment and snatched up Lynch's gun from earlier.

And then he shoved it into the asshole's mouth.

I turned Colt's head away and held him to my chest.

But I couldn't do the same for myself.

I just couldn't look away.

I needed to see this.

As sick as it was, it was the closure long denied.

His demise had to be by our hands.

Levi must've sensed it from me, because he looked out at me.

I gave a nod.

And then he turned back to a violently bucking and freaking out Lynch, and pulled the trigger.

Blood and brain matter exploded everywhere as the demon died right before our eyes.

Gone.

Defeated.

Fucking over.

A choked sound left me.

After all this time, I couldn't believe it.

It was done.

Emotion took me over so quickly that I couldn't get a handle on it.

Tears were streaming down my face in the next moment and I was sobbing hard.

Colt tightened his hold around me, uttering words of comfort.

And then Levi and Mason were also there quickly wrapping themselves around me.

In that moment, I'd never felt so safe and loved.

I've never felt such peace.

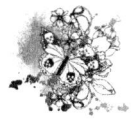

Epilogue 1
~BRIANNA~

One Month Later

God, he was so sexy.

And he was really in his element, rocking out, putting his charisma and his heart and soul out there for all to see.

So bold and brave.

So kicking major ass for the record execs that were here tonight for his performance.

Mythic Cry was killing it!

I watched from backstage of the trendy club as he worked the crowd to his will. He was a natural front man, right up there with the greats. People couldn't take their attention away from him for a moment when he was performing.

And it was going to finally pay off for him in the best way.

Levi and Mason had their arms draped over each of my shoulders as we looked on watching Colt do his thing and bring absolutely everything he had to the table.

He'd had a ritual before performing of kissing each

one of the tuning pegs of his guitar, but we'd accidentally added another tonight.

Me, Levi and Mason had just intended it as a one-off to help get Colt into a calm state because he'd been unusually nervous as the stakes were high tonight, something he wasn't used to with his music. But then he'd claimed it was now going to be an actual ritual—the four of us fucking in his dressing room.

Well, I was never going to turn that down.

Whenever the four of us came together it was so amazing. It made us all feel alive.

As did the fact that Mason was doing what he loved now, Colt was on the verge of skyrocketing to the next level with his music, and Levi and I were free of those awful shackles of our past.

I caught sight of Colt's parents in the front row. His dad, Oakley, was head banging to the hard-rock beat, while his mom, Lena, was dancing it up. The two of them were so uninhibited and upbeat people. We'd had dinner with them a week before the show and it hadn't been a nerve-racking thing meeting them at all. It had actually been fun. We'd had a barbecue in their villa-style home. They hadn't batted an eye about the four of us being together, they'd just been happy that their son had a whole lot of love in his life. We were all getting together after the show for drinks too tonight and I was looking forward to it.

Speaking of parents, I was having dinner with my dad in a couple of days at one of his diner chains. We'd made a deal to do it every couple of weeks and it had been great. We'd basically been getting to know each other again as the people who we were today.

As Colt finished one song, then got ready for another, having some whispered words with his hired drummer and bass player, joking around and looking so happy, commotion from down the backstage corridor caught my attention.

A flash of purple hair caught my eye a moment before *she* came into view.

Yes! She'd made it!

"Chloe!" I cried, easing from the boys and running to her.

We ended up meeting in the middle and throwing our arms around each other.

"Sorry I couldn't make it for the start of the concert," she said, as we pulled back. "I really had to get my final dress done for the upcoming fashion show we're putting on at school."

"No problem, he's only halfway done, there's still a lot to see. And the important part is we get to see each other."

We'd set things up now where we constantly kept in contact via video call and texts, while also meeting up in person every few weeks. Either she came to me, or I went to her in the City of Tolhurst. Sometimes the boys would spend time in the city while I was with Chloe, and then the four of us would head to Roman Knight's mansion for a catchup dinner, which had also become a regular thing now.

"Nice seeing you again," Levi said, coming to greet her with Mason staying closer to the stage so he didn't miss a thing when Colt started up again and launched into another song.

He offered his hand and she took it, the two of them smiling at each other pleasantly and shaking firmly.

They'd buried the hatchet, thankfully.

He'd actually apologized genuinely and she'd admitted that things were better for her career aspirations being at the design school in Tolhurst. It had come out that he'd actually been the one who'd gotten her accepted too.

There it was, him doing questionable things for the right reasons and having a heart about it all, actually caring even then.

Levi Knight was definitely a complicated person, but I was more than equipped to deal with it. The others had their things too and hell knew so did I.

But together, we were just right.

We functioned perfectly.

Powerfully.

And completely.

I brought Chloe back to my spot that viewed the stage, with Levi following over, then we all stood together in perfect harmony as we watched Colton continue doing his thing, his lyrics rolling through me with that powerhouse voice of his doing them so much justice.

"I remember the nights I couldn't sleep/ The nights I was screaming out your name/ The memories made me weep/ They had me twisting the sheets in fucking pain/ Whiskey eyes pulled me through/ Your memory took the chill out of the night/ Even in my worst nightmares, I'd see you/ Like a dark angel, you shone the way with your light."

The fact that it was about Levi and me just added a whole other beautiful element to it all.

Next on his set list was *our* song, *Vicious Things*.

I couldn't wait.

Having our love come to life in song like that, it was another level.

And I'd cherish every moment of it.

It was all so amazing.

Spectacular as Levi would say.

I sank into it and let it all roll over me.

He'd done it!

Colton Sharp as *Mythic Cry* was the latest signed client of *Rock 'N' Ruin*, a heavyweight record label!

They specialized in representing hard-rock and alternative rock acts.

I grinned as he skipped through the parking lot, unable to keep still at all because he was so excited and hyped up.

His parents had taken off home to their villa in the City of Tolhurst, and the four of us were headed back to the mansion in Stonewell to celebrate in our favored down and dirty way.

"I can't believe it!" he said, spinning around to face us and bouncing on the balls of his feet.

"We can," I said.

"You worked so hard to put that act together and your performance was incredible," Mason told him.

Levi slapped his back. "You deserve this, brother. You're spectacularly talented and you've been working toward this your whole life, since you were a boy."

"Yeah," he said. "I have. Shit! It's actually happening!"

We all wrapped ourselves around him, crying congratulations and showing him all the love and celebration that he deserved.

And now there was nothing dragging that down or dampening it.

Ever since the takedown of that psychopath, Malcolm Lynch, a weight I'd borne for six whole years had been lifted right off me. Taking him down like that really had made me feel like me and Levi had taken our power back that had been lost in that hellscape.

I felt vindicated in a way.

Lethal justice had been dealt out and *Osiris* and its maniacal leader was no more.

They'd been wiped from the face of the earth.

And now that dark and twisted time was fading into oblivion.

Now Levi and I were able to sever ourselves from it and belong to the present—and our plans for the future —instead.

It all took me over and I shifted position and held onto my boys.

"Here's to the future!" I cried. "It's now brighter than it's ever been!"

Epilogue 2
~LEVI~

Two Years Later

"Your pain tolerance really is spectacular. Jesus, brother."

I blinked at the sound of Mason's voice, coming back from zoning out to see him eyeing me as he paused inking my ribs with the best design fucking ever. Not just because he'd designed it and he'd really come into his own, creating some incredible artwork over the last couple of years that he'd been learning and working at *Inked Zoners*. But because of what the design represented.

I'd wanted to make it even more special by getting it done on my ribs.

Painful to the uninitiated and the experienced alike.

It was worth it, though.

To me, the way I was interpreting it for my life, the ribs were what protected that which enabled you to breathe, that safeguarded your life force, basically. After everything I'd been through and after what we'd all gone through two years earlier, it held a shit-ton of symbolism associated with that.

"Yeah. Still got it," I said, grinning out at him.

He put the needle down and rolled back on his chair. "Let's take a ten-minute break."

I sat up carefully. "Perfect. It gives me some time to return a couple of emails."

"You know you're supposed to be clocked off for the day, right? It's after seven, brother."

"You're one to talk."

"Well, I made an exception for you."

"Sure that's all it is. It can't possibly be that we're both being workaholics right now and pushing ourselves to build our lives."

I snatched up my phone from a side table and started responded to a couple emails that had come in. I mean, they could wait until tomorrow, but why put it off when I could get it done now?

"And because we love our jobs. Your dad having you head his computer engineering division lets you show off your incredible skills every day and do that high-level problem-solving that you love sinking your teeth into."

"There's that," I said, typing away. "And the fact that we're finally about to take a vacation together, all four of us."

"Fuck me, the last time was up at the safehouse. Not exactly a proper vacation."

"Private island paradise is more like it."

"Thanks to Colt and those high-flying contacts he's made as a big-time rockstar. Can you even turn on the radio anymore without hearing one of *Mythic Cry's* songs?"

We both chuckled. "I know. It's incredible for him."

I looked up as he leaned back in his chair. "Fuck, Lev, I'm so glad you're finally getting this done today. Me and Colt have had to hide *our* tattoos and the only way was to forgo fucking."

I finished off my emailing, then put my phone back on the table, looking out at him, giving him my full attention. "Fortunately, Brianna bought it because we've all been so busy. You and me with our stuff, Colt recording his next album, and our woman launching her app development business."

"I can't hold out much longer."

"A couple of days for this to heal a little so it's not red-raw and more dried blood than ink, and we'll be good to go."

"Unless I try to persuade Bree that we don't all strip naked to sleep surrounding one another after fucking?"

I laughed. "Yeah, good luck with that. There's no way. As soon as she thought of doing it regularly like that, it became permanent, She loves it, the skin-on-skin, the intimacy of it, being close to us with nothing between us." I shoved my hand through my hair. "Sorry I had to delay getting mine."

"Nah, I completely get it. You only graduated a year ago and started working at *Knightsridge*, you had a lot to cover and to learn before you took on the newest division, and once you did it was chock-a-block getting your new, handpicked team in shape and all that. The point is it's happening now and we've only got about an hour left to finish."

"Perfect. Ready to get back down to it?"

He rolled forward on his chair. "Yeah, let's do it."

I assumed the same position on my side.

After a few moments of the grating pain, I was able to zone out.

These days, when I did, it wasn't the demons that I saw.

I rarely even saw them in my sleep now either.

Nah, it was all sugar and spice and all things nice now.

Excitement.

Happiness.

Hope.

Love.

So much of that last one.

Because of Brianna, Colt, and Mason.

Because of our foursome and how spectacularly it was functioning now, how we all melded perfectly as one, how we were intrinsically linked, how we were immersed fully in one another's lives and supporting each other's endeavors, pushing and encouraging each other in the best ways too.

Our lives we'd set out to build since Stonewell U were coming along nicely.

Everything was falling into place.

—

I leaned against my Harley in the courtyard of our home in Stonewell.

We'd decided to stay here after graduation because the place meant a lot to us.

It was where things had changed for all of us, where we'd first come together as our foursome. It was off-campus so we were fine in that respect. It also wasn't far from my work in the City of Tolhurst, Colt's record company also there, and Brianna's app development firm. The tattoo parlor Mason worked at was in between both, so that worked out well too.

We'd disbanded *Hex* because we were no longer at Stonewell University. But, speaking of underground organizations, Brianna was still operating *Vixen*. Right now it was geared toward ensuring her dad was all right, given how many enemies he had from his old club days. No one had made a move, but as the cliché went: a good defense was a good offense.

Besides, although there were no immediate issues, she'd taken my advice to heart about keeping *Vixen* operational to safeguard all of us and those whom we loved.

"When the world is at peace, a gentleman keeps his sword by his side."

That Wu Tsu quote was something I'd taken to heart *and* still took very seriously.

Definitely words to live by in our complicated world.

I looked out down the private drive waiting on Mason's Porsche to come down the way with Brianna and Colt inside.

The two of them had gone to visit *Rock 'N' Ruin's* recording studio where our little rockstar was spending so much of his time. He'd convinced Brianna to re-record the duet, *Until You,* with him. Unfortunately, I'd had a situation at work so I hadn't been able to make it there on time.

I'd ridden here like a fucking maniac right after instead, not wanting to be late to the house as well. Now I'd gotten here first, an hour or so ahead of them, absolving myself from the other thing.

My phone buzzed and I pulled it from my black designer jeans to find a text from my dad.

Dad: You're still signed into the server. Clock off.

I frowned down at the message. *What?*

Levi: How do you know that?

Dad: Just checking in every now and then.

Levi: Should I be touched or offended?

Dad: Both. LOL.

Levi: LMFAO.

Dad: Seriously, though, clock off, son. Enjoy your vacation.

Levi: Ok. Thank you, Dad.

Dad: You're doing great, by the way. So great that when you get back you and me are going to celebrate big.

Levi: I can't wait.

Dad: Have fun, son. Love you.

Levi: Love you.

I was just about to slide my phone back into my leather jacket when it buzzed with another text.

Brianna: Almost home, lovely. Can't wait to see you. Been a couple of days with you coming home so late and me leaving at the crack of dawn.

Levi: I'm here now and will be for this next week of our spectacular vacation.

Brianna: I'm so excited. Just the four of us, no distractions?

Levi: I promise.

Brianna: Me too.

My phone lit up with Colton opening a group chat.

Brianna and I entered and then he was messaging us right away.

Colt: Lev! Five minutes out now. Island vacation here we come!

Brianna: We are fucking first.

I smirked.

Levi: Are we now, baby?

Colt: Damn, cutie.

Brianna: We absolutely are.

Levi: It's on. Hey, aren't you two right next to each other in the car?

Colt: I wanted my own input, hence using two phones.

Levi: I see.

Brianna: Mason asked if you already packed your stuff for vacation?

Levi: I packed for all of you. I've been here for a while.

Colt: Wow. Thanks, brother!

Levi: No worries.

Brianna: Look at you being so organized and on the ball these days.

Levi: The new and improved me. Does it turn you on, baby?

Brianna: Absolutely.

Levi: Mmm, knowing that is getting me hot.

Colt: You're always hot for her.

Levi: Right back at you.

Colt: True. I'm a dirty fucking slut for her.

Brianna: Levi, don't work him up while we're in the car. He's giving me the eye right now and he just sank his fingers into Mason's hair while he's driving.

Levi: Down, cupcake. Keep your frosting on.

Colt: Frosting! Too funny!

Brianna: HAHAHA!

Colt: We're pulling onto the private drive now. See you in a few seconds, Hellraiser.

Levi: Right back at you, Maverick.

Levi: And my Wildflower.

Levi: Colt, tell Scourge it's time. Before we even head into the house. Because the second we do, Brianna's gonna be all over us.

Brianna: Hey. Well, it's true. It's been way too long.

Colt: Fucking right, my cock has been hating me. And Lev, got it. Just told Mason. In code, of course, so our little Bree doesn't get tipped off.

Brianna: Tipped off to what?

Levi: Dammit, cupcake.

Colt: Well, she's right here.

Levi: You could have whispered.

Colt: Sorry, too excited to keep my voice down. Besides, we're almost there anyway.

Levi: See you in a moment then.

I left the group chat, then pocketed my phone in my jacket.

Not a few seconds later, I spotted the Porsche coming down the drive.

Well, *hurtling* down it. Mason was eager as fuck. I couldn't fault him there, we all were. The need was burning in my fucking veins. My cock was already rock-hard with the anticipation alone of the four of us finally coming together again.

Before long, they were pulling in right beside my bike.

Brianna and Colt were out of the car first and bolting over to me.

Colt ruffled my hair. He kept doing that now after seeing my dad do it to me a couple of years back when we'd stayed at the Knight mansion. I laughed but it got caught in my throat when Brianna slammed into me, wrapping her arms around me.

She planted little kisses all over my hair, my cheeks, my throat, my chest.

"Missed you too, *Wildflower.*"

When she eased up, I went to chase her lips, but Mason cleared his throat.

"First thing's first, Lev. You kiss her again and that'll be it, all roadblocks down and some epic fucking underway."

"Right," I said, taking a couple of much-needed steps back from her instead.

He and Colt came to stand either side of me.

Brianna stared between us curiously. "So, what's this surprise Colt alluded to?"

"Something ace!" Colt exclaimed in his usual no-holds-barred excited way.

"Ready?" Mason asked us.

"Shit, yeah," Colt cried.

"Fuck, it's on," I said.

He nodded, and then Mason turned around and lifted up the back of his *Inked Zoners* t-shirt with the bold zigzagging black and gold design to reveal a special tattoo across his upper back.

Colt pulled down his leather pants to reveal the same on his upper left thigh.

And I raised my crimson tee to reveal mine on my ribs.

We now all shared the same tattoo.

Mason had taken inspiration from Brianna's watercolor butterfly tattoo on her arm. He'd actually used the same butterfly like I had with the nightlight in the design. And he'd incorporated several other elements meaningful and special to our foursome. Wildflowers were interspersed throughout the design to represent her—dandelions, daffodils, lavender—and a Les Paul guitar for Colt, a tattoo gun for Mason, and a keyboard for me. Across the different elements was the word *Brianna* in a striking script font.

He'd designed something so intricate and edgy that really spoke to our love for her.

"Oh my God," Brianna breathed.

She came to each of us in turn and traced her fingers over our tattoos.

"I can't believe it. This is amazing. The best present I've ever gotten. You guys are so sweet! So incredible! *Thank you!*"

"Of course," Mason said, as we all fixed our clothes. "You deserve nothing less, dark angel."

It wasn't over yet, though.

He pulled a piece of paper from the back pocket of his distressed gray jeans and unfolded it, holding it up for her to see. It was the same design, except with our names scrawled across it in a script font.

"If you want," I told her.

She didn't even need to think about it, didn't even hesitate. She grabbed the paper and pressed it to her chest. "I'd love to! No question!"

"We'll set an appointment after vacation then," Mason said, grinning from ear-to-ear like Colt and me were.

"Speaking of vacation, let's get to the fucking, then we'll head out," Colt said. "I can't wait any longer."

"Me neither," I said, my words coming out as a growl.

In the next moment, I lunged at Brianna and threw her over my shoulder.

She squealed as I carried her toward the mansion, Mason and Colt chuckling as they followed over.

I smiled to myself.

This was it.

Our lives.

Our amazing lives.

Our spectacular foursome.

Things had come a long way.

We had as a unit.

I had as an individual.

I wasn't just a whole lot of damage anymore.

I was hopeful.

I was happy.

I was most definitely loved.

And, above all, I was at peace.

THE END

Want some dark academy RH paranormal romance? Check out ELECTI ACADEMY

Or dive into dark mafia RH, COVETED KINGDOM

Mythic Cry Lyrics

Until You

I've been standing in the shadows.
Willing the blackness to pull me in.
A place where nobody else knows.
I'm barely holding on, barely surviving.
It was easier not to open my eyes.
It was easier not to feel a thing.
Until you.
You came into my life like a hurricane.
You eased away the pain.
Until you.
You chased away the gray skies.
You opened up my life.
Now I can breathe without it hurting.
I'm finally learning.
Until us.
Until me.
Until you.

Vicious Things

Dangerous, feral, ruthless.
Far from toothless.
Dark horses to the rotten core.
We collided with a ball of sunshine.
Made for one hell of a war.
Pink bubble-gum, cotton candy.
On the surface that's what you'll see.
But there's a whole lot more underneath.
Vicious things tangling in the night.
She was made for one hell of a fight.
Fuck it, she was born for this.
Born to be merciless.
Girl's got claws and she'll sure as fuck bite.
Vicious things walking into the light.
Girl's ours now and we make a real sight.
Stay here.
Stay, my dear.
Vicious things like us belong right here.

Headstrong
Like a thief in the night
You tried to steal me away
From everything I'd been leaning on.
You thought you could handle it
That I was just another play
Too bad you didn't count on my might.
Watch out.
Watch me.
I'm coming for you.
Beating you at what you do.
Meeting you at the peak you thought only you could meet.
You see, I'm headstrong.
Headstrong.
And you're dead wrong

Thinking I was someone you could step on.
Headstrong.
I'm headstrong.

I Remember

I remember the nights I couldn't sleep
The nights I was screaming out your name
The memories made me weep
They had me twisting the sheets in fucking pain
Whiskey eyes pulled me through.
Your memory took the chill out of the night.
Even in my worst nightmares, I'd see you.
Like a dark angel, you shone the way with your light.
But you can't admit
That you were there.
You can't commit
To what's fair.
I can't let you run
I'm under the gun.
I've waited too long
Baby, don't fucking run.
I'm sorry, I never meant to hurt you.
Anyone but you.
Can't you see what you do
I just needed you to remember too.
Remember me.
Remember you.
I just needed you to remember too.
I just needed you to remember.
To remember too.

Connected Series

VICIOUS THINGS & COVETED KINGDOM

VICIOUS THINGS
Brianna, Levi, Colton, Mason
THEY BREAK BEAUTY
WHEN KINGS FALL

COVETED KINGDOM
Caterina, Nico, Emilio, Julian
WHERE THE WICKED REIGN
VICIOUS LITTLE PRINCESS
THEY MAKE MONSTERS

———

WALKING WITH MONSTERS & TWISTED TORMENT

WALKING WITH MONSTERS
Aurora, Asher, Killian, Jonah
LOCK UP THE DARKNESS
SCARS RUN DEEP
BURN IT DOWN

TWISTED TORMENT

Skylar, Bastian, Caleb, Caspian
WRECK ME
HATE ME
CRAVE ME

Leia King Library

OMEGA FALLS

IMMORTAL PASSIONS
IMMORTAL BURDEN
REIGN OF THE BEAST
FALLEN ANGEL
OUT OF ASHES

IMMORTAL FLAME
HARBINGER
LEGACY

KING

About the Author

Where Damaged Heroes and Badass Heroines Collide.

Leia writes edgy and emotional stories across multiple genres. She enjoys crafting flawed heroes with a dark side and strong women who hold their own.

Printed in Dunstable, United Kingdom